I0525495

Magic Rules

Sylvie Janes

Copyright © 2023 by Sylvie Janes

Book cover design by Sarah Waites of Illustrated Book Cover Design

All rights reserved.

No portion of this book may be reproduced in any form without written permission from the publisher or author, except as permitted by U.S. copyright law.

This book has been written in Australian English. It's not the same as American English, we use extra U's, few Z's, and some of our terms don't mean quite the same thing as they do in the US. Sorry about that. If you do find a typo, and I'm sure there's a few, no matter how many times this book has been edited by professionals, please let me know. sylviejanesauthor@gmail.com is the best way to contact me. Thank you so much for reading my stories. I hope you like them.

CONTENTS

Dedication   V

1. Chapter 1   1

2. Chapter 2   13

3. Chapter 3   24

4. Chapter 4   34

5. Chapter 5   48

6. Chapter 6   64

7. Chapter 7   79

8. Chapter 8   93

9. Chapter 9   106

10. Chapter 10   118

11. Chapter 11   129

12. Chapter 12   143

13. Chapter 13   154

14. Chapter 14   170

15. Chapter 15   183

16.	Chapter 16	195
17.	Chapter 17	208
18.	Chapter 18	218
19.	Chapter 19	228
20.	Chapter 20	240
21.	Chapter 21	251
22.	Chapter 22	263
23.	Chapter 23	274
24.	Chapter 24	288
25.	Chapter 25	310
26.	Chapter 26	322
27.	Chapter 27	334
28.	Chapter 28	344
29.	Chapter 29	353
Acknowledgements		365
About the Author		366
Also By		367
Chapter		369

A genuine thank you to those who love the stories.

1

— · —

I dragged myself through the Swift Security office door as driving sleet pushed at my legs. It'd been a horrible night.

"Look what the cat dragged in." Marg stood behind her desk. The low hum of a large heater churning out warm air around her set a homey tone to the room. She had been warm and cosy all night. Unlike me.

"I feel like I've been regurgitated by a cat," I replied with a waspish snap to my tone. I handed her back the keys to the patrol car before I held my hands out to the heater on the desk. My fingertips were white. Where were my gloves? Probably at the bottom of the pile that lived in my cupboard.

"A few alarms go off, did they, Lucy?" Marg's fingernails clacked slowly on the keyboard as she logged my routes into the system like always.

"Those stupid buildings need upgrades. I swear tonight was out to get me. The owners need to invest in new alarm systems. Or else demolish the buildings," I muttered, turning my hands over, warming the backs of them. My fingertips tinged slightly pink as I waited for Marg to finish her routine. Give me warmth and somewhere snuggly to hide. I was spent.

"You going to clean up here, or head home?"

I pushed a few strands of hair back from my face, even my hair was cold. The brown mess I'd tried to control with a braid seemed to have its own agenda tonight. "Rain's not going to stop, so I'm heading home."

"Still at Coven House?" Marg asked.

"Yep. Until I get my own place. Had little luck with that lately. Who upped the rents all of a sudden?"

"The mayor's been doing dodgy stuff, think he's trying to re-vamp downtown, again." Marg smiled slightly as she turned and caught my gaze. Her over plucked brows were still a little furrowed as if the weight of running Swift Security rested on them. "Do you want a lift?"

"Buses are still running. I'll catch the next one."

Getting a lift would mean listening to either John or Henry, my co-workers, complain about life, aging, how it used to be better, kids these days and that sort of thing. I'd rather avoid interaction as much as possible. The bus drivers always picked me up, didn't ask questions and dropped me off without comment.

"Okay, be safe out there. It's not a nice night," she replied.

"I'm not a nice person." I waved the fingers of my hand in a half-salute as I headed back out into the squall.

"I'll be the judge of that," she called out as the door slammed behind me.

I pulled my hoodie tighter and trudged into the face of the rain. Wayland City did nothing by half. If it was going to rain, it was going to be skin blisteringly hard rain that came at you sideways so it could get up and into your face. People didn't bother with umbrellas here. They were the first thing the rain and wind attacked. I hunched further into my jacket and hopped over puddles that were threatening to engulf the sidewalk. I made my way to the bus stop. I had three minutes before my bus would turn up. I stood to the side of the bus stop where the wind wasn't so harsh and shuffled my feet back and forth to keep warm. The squally wind had kept the most sensible people indoors, snuggling under deep blankets with those they loved. I wished that I was one of them.

Lights came towards me, too low to be the bus, so I hunched even further and turned to protect myself in case of a splash. A car slowed as it passed me, completely missing the puddle and kept going. Great, the weirdoes were coming out even on a night like this. The car turned the corner and I went back to concentrating on keeping as much warmth as I could in my body before the bus came. I shivered, come on bus. A large arm wrapped around my neck, dragging me backward. I let out a squawk that was cut off as my windpipe crushed under the pressure.

A male grunt greeted me as I fought to get free. I lifted my feet up as I had been taught as a child to put all my weight onto the attacker, his arm loosened, allowing me to suck in a quick breath.

"Shit," I blurted out before a dark blur raced towards me and threw the man that had grabbed me over against the wall. I fell into the icy puddle with a hard splash, soaking my jeans completely.

Detective Nichole Pearce stood seething at the attacker, her eyes red and glowing. Her fists clenched beside her as if she was getting ready to start the fight. Looking up at her, I couldn't help but be intimidated. She wasn't all that tall, but kick-arse determination made her seem like a giant. If I wasn't soaked already and tired, I would have made some witty remark to Pearce. Instead, I groaned and knelt in the puddle to stand up. Pearce zipped beside me with vampire speed and held her hand out. I waved her away.

"I got this, don't want to get you muddy." My knees creaked again as I groaned at the ache in my legs. I guessed that a large bruise was already forming on my backside. I'd hit the footpath hard.

"Can't you ever stay out of trouble?" Pearce growled at me. Her short blonde hair was tied back in a no-nonsense cop way. Detective Pearce had until recently been an upstanding member of the Wayland Police Force, that was until her then partner revealed he was a witch hunter and killed her while trying to kill me. Rory had brought her back to life as a vampire, against my better judgement and now Pearce was here, throwing weirdoes to the wall on a dark and squally night. No one had asked her if she wanted to become a vampire and I think she was working on deep-seated issues of resentment, hence the tossing of fully grown men. Or maybe that was just Pearce, she always had a short fuse.

I rubbed at my lower back then tried to push any excess water off my pants. It was futile. I was fully soaked and freezing through. "What did I do?"

"You attract the freaks and weirdoes," She stared at the downed man as if he had singlehandedly made her night worse than it already was and he was going to regret ever starting anything.

I stared at her through the rain and sighed, pushing some of the excess water down my jeans. "I know."

"That's the second attempt on you in the last few nights. I'm going to kick Rory's arse for this," she replied.

Rory was on a lot of peoples hit list lately. I could name a thousand things that might have pissed Pearce. It was too much work to figure it out on my own.

"Why's Rory in trouble?" I tried to wring the water from my braid, but it didn't help the situation. My fingers were back to white and cold.

"I've pulled Lucy Duty," she spat the words as if they were the most distasteful things in the world.

"Lucy Duty?" I wiped my eyes. My hands were back to freezing now. I probably should have taken Marg up on her suggestion of a ride home. I blinked up at the rain, it had mutated into sleet. Great. Just more fun.

"Yes, we take turns keeping an eye on you."

Sleet collected on her short blonde bun. She paid it no mind. Since turning into a vampire, Pearce's winning personality had gotten more efficient. I'd have to thank Rory once more for this delight.

"So, what did you do to pull Lucy Duty?"

"I may have hit a few people," she mumbled as she stomped over to the unconscious attacker. ser

I followed her, curiosity getting the better of me. "Rory hits lots of people. Why punish you?"

"They were important guests." She knelt and rummaged through the unconscious man's pockets.

"What did they do to piss you off? Other than breathe wrong?" My sarcasm reinserted itself into the conversation. I turned as the bus zoomed past my stop. The puddle exploded up in a dirty wave of slush, coating me. "Damn it."

Pearce snorted at the disaster. Just great, now I'd have to wait another half an hour before I could get the next one.

"It's not important. This is the second time I've had to save you from disaster in the last few days."

"Why, who's after me?"

Pearce shrugged. "There's been a couple of guys shadowing you on your shift. She bent down, pulling a wallet out of the guy's jacket. "Amateur."

"He had his wallet on him?" I shook my head.

"Nothing to worry about." Taking the money from his wallet she threw the rest back at his face.

"Isn't that stealing?"

"He hurt you and you're worried about money?" Pearce's voice took on a gravelly tone, her eyes still alight with vampire glow.

"Well, you are a police officer." I shrugged, the thought of Pearce not following procedure was wrong.

"Lucky for you. I spotted this guy tailing you back at the last stop on your route. Didn't know why he didn't jump you then, would have been easier to get you in the abandoned building." She kicked the guy in the guts. "He'll be out for a while."

"Don't you want to take him in for questioning? You know, make sure you find out why he attacked me?" I kept my voice low. Pearce wasn't a vamp I wanted to piss off. Besides, she'd saved me a bit of a headache. I'm sure I would have fought him off eventually, maybe.

"Nope, he's one of a long line of bounty hunters out to get you. Someone put a big bounty on your head." She strode back over to the bus stop.

"Why me?" My stomach dropped, I would never be safe. I thought by hiding in Wayland City I could live a semi-normal life. Her words ripped that thought away.

"Probably because you're a pain in the arse." Pearce flicked her short blonde hair back from her face.

"No, tell me how you really feel." I'd feared Pearce originally, especially of her no-nonsense cop attitude and her thousand-yard stare that cut through all the bullshit.

"The real hunters haven't turned up in Wayland yet. I'm waiting for them. See how good they are."

"You're using me as bait?" Indignation churned within my chest, creating a small fiery warmth that spread to my neck and face.

"Of course, we are." Pearce shot me a glance, her facial expression betrayed her thoughts of me being a total idiot.

"Who's we?" I clenched my fists, knowing her answer but needing to hear it.

"Rory, obviously, but also the witches and the hot shifter," Pearce replied.

"But you're a cop. Don't you have work to do?"

"Well, the captain has me in charge of a new task force," she replied. "So technically I'm working."

"Are the police in on this too?"

She shrugged one shoulder.

"Everyone knows about this bounty, but me?"

"Your boyfriend is trying to track down who's set it and then he said he was going to rip their entrails out through their nose. I like his method."

"You can't rip anyone's intestines out through their nostrils. It's physically impossible," I replied.

"I have never tried. If he's going to, then I'll bring the popcorn."

"Well, thank you for saving me from this idiot, but I've missed my bus. So now I think I'll shuffle home." I put my hands in my sopping jacket.

"Why? I've got this guy's keys." She jingled the aforementioned keys in my face.

"You can't steal his car." My protest was half-hearted, my shivering changed my mind. The icy sludge coating me smelled of petrol and dirt. I tried to flick most it away, it did little good.

She shook her head. "You know, you have the weirdest set of morals I've ever encountered. Yes, I can steal the car from the guy who attacked you. Get in the freakin' car."

The sleet had turned harder and icier. If I didn't know better, I thought it would snow. But it never snowed in Wayland City. Just sleet and slush.

"Fine. But don't leave it at Coven House. I don't want them associated with this."

"No chance. Raoul will love this one." Pearce shot me a toothy grin.

Shock rattled through my body. "Pearce, did you just smile?"

"Fuck off Driver, get in," she snarled.

"What's Raoul got to do with this?" I was sitting on the deep lambswool seat cover.

"He's got a chop shop going, always knew it was one of them."

"Raoul? As in flamboyant bartender, maker-of-the-cock-tails-extraordinaire Raoul?" Of all the people to have a chop shop, he'd be the last on my list of suspects.

"Yep, guys' a car nut." Pearce revved the car to life and took off at an astounding speed that had me hitching my breath and gripping the door handle.

Pearce saw my reaction and laughed.

"I swear this night is weird. I've seen you smile and laugh in less than two minutes. If this is a nightmare, I want to wake up now," I mumbled.

"Shut up Driver, you can always walk home." She took the corner way too fast for a mortal to handle.

"I think these newfound vamp reflexes need to be worked on Pearce. You can drive slower you know," I replied, still gripping the handle.

"No chance," she replied, as she floored the accelerator to make it through another major intersection as the lights changed. The car's suspension bounced and almost sent me hitting the roof with my head.

"I don't think I like this new you." I tried to push myself through the seat to stabilise.

"You and Rory both."

"You're sticking it to him, aren't you? Can you do that? You know, because he's your sire and all?" I had been meaning to ask that of Rory for weeks now, but he always skirted the conversation away from Pearce.

"Technically, I don't have a sire. He used your blood and his combined, so he has no claim on me."

"Are you saying I'm your sire?" The thought of me having command over another being was preposterous.

"No. I have none. Basically, in the vamp world, I'm self-made." Her fangs flashed for a moment in the dim light of the car.

"That's a good thing?"

"Not according to his highness. He assigned me to watch you and keep you safe. I don't have to follow his directions, but I was curious who and what would come after you."

"I'd rather be left alone to live an uncomplicated life, if anyone's asking."

"Fat chance in hell on that one. People have been sharing stories about you and it's got out that you're a metalsmith. Some big names are gunning to get control of you." Her hands gripped the wheel tighter.

"They're delusional if they think I'll do anything for them."

"You would eventually. They'd break you. They always do." Pearce's dark tone was worrying, as if she'd encountered these types before and wasn't happy with the outcome.

"Do you have any idea who's behind it?"

"Not yet. That's why I'm trailing you. Do me a favour, though. Just go home and sleep. I have a thousand things to do today and I don't have time to save your butt every three minutes."

"But it'll be daylight soon...you're a vampire." I waved my hand at her and then at the lightening sky.

"Dayish-walker." Pearce pointed at herself.

"What the hell?"

"Yep."

"No wonder Rory's pissed at me and you. You can go out in the sunlight." A mix of wonder and terror flowed through me. Having vampires around was one thing, but having one that could go anywhere at anytime, especially it being Detective Pearce was a true nightmare.

"Sort of, I can go out a bit but not direct sunlight. I burn like I'm a redhead in a tropical resort within a few minutes, but I don't crispify like the others do. That's why I'm still on the job." Try as she might, she couldn't keep a smidge of spite out of her tone.

"Oh, yeah, congratulations on the promotion."

She shook her head. "Stupid dickheads still won't listen to me, though."

"Why? Because you're a vamp?"

She gave me an expression full of derision. "No woman has ever had the top job in this city. And the establishment has told me in no uncertain terms that's not going to change soon."

"Oh."

"Anyway, here's your place. Stay home. Let me work, or I'll let the next dickhead do some damage before I rescue your lily-white arse."

"Whatever." I stepped out of the stolen vehicle. "Tell Raoul I said hi."

Pearce screeched off without replying. She was growing on me. Still an absolute bitch, but at least her motivation to fix Wayland was in the right place. I sighed and trudged up the gravel path to Coven House. The wind and rain had died down. I didn't know whether it was a let up in the sky or a hex that Josie had wrought around the house. I was cold, drenched and ready for a hot bath and bed.

I was not ready for Cole to be pacing the kitchen like he was about to rip the kitchen bench top in half with his bare hands.

"What?" I didn't bother to put my bag down.

"Jessie's gone missing,"

2

"When?"

"A few hours ago. She's been out of sorts for a few days. Brad tried to talk to her, but she won't speak. She went to bed and then when her mother checked on her at twelve she wasn't in her room. The pack is searching for her," Cole stated.

"Okay, where are we headed?"

Cole took in the state I was in, then frowned. "You need to get dry before you do anything. You're hypothermic."

I shook off his judgement. "I don't care. We need to find Jessie. She could be anywhere."

"Go shower. I'll make some calls."

"Cole." I stood my ground, hands on my hips. Trying to out-stare a shifter was quite hard but if you practiced long enough, you could stand a chance. Unfortunately for me and the night I'd had, I stood no chance.

"Lucy, you can't help if you're exhausted and collapse. You'll be dead weight, so go get changed, eat something and we'll go." His eyes flashed electric blue.

I stood staring at him. When I regained the ability to speak without starting one hell of an argument. "I suppose I'll go get changed then."

"Lucy. Sorry. I'm worried. I shouldn't take it out on you." His eyes were back to his normal steel grey. "Jessie is everything to our pack."

"I understand. Let me get changed and we'll go."

"Do you think the witches could scry her?" he asked.

I scanned the kitchen. Josie would normally be up at this time of the morning, but I guess she'd given them some alone time knowing that something was amiss.

"I guess it wouldn't hurt. Where's Josie?"

"She's downstairs with some witches."

I nodded. "Go ask. I'll be back in a minute."

I left him still standing forlornly in the kitchen as I hurried to my bedroom to change. I ended up taking slightly longer than I had hoped when I realised, I hadn't done my washing that week and had to search through my wardrobe for a clean t-shirt to wear under my jacket. I noted to myself that I would have to get more organised. The past few weeks were hectic, but hygiene shouldn't be compromised, especially when I was interested in a shifter.

When I came back to the kitchen, I found Josie making Cole a hot chocolate laced with a few extra herbs to help calm nerves. The two were whispering low, as if to keep others out of the conversation.

"I'm ready. Where do we start?" I took the jug from Josie and pouring myself a drink too.

"The pack has searched the houses and areas she normally goes to. We've checked the surveillance footage. No one came into or left the house that wasn't supposed to be there. We don't know if she's been taken. There's no ransom demands." Cole's grip on the mug tightened. I put my hand over his and waited until the wolf calmed within him.

"Do you want me to call the ghosts? They are always with her. Maybe they know."

Josie wiped down the bench top, before pausing and staring at me. "Aren't they scared of you?"

"I can command them if I want to, I don't usually. It's not pleasant for them or me. But this is Jessie we're talking about."

"Do you need anything for it?" Josie hung up the tea towel beside the sink and came forward.

We'd been working together on magic for the past few weeks, trying to teach each other our specific brands of magic with little success.

I rubbed the sides of my arms. "I'll go do this. They won't come if anyone else is in the room."

She nodded and gave a tight smile then addressed Cole. "If you need us, the coven is at your disposal."

He nodded and remained focused on the cup still in his hand.

I leaned in to him. Nothing I said would help ease his worry, but as a wolf I knew he responded to touch more than words.

"Help us." His words were tight, as if he'd fought to keep from saying them.

"Pack." I reminded him.

He nodded as I left him alone at the kitchen bench. Hurrying down the stairs to the practice room, I noted the lights were still dimly lit throughout. Young witches were impressed with how spooky the lighting made the room. It didn't matter to magic either way. I turned the lights up and stood in the middle of the room centring myself. With a long exhale, I let my magic loose. Thick dark tendrils of black and purple magic streamed away from me, stirring the dust at the edges of the room. Someone had been playing with fire and hadn't cleaned up the ash. I'd have words with the witchlings once this was done. No need for an untidy space. I shivered at the thought. My subconscious voice sounded an awful lot like my grandmothers. She was not someone I aspired to be.

"Where is she?" I pushed my voice into the beyond. As the daughter of death, I had an inroad into the afterlife and could call people who had died to me. The result was I'd get a migraine and a bloody nose for the effort, so I rarely used the power. It was too much work for little reward. Jessie was a different matter. I would do what it took to get her back.

"Where is she?" I asked again and waited for someone to heed my call.

"Lucy?" Jessie's voice was soft, fractured, as if she was talking through an old-fashioned walky-talky that was running out of battery.

"Jessie. Where are you?" I called.

"They're not here," she said with a faint wail.

"Jessie, listen to me. Where are you? I'll come to you and then you can tell me all about it." I opened my eyes into the nether realm. Scenes flittered past me of other lives lived. I shooed them away and focused on where Jessie's voice was coming from.

When you enter the afterlife, the first thing that's noticed is that everything had a worn out look to it. Colours weren't vibrant like in life and there was a static haze across it.

"Jessie," I called again.

"Lucy." Her voice sounded louder now.

I turned my metaphorical head and focused on a bright spark of yellow and red light to my left.

"Jessie." I raced towards her through the realm. "Where are you? Are you hurt? Did anyone take you?"

"No. I had to find my friends. They're not here. They said they wouldn't leave me. But they are gone. They're not here." She wailed again.

"I'm going to come to you. Let me in." I reached out my hand.

"Okay."

I took two steps forward and hit a barrier. Jessie was curled up under a marble bench that looked to be in a park. "Where are you, Jessie?"

"In the cemetery."

"Oh."

Jessie had survived a lot in the past few months and had been changed. One of those changes was she could now talk to the dead.

"Lucy, they've been taken. Help me." She started crying again.

"I'm coming, don't move." I pulled myself back to my body and clenched my jaw as the inevitable headache descended sharply. I hissed and took the stairs two at a time to find Cole.

Josie was there with a shot glass full of some green liquid. I grabbed it without hesitation and gulped it down. Her medicine tasted like garbage, but it worked.

"She's at the old cemetery, near Kingsgrove. Do you have anyone near there?"

Cole shook his head. "No, we're the closest. How did she get so far?"

"Jessie's been hiding a few things from us, but she's safe for now. Let's go get her."

Josie didn't offer to come with us. I guess she could sense how close to the edge Cole was. I nodded at her and grabbed Coles keys before he could get them off the bench top. That brought him back to reality.

"No, I'll drive," he growled.

"You sure you don't want me to drive you?" I skipped out the front door.

"Lucy, we both know what you're doing and I'm grateful that you are trying to distract me, but for all our sakes, give me back my keys." With one quick movement, he'd covered the distance between us and snatched his keys from my upraised hand.

"Well, if you say so."

The drive was quick. Neither of us spoke. I kept sending out little tendrils of magic to check on Jessie. She wasn't crying anymore, but she was still hunched up under the bench. The night was cold and even as a shifter, she was shivering. When we stopped the car, there was a flutter of magic near us. Magic sent ripples through the air when it was used that other practitioners could sense. I turned and tried to see where it was coming from. Cole halted mid-stride as I scanned the area.

"You okay?" he whispered.

I tilted my chin upward. "There's something."

He grabbed my hand. "We'll deal with it later. We need to get Jessie."

I nodded and took the left path into the older part of the cemetery, where the mausoleums were situated. Jessie sat up when she saw us. Her tear-streaked face haunted with sorrow. Cole got to her first and wrapped her up in his arms, growling low and insistent. This set Jessie off crying again. I gave the two a minute before I spoke.

"Jessie, are you okay?"

Such a stupid question, really.

"No. They are gone. Someone's stolen them." She hiccuped.

"Who stole them?"

With her head buried into Cole's shoulder she whispered. "I don't know. They're all gone."

"Let's go see what we can do. We'll find your friends and get them back."

"Okay."

Cole carried her back to the car. I sat with her as he sent a quick text to Brad, Jessie's father, telling him we had her. Jessie's hands were cold. I took both in mine and sent a bit of magic through our touch to warm her up. She giggled and shook her head.

"That tickles."

I winked. "How'd you get here?"

"I walked. The shadows are quicker."

"Have you shadow walked before?" I kept my voice light. She didn't need to know the fear coursing through my body like a freight train thundering down a track. I could freak out once I was alone.

"No, but I had to find them. I've called them for weeks and they're all gone," she sighed. "Someone took them from me."

I nodded. "I'll find them and deal with it."

She bared her teeth in a wolfish manner. "No, they're mine to deal with."

"How about we work together? But not until you explain to your father why you scared him and your mother half to death," I replied.

At my words, her face dropped any semblance of determination. "They're going to be so mad at me."

"I think they'll be glad you're safe," I replied, then put my finger across my lips before she could say more as Cole slid into the driver's seat.

"They okay?"

"Relieved. I think it's going to take a little while to sort things out." Cole started the car. The muscles behind his brows tightened as if he was making important decisions. He didn't want to think right then.

"Okay."

Pack business was not my business. I had been made an honorary member, but I wasn't a shifter, so I didn't get the politics behind decisions made. To me things were more black or white.

But knowing Cole, he was dealing with many shades that brought on the frown.

Jessie took that moment to sneeze, which sent Cole's frown deeper into his brow.

"Bless you," I said automatically then put my hand to Jessie's forehead. She wasn't running a temperature. "You feeling okay?"

"Yeah, the cemetery had some dogwood and milk thistle. I'm allergic," Jessie muttered.

"You didn't stay away from them?" Cole rumbled.

"I was trying to find my friends."

He let out a frustrated sigh. I place my hand on his forearm and gave him a small shake of my head. I settled my hand onto his lower thigh as he drove, hoping the warmth and pressure would help him control his temper.

"Can you tell us when they started disappearing?"

"Two weeks ago. The older people, the ones in funny clothes, stopped showing up," she replied. "Then less and less came until none of my friends were left."

Cole bit down on his bottom lip. I squeezed his leg lightly. Now was not the time to argue with her.

"Okay. Have you tried to find them elsewhere?"

"I've tried all over the city. There are no departed around." There was a slight tremble to her voice.

"That's not good." I tried to use soothing tones, if I came across too harsh it might set her off again.

"I thought they might hide from the wicked lady."

My heart thumped to the bottom of my chest. "What lady?"

"She hides around the place and runs from me." Jessie thumped the seat beside her.

"Jessie," Cole rumbled.

"Yeah, don't hurt Cole's car, Jess. He's particular about the seats," I blurted, trying to stave off anything else he was about to say. I squeezed his leg harder.

"He can't feel that you know," Jessie said.

"What?"

"You're trying to stop him going off at me like he usually does by touching his leg," she said with a matter-of-fact attitude. "He likes you touching him, but he's going to yell at me anyway, so we may as well get it done in the car. My parents will yell at me more."

"Cole will not yell at you. You were looking for your friends. He would do the same."

"You don't know the Sigma." She blew out a hefty breath at the end of her words.

"Sigma, schmigma. Cole won't say a word, because you and I need to figure out if the wicked old lady took your friends and how I'm going to get them back for you."

Jessie started giggling.

"What's so funny?"

Cole gripped the steering wheel. The set of his jaw let me know he was ready to turn the car off and yell.

"You commanded Cole. You're his alpha." Jessie burst into full-blown laughter.

I gazed over at Cole, then back at Jessie and shook my head. "I don't get it."

"Leave it," Cole rumbled.

"Jessie, why are you laughing?"

"I wish my friends were here. They could explain it better. Old Mr Sims was alpha of the pack years ago. He knows the law. He doesn't like some things my dad has been doing. Says he'd never have allowed it in his day. He'd tell you."

"Am I breaking a law or something?"

"Nope, not at all. It's good for Cole," she replied.

Cole pulled the car up out the front of Jessies home. A blur raced to the car. Before I could get wards up to fend off whoever was attacking us, Jessie yelped and was pulled from the car. Cole placed his hand on my arm as I recognised Brad and his wife, engulfing Jessie in their arms. I nodded silently. Parenting was hard, especially when your daughter could walk in shadows.

3

— · —

Waiting in the car while Cole sorted out pack business was comfortable; the leather was soft and smelled new. The seats were heated and my bottom and lower back were happy. My fingers were still cold. I slid them under my legs to help warm them up. I figured the pack might not like me interfering again. I'd helped rescue Jessie before and both times I sensed it was partially my fault that she was attacked and abducted. Jessie had been attacked by Wraiths who had drained her life force and I had had to pull her back from death, which had caused a mutation in her abilities.

She'd been born a shifter, but now she was a shifter who could talk to the dead and apparently walk in the shadows. A shiver rolled through my shoulders as I imagined her father getting that news. Brad was the local alpha of the shifters. He had enough to deal with, without having a daughter who could disappear at whim walking through the shadow realm. I hadn't tried to walk through it much myself. Every time I tried, I ended up having a good old conversation with Dad.

One of my parents is Death. It had made a bargain with my earthly mother to help her stop the Blood Witches unleashing hell on Earth and in return it had implanted me. So, my Dad was Death. I still had yet to work out the actual biological absurdity of such an event, but I took it at face value. Death said I was part of it and who was I to argue? Being the daughter of death had its perks. If I tried hard enough, I could bring people back from the dead, like Jessie, but I found it altered them in ways I had no control of and sometimes that wasn't a good thing. I rarely used the powers. I preferred to punch people who annoyed me than using my magic.

Cole opened the car door again and slid into the driver's seat. The fragrance of chocolate and wood-fire followed him. It set my stomach gurgling. It reminded me that I hadn't eaten since the start of my shift many hours before.

I rubbed at my belly. "Sorry."

Cole's eyebrow raised and then he gave me a knowing smile. "Let's stop at the Shack and get some food."

"You read my mind." My stomach gurgled once more in agreement.

Wayland City had many features that the mayor tried to sell to tourists, including a revamped waterfront which housed new shops and restaurants. However, the best kept secret was a little café by the bay that had an old neon green and pink sign flickering in the dark of night. The Sugar Shack was frequented by night owls and police in equal number. It served the best doughnuts in the world and had as good burgers and fries. Plus, as a security guard, I received fifty percent discount. It ended up being a mainstay in my diet when Josie wasn't cooking massive feasts at Coven House. We pulled into the deserted parking lot and made our way inside.

Emerald, the usual waitress, wasn't working. Marty, the owner, was in the kitchen frying onions and something barbeque-y that set my tastebuds on fire. I clanged the little bell on the counter and offered him a big grin when he came out to the front.

"Whatever you're cooking I'll have a double."

Marty's crooked smile greeted me. "Stack Burger Deluxe?"

"Yes, thanks."

Marty glanced at Cole, sighed and grumbled something about shifters I couldn't hear. I sent Cole a querying look, but he remained steadfastly indifferent.

I slid into my favourite booth. "What's that all about?"

"He thinks I need to eat more vegetables," Cole grumbled.

"Veges?"

"I'm bad for the business because I don't eat the greens," he replied.

"Greens are good for you." I stacked all the innocence I could muster in my tone.

"Shifters don't need them."

"Everyone needs greens. Your bowels will thank you."

"Shifters don't eat greens," Cole grumbled again as he stared into the kitchen.

Marty clattered around and eventually came back out with our meals.

"This looks so good, thanks Marty." I stared at the deliciousness Marty placed in front of me.

Cole nodded once at the plate Marty set in front of him. Steak was stacked high on the plate, no sauces or greens to be seen. Marty shook his head and headed back to the kitchen.

"Do you want any sauces or fries or anything like that?" I took a big bite of my burger.

Cole gave me a deadpan stare and cut into his plain steak, the middle of which was red and flowing with juices.

I chewed and swallowed my food then sent him a quick raised eyebrow. Cole was big enough to defend himself. "Okay, be like that. Greens would go well with it, though."

Cole shook his head and kept slicing into the meat on his plate.

We ate in silence. The pineapple Marty had slipped into my burger was cooked to perfection. Its juices slid down my chin.

Cole reached out and wiped the remnants away with his finger, a burgeoning smile accompanying his gaze.

"What?" I grabbed a serviette to dab the rest of the mess on my face. "That's how you can tell it's good. The messier I get the better the meal."

"I'll remember that."

A blush flushed through my cheeks at the way he stared at me and I glared furiously at my food, trying not to let my imagination run wild. It didn't need any encouragement and I'd been having a hard time keeping my thoughts focused when he was around. So, I ate my last chip and sat back with my stomach sated.

"Jessie can shadow walk."

Cole grumbled and pushed his plate away. "I figured as much."

"It's dangerous. If you stay in the shadow world too long, you can forget yourself and get lost." I wasn't an expert at any rate, but every time I'd gone into the realm between the living and the dead I didn't stay long. It was spooky. Things were there that I did not want to meet and so I kept my time short and sweet.

Cole nodded for me to continue.

"The ghosts are gone from this area. I can smell it. Well, not smell, but sense, they're not around anymore. They usually give off a vibe that you can tell when one is near, but nothing. Something or someone has cleaned Wayland City out."

"And you think your grandmother is involved?"

I was about to answer when Marty came back out of the kitchen with a stack of doughnuts and placed them in front of me.

I gave him a grin as I tidied my plate for him to take. "Marty, this was the best burger I've had, thank you."

"You'll enjoy these." Marty shot Cole a suspicious glance.

I gave Cole a quick glance and then looked back at Marty. "Do they have hidden greens in them?"

Marty stopped lifting the plates and looked as if I'd given him an idea. "No, but I should."

"Always happy to help." I poked my tongue out to Cole who was looking dangerously like I'd crossed the line to interfere with his food.

"They wouldn't even know, would they?" Marty chuckled. A grin placed firmly back on his face as he walked the dishes back to the kitchen.

"I had to." I picked one of the hot doughnuts up off the plate.

Cole sighed and watched me consume the glorious sugar-coated delight without a word. I couldn't tell if he was tired or frustrated.

"A penny for your thoughts." I finished the first doughnut and then picked up another. This time I picked it apart before taking my time inhaling it.

"I don't know what's the right thing to do." Cole's voice barely made it across the table to me.

"One foot in front of the other."

He nodded.

"You could help me eat these." I pointed at the stack I'd barely made a dint in.

He sighed again; the tension easing in the muscles around his eyes as he picked one up.

"Careful, they're more-ish."

He offered a quizzical look.

"You take one and then you have to have more, so more-ish." I scrunched my lip returning his look. It was the easiest thing in the world to understand.

His shoulders relaxed as he grabbed a second doughnut.

A cold menace rolled through the air towards me, sending me instantly into fight-or-flight mode. Cole was even faster on his feet than I. His irises blazed sigma blue as a pot clattered in the back. We turned as one to see Marty backing out of his kitchen, his head shaking in disbelief.

"Marty, it might be time to close up." I grabbed every bit of cutlery I could ready to meld it into a makeshift weapon.

Cole didn't need weapons. His training kept him ready for a fight at any minute. He strode toward the kitchen, his shoulders square, his feet light, ready to deal with anything that came his way. I pushed some of my energy into the metal I held in my hand and formed a sturdy little knife, not long enough to be called a sword. Both sides of the blade were razor sharp. I nicked the inside of my left arm and merged my blood with the blade. It would last longer now. With a heated breath, I strode directly after Cole.

Anger rolled through the kitchen, but I couldn't pin point where the creature was. It flittered sideways, then back again. Poltergeist. Someone had contaminated the remnants of humanity and left only rage. I tapped Cole on the shoulder and he stepped aside without a word.

"Okay, come out." I centred on acting bored as if I had better things to do with my night than deal with their ghostly crap.

A knife came hurtling towards me from the left side of the room, but dropped a metre from my body.

"Really? You know before you couldn't even move a single thing, now you've changed you can pick up knives?"

Another followed in its wake. It didn't make the distance.

"Come to me," I commanded, my voice dropping as I gathered my parents' power into the centre of my chest.

Several pans fell. Luckily they were too heavy for the entity to throw. Marty only used the best cast iron skillets for cooking.

"Come to me." I didn't not raise my voice.

I could feel the shades' reluctance pushing at the edges of my mind, yet it had to comply. Death magic couldn't be ignored.

Its body coalesced in front of me into a grimy grey cloud that resembled a shade I'd seen Jessie talking with weeks ago.

"You're the alpha," I stated.

The shade nodded and then his face changed as if he was gripped by pain and his wolf emerged snarling ready to fight.

Cole stepped forward, his face stern. I put my hand on the top of his arm and shook my head.

"I can stop the pain. Come through me. You deserve to rest."

The wolf and man stopped struggling long enough for me to see the binding on its form. It resembled a black sludge at the edge of my vision when I stared at him. I'd seen this before, blood magic.

"Come through me."

The binding flared. Even blood magic could not overcome death. I pulled deeper from within me and reached out to the shade. He took my hand and passed through. As he did so, I caught glimpses of his life. He was a pack leader nearly a century before. He'd known Cole as a pup. He had died fighting blood witches and had been snared a week ago by another one. His wolf gripped my mind, sending a warning not to trust anyone, but before I could ask the two of them faded into the netherworld. If I wanted to, I could race after them but the cost on my body would be exhaustion for days and I couldn't afford to lose any energy. I still slumped back and was grateful Cole had caught me before I tumbled to the floor.

"Well, don't that beat the shit out of things." Marty looked into the kitchen, a frying pan raised to protect himself.

"Yep, beats the shit out of me." I leaned further into Cole's chest. I could snuggle there for hours if I wanted to but the thoughts the alpha had given me were alarming. Snuggling would have to wait. The burners were still flaming away. Someone should turn those off, but I didn't voice my thoughts.

"You do this often?" Marty asked.

"Nope, this was a first, but hey if you know of anyone that needs a ghost busted, I'm your man."

Marty let out a chortle and then a long whistle. "For a bloody ghost, it did a bit of damage."

"Nothing that can't be fixed." I stepped past him and found the first chair then plunked myself into it.

"I think you need some sugar," Marty stated matter-of-factly.

"Always." My answering smile didn't have the same enthusiasm as it normally would when faced with that statement. My legs were beginning to shake even as I sat. Exhaustion caused by ghost hunting was new.

Cole pulled out the chair beside me and sat, his eyes full of questions that he knew not to ask when Marty was still in the room. I sighed and placed my forehead on the countertop. It was nice and cold. I could nap right there.

"You need to take her home, out too late as it is." Marty faced Cole with a hint of disapproval as he rustled a paper bag.

Cole remained quiet as I looked up. Marty held a bag full of doughnuts.

"I can pay you for those."

Both men stared at me as if I'd grown a second head. Cole stood and held out his hand for me, taking the bag of doughnuts in his other hand.

"Girl you saved me a hell of a lot of money getting rid of that ghost. The least I can do is pay you in doughnuts," Marty said.

"It was nothing." My legs were shaky as I stood.

"Go home, get some rest, ghost buster. You deserve it," he replied.

"I could get used to that name. Better than what some people call me."

Marty focused his attention on Cole, kindness melting off his face into stone cold meanness. "Take care of her."

I half expected Cole to roll his eyes like a rebellious teen talking to his girlfriend's dad, but he dipped his head in acknowledgement and steered me out of the café without a word.

"He doesn't like you," I whispered as we drove away. "What did you do? Insult his cooking?"

Cole's annoyance drove across his face and settled his darkened brows into a frown.

"You did. You insulted Marty's cooking. Oh boy, it's lucky I was there or you might not have been served."

"Something like that," he replied.

I would wait and find out the story. One thing about me, I didn't let go of a good tale. And with Cole, I was obsessed.

4

_ . _

Instead of taking me to Coven House Cole drove to his place. I woke up as he pulled into his garage.

"Have I told you I love this car?" I grumbled as I got out.

"Many times."

Cole held my hand as we took the stairs up to his living room. It was a chivalrous gesture but comforting at the same time. The way my legs were feeling I probably would have accepted him carrying me up the stairs like some medieval knight intent on taking my virtue. The thought almost had me in giggles. Chain mail would look good on him.

The living room was softly lit. The fireplace had turned on automatically when we entered the room. I grabbed the big fluffy blanket on the edge of the couch and curled up on it. I should invest in better blankets myself, but I hadn't gotten around to it yet. Too much time training the new witches to even think about shopping for blankets and clothes.

Cole had left me on the couch while he boiled the kettle. The bag of doughnuts was a little too far for me to reach without having to take my arms out of the fluffy blanket. I tossed up the idea of leaving its embrace for the sugar and then quit. The blanket won the fight and I laid back against his leather couch, watching the flames dance in the fireplace.

"You okay?"

"Hmm? Yeah, you know, it takes the energy out of you." A smile came to my face as I saw what he held in his hand. "For me?"

I let my arms emerge from the blanket and took the mug from him. Chocolatey goodness assailed my nose. I took the time to reach over and bring the bag of doughnuts to me as well. Marty had filled it with Pete's favourite type Double Choc Caramel. If this didn't give me energy, it surely would give me diabetes. I bit into one and closed my eyes.

"You want to tell me what he said," Cole said after I'd swallowed my mouthful.

"The alpha? How'd you know?"

"You got that sad air about you when he passed through. I knew he told you something you didn't want to know," Cole replied.

"He was alpha when you were little. He remembered you fondly, I think. He was killed by blood witches, the first time. His life wasn't finished and he stuck around to protect the pack."

Cole nodded as I took a sip of my drink. "I am pretty sure my grandmother turned him poltergeist." I tried to stop the waver in my voice.

"We knew she was coming."

"Yes, we did." I let out a long sigh. "His wolf told me not to trust anyone."

Cole's eyes widened at my words. "His wolf?"

"Yeah, he was pissed about the blood witch thing. He was the one throwing stuff around."

"I thought when you die, the wolf," Cole's words faded off.

"Nope, you are together for eternity. Kind of neat, huh?"

It was Cole's turn to sit back in shock. He rubbed at his eyelids.

"Anyway, his wolf told me not to trust anyone, that there's more going on than we know," I replied. "I think she's keeping the other ghosts in reserve. She couldn't control the wolf part of the alpha, so they escaped to warn us."

"Shit."

"Indeed. Anyway, my grandmother is in town. She's going to make life hell for everyone and she'll try to kill me first chance she gets." I took another big swig of drink then pulled the last of the doughnuts out of the packet. I offered it to Cole and he shook his head. More fool him. These were the best.

"What about the witch hunters?"

"I don't know. We're going to have to find out." I swallowed the mouthful of chocolate before continuing. "We don't want a pack of witch hunters attacking supernaturals when we're trying to defeat the Blood Witch Queen."

Cole leaned further back on the couch. I snuggled closer after putting my empty cup on the table. Cole had frowned when I'd missed the coaster and I'd rolled my eyes at him and put it on the coaster proper. For a wolf, he was awfully fussy.

"You know, you could turn wolf for me so I could be warm," I whispered up at him.

"I know how to make you warm." A mischievous grin started in the corner of his mouth.

"Are you threatening me with a good time, Mr Sigma?"

He leaned closer, his lips almost touching mine as his gaze bore through me, seeking permission. My breath hitched as the rest of my body eagerly responded to the scent of him. If he didn't move faster, I would have to jump him and have my way. My nether regions agreed. I reached my arm around his neck to pull him closer when a booming on his front door rattled me enough that I head-butted him instead.

"Who the absolute hell is that?" I threw off my blanket.

Cole moved faster than I could and was at the door before I stood. The man could move fast when he wanted to. A part of my brain wanted to complain about fast movements and slow seductions, but then I saw who was standing in the doorway drenched from the winter rain. Raoul, usually so impeccably dressed, stood waiting for me to reach the door.

"What's happened?" I asked.

Cole stood with his hand still on the door as if he was of two minds regarding slamming it in the vamps' face.

"Metalsmith, I need your help," Raoul stated. "You can't tell the King."

"Rory?"

Raoul nodded. "We need your special skills."

I frowned. I had many skills, some of them included eating a hotdog in less than ten seconds and being able to pick locks in under three. I scratched at the back of my neck. If Rory wasn't allowed to know what was going on, I knew that it was trouble.

I turned to Cole. "Can you let him in?"

Cole hesitated.

"I will not enter. I will await your decision here," Raoul's urbane tone had a courteous edge, as if he was simply waiting for a Sunday lunch invitation and not standing in the squalling rain waiting for our answer.

"Oh, right. Look I've only just got home, I'm buggered. Is it that bad you can't let Rory know?"

"He has beheaded people for less." Raoul would not meet my gaze.

"Fine. Let me get my things." I leaned a hand against the door.

Cole put his hand on my forearm, stopping my movement.

"The sun is about to rise. She has had no sleep. Think carefully about what you ask her. Is it that important that she must go now?" Coles voice was deeper than usual. If he used that voice on me, I would cave and do whatever he told me. Daddy vibes galore.

"I would not come if it were not dire," Raoul stated.

Cole nodded and shut the door on him. "Let's get our things."

I frowned. "Our things?"

"Where you go, I go." He glided over to the table and grabbed his keys. Shifter movement was so natural, not like my uncoordinated mess.

"I want to go to bed and drown in pillows and blankets and stuff," I deliberately left out what type of stuff I'd like to be doing.

He walked to the closet in the hallway and pulled out a coat then handed it to me. It was wool, but the inlay was soft and snuggly. I put it on.

"Where do you shop? This is amazing."

Cole gestured to the garage, all those stairs. I sighed and started down them, then focused my attention on to him.

"Shouldn't we tell Raoul we're coming?"

"He heard, he'll be at his car to guide us where ever we need to go," Cole replied.

I nodded and strode to the car. Cole had several in his garage. For an underground lair, it was brightly lit. I thought about suggesting he dim the lights to make it more menacing, but my body was too tired to voice any sarcasm. His car for this early in the morning was a black SUV that had reinforced everything. I had hoped we'd take my favourite with the custom seats. He'd opted for the security vehicle instead. One day I'd get my own car, but so far, I'd managed without one. Cars were useful, but they cost a lot in upkeep and I was barely making ends meet as it was.

I shut my eyes for a minute, comfortable knowing that Cole would get us to wherever Raoul needed us to be, but then Cole woke me up.

My tongue was parched as I pushed my head away from the window. "Was I snoring?"

"Only a little," Cole whispered as a wry smile pulled at the edges of his tired eyes.

"Damn it, Cole. I don't snore." I wiped the drool off my face and then replaced it with a yawn. I needed a good night's sleep with no interruptions from vamps, ghosts or worse.

"We're here." Cole turned the car off.

"Where's here?" I looked out the window, reluctant to move from the warm leather seat.

We were outside a dark warehouse that would make the perfect horror movie set. Isolated, dingy, with metal chains hanging from the rafters. Truth be told, I was safer here than anywhere else. The metal surrounding me called to me. I could make so many amazing things with it. I willed my fingers to stop itching and undid my seatbelt.

"Chop shop, I'm guessing," Cole replied.

I opened my door and stepped out as Raoul turned the lights on. The place was a mess. Half disassembled car bodies were strewn across the floor. Dark patches of ash scattered across the floor.

"What are those?" I asked no one in particular.

"Remnants." Raoul had a sharpness not usually present in his urbane tone, as if someone had hurt him badly and he was trying to remain calm and failing.

"Of what?" I stepped up to one and scuffed the edge of the ash with the toe of my boot.

"My friends." Raoul walked past me not looking at the floor. His tone held sorrow and frustration in equal parts.

I pulled my foot back. "Sorry."

Raoul made his way around the piles and beckoned me into the office on the side of the warehouse.

I wondered if I should wipe the ash off my feet. An icky sense of betrayal swept over me knowing I'd kicked his friends remains around.

"Who did this?" Cole's voice was low and calm, his shoulders taut, as if ready for a fight.

"We thought it was witch hunters, but they would have left a calling card. Instead, we're left with piles and nothing else," Raoul said.

"There's been more than one of these attacks?" I took a seat behind the desk.

Raoul nodded. "This is the third. They started happening about two weeks ago."

"What's his majesty doing about it?"

"The King is busy right now." Raoul refused to meet my gaze.

I leaned back in the chair, put my feet up on his desk and folded my hands over my belly. "Spill."

Raoul looked at me with the type of fake, innocent gaze that only guilty people can give. His gaze then progressed to my feet on his oak desk and a tightness came to his eyes. He turned away, thinking I'd not seen.

I put my feet down, no need to upset the vampire further. "Rory would go out of his mind if he knew his people were being slaughtered like this. I counted five vamps dead out there, probably more. And this is your third attack, so you're losing people. You asked for my help, so spill your guts and I'll see what I can do."

Raoul pushed his hand through his damp hair as he paced the room. "We can't work out who's attacking us. If we knew where it was coming from, we could prevent it. Joseph thinks that it might be rival vamps trying to move in on our territory."

"Not possible." Cole crossed his arms as he leaned against the side of the desk.

Raoul nodded. "I know. Then we thought it might be the hunters. They'll kill us as easily as they kill witches. But there's no evidence for them. And the humans don't have the capabilities of taking out a full-grown vamp, not unless someone's helping them."

I winced. Of course, someone would help them. I knew who that someone was. She was the type of person who would use anyone or anything to achieve her goal.

"You know something?" Raoul's words were clipped with pain as if he thought I had betrayed him.

"My grandmother. She can do this and worse."

Raoul frowned. "A Blood Witch? Why wouldn't she turn them into Wraiths?"

"She doesn't need their power, she's siphoned the dead recently and she would have taken some of the energy from your people, but making and keeping Wraiths takes time. This was a fast attack. None of your men would have known she was there. It was over before they could blink."

"You can do this?" Raoul's look of terror worried me.

"I wouldn't. Only those who are desperate delve into this type of magic. It has...unforeseen consequences." Like your skin splitting open and your flesh necrotising as you try to wield the magic. I shivered. I'd seen it happen once to a witch who'd been desperate to get away from my grandmother and her punishment. It turned out that by wielding the magic she killed herself anyway and did no damage to the council at all.

"Then how has she survived three attacks on our people?" Raoul had come to a complete stop. If I didn't see his mouth move, I'd thought he was a marble statue.

"She's found a way. Adapt, improvise, overcome. Gran is the best of the best in dark magic." A shiver rolled down my spine.

"Why haven't you told your master?" Concern radiated from Cole as he placed himself between Raoul and me.

"The King has been trying to sort out other issues. This seemed like witch hunter work or similar. I had no idea." Raoul moved towards the cabinet near the door.

"He needs to know."

Raoul nodded, pouring himself a drink from an old decanter. The odour of zinc and iron was strong. The vamps were using synthetic blood again, or at least this one was.

"We've lost twenty of our people. No, twenty-five." Raoul took another swig. His lips stained by the liquid.

"How many vamps are in this city?" I ignored the worried look Raoul gave me before continuing, "do you want me to tell him?"

Raoul put his drink down, his shoulders sagging. "I have failed him."

"You know who would be good at working out what's going on?"

"You can't ask me to work with that woman," Raoul replied, before I could even suggest a name.

"Detective Pearce is a good cop. And what do you have against her?"

"She is a nuisance, changing our ways." He waved his hand in the air.

"She's acerbic, likes to swear, but you should be used to that. Weren't you a soldier?"

"I had hoped you could help me." Raoul's face fell, he looked like he was fated for true death.

"Don't be a misogynist Raoul. She will help, she'll do it to piss Rory off, of course. But she's our best bet."

I moved closer to him, skirting around Cole who tried to block me with his large shoulders. Raoul had again frozen on the spot.

"My grandmother will wipe out every vamp in this city, every shifter, every witch, every human to get what she wants. We need to know how she's found out where your people are and how she can attack without warning and kill so many. Pearce is our best hope." I crossed the room to him.

He shivered as if I'd poured ice water down his back. "She's so..."

"Good at what she does," I finished his sentence for him.

Yes, Pearce was a bitch who would cuss a person out for every mistake they'd ever made and make them feel like absolute garbage for not improving themselves. But I'd seen that deep down she could be kind. Deep, deep down.

"We'll need to inform the pack." Cole's soft voice came from behind me.

It hadn't surprised me that Cole had shifted to being close enough that he could rip off the vamps' head before I got a single word out should I need him. He also was good at what he did. Not that I needed his help. But it was nice to know I had backup.

I tried to stop the yawn from escaping, but I'd been on my feet for twenty-six hours and I desperately needed a proper nap.

"I need to go home. I'll sleep and then we'll work on this. She's not going to strike again tonight. She'll need time to regroup. Tell Rory. I can't believe he doesn't already know."

"He's having some troubles and this would push him over the edge," Raoul whispered.

"What troubles? Why hasn't he told me?"

Raoul glanced pointedly at Cole, who raised his hands and stepped outside without a word.

"There are other vampires in the world. Word has got out that there is a cure." Raoul's voice was barely a whisper.

I knew Cole could hear every word we said but he'd attempted to go outside the office and that was a nice gesture.

"Cure?"

"To being a vampire."

This time it was me raising my eyebrows to new heights.

"No, there's not."

Raoul took a breath, which he hardly ever did, as if he was being incredibly patient, trying to explain something simple to someone who didn't get it. "The book you showed him. There was a passage regarding mortality and restoring vampires."

"I don't remember that." I scratched the back of my neck.

"Word got out and now the older vampires are involved. Rory has been trying to stave them off from coming to Wayland City to find the cure," Raoul said. "Some want it for themselves, some want to get rid of it permanently so it can't be used against them."

"What is this cure?"

"It involves you," he replied.

"Of course. When has anything of earth-shattering importance not involved me lately?" I scoffed but deep down my stomach roiled at the thought of being the centre of attention of some of the world's oldest and deadliest creatures. I wanted to go to work, come home and sleep.

"You are Death's daughter. You can resurrect the dead," Raoul said. "Your blood changes us."

I gave a little huff and pointed at the tall man. "You're still you."

"I'm different." His sigh held a note of worry. "I can no longer drink. I have been reduced to this."

He pointed at the bottle of synthetic blood I'd seen earlier.

"So, I tainted you? I'm sorry."

He shook his head. "You don't understand. It's a good thing. I have struggled for centuries with what I am."

I followed Raoul as he walked from the office to the open doorway of the warehouse that our cars had come through. The sun was rising on the horizon and I wondered if I should step in and stop him from doing anything stupid.

As I came up beside him, I noted that Cole was still leaning against his car. He had made calls, of that, I was sure. Now he was sending me a quizzical look as Raoul waited for the first rays of the morning to pierce through the cloud bank over the water.

I placed my hand on Raoul's arm. "Come on. There's no time for this. You have a job to do and I need to help you fix this mess."

"Wait." He placed his coldish hand over mine. "Just wait."

My heart sped up. "Joseph is looking for you right now. We can't keep him waiting." Joseph was his partner. The vamp, formerly known as Slayer, would skin me alive if I let Raoul commit suicide by sunlight this morning. I pulled at his hand. He let go and placed his arm around my shoulders in a friendly gesture.

"Watch." He had a beatific smile on his face.

"No, no. You're going to get me into trouble. Rory will kill me. Joseph certainly will as well. You come back inside."

It was hard to move a vampire when they had set themselves to a task. I peered over my shoulder at Cole who had dropped his phone and was about to leap towards me when the sunlight hit us like a floodlight on a darkened stage. I turned in fear, looking up at Raoul, worrying that his skin would smoke any minute now.

Nothing happened. He stood perfectly still, his eyes wide open, the rays of the sun hitting his skin and not burning.

"What have you done?" I pushed myself away from him as Cole reached my right arm and swung me around set to fight the vamp.

"You did this. You changed me." Raoul's tone was full of worshipful devotion.

I stood staring at him over Cole's shoulder. The full impact of my donating blood to save Raoul from ultimate death hit me.

"What have I done?"

5

Raoul let out a deep sigh and turned back to me all business. "I never thought I'd see sunlight again."

"Well, you're welcome, I guess. I didn't know. I didn't want you to die, you know?'

"It's something we've tried to keep quiet. That's what his majesty is doing. The others think there is a cure, a potion or something that can help them. If they knew it was you..." His words trailed off as Cole flexed his muscles.

"Well, I'm glad he's keeping me on the down-low. I don't know how I've done this."

Cole still had me wedged behind him and the vamp. It was a gracious thing to do, but I didn't need saving right then. Raoul was anything but a ravenous monster out to get me. The look he sent me was of devotion.

"I have no answers either. When I came to, I knew something was different. It wasn't until I tried to feed a week later that I found I couldn't. I eventually took myself off to face the sun. I'd let everyone down. Then when the light didn't burn me, I knew. You'd saved me."

"I didn't save you. You didn't need saving. I gave you some of my blood to keep you from dying," I said. "I'd given a drop to Rory before that, but it didn't change him."

"Yes and that's the thing. You hadn't used your magic much before you gave him your blood, but you'd changed somehow when you helped me." He moved out of the sunlight and strolling over to his car.

"I don't know what I did differently."

"Well, we need to keep you a secret. No one knows, except my King and Joseph," Raoul replied.

"See that it stays that way," Cole growled.

"Ah Sigma, she is a delight in my old age. You misunderstand me, I would never harm my saviour. But there are others out there that if they got wind, they would wipe out this city to get to her."

With a shiver, I stood taller. "Well, they'd have to get through my grandmother first. We need to make sure that we stop her before your marauding vamps get the chance to have a bite."

Raoul gave me a baleful stare and eventually blinked before letting out a huff of breath. "I will talk to the Detective."

"She's our best bet." Another yawn escaped me.

"Go home Lucy."

I nodded and let Cole guide me to his car. It had been a long day, night, time period. I needed sleep before I could work out how to stop my raging Blood Witch of a grandmother from wiping out all I loved and held dear. If only I could click my heels three times and this whole thing would be over. I had tried clicking in case about a week ago, but nothing had happened. Luckily, I had been alone. No need for anyone else to think I might lose my marbles.

I had Cole drop me off at Coven House. While I would love to spend the morning with him. I needed sleep and he was far too tempting for me to get any sleep. My libido hated me, but I slept like a log, right up until a boom echoed throughout the house.

"I'm up, I'm up!" I rolled out of my bed and crawled across the floor to reach my machete.

"Sorry," a voice yelled from underneath my room.

The trainees were at it again. Maybe I should have gone and hung out with Cole. I rolled onto my back and decided I could camp there for a few more hours sleep. My door creaked open and Josie stuck her head around with a sheepish grin.

"Um, did we wake you?" She held out a double hot chocolate that appeared to only have sugar in it and not some herbal remedy she was usually trying to chuck down my throat.

"Yes." I sat and scratched at my head. I think I hit it on the floor during my flight from the covers.

Josie crossed the floor and gave me the drink.

I sniffed it with caution. She'd caught me one too many times with her sneaky herbal remedies for me ever to trust her fully with beverages.

"It's chocolate. Quit worrying." She crossed her arms under her ample bosoms. Her outfit held them in place, just.

"You never know." I took a hesitant sip. It was good. Dark choc with a creamy smoothness that hit the spot. "What were the kids doing?"

"They tried to use circle magic." She blew a stray strand of red curls out of her eyes.

"How did it go boom?" I took another gulp of my drink and crossed my legs. My machete was still beside me, so I pushed it with my free hand under my bed. There were quite a few weapons stored there. I had thought I'd meld them all so no one would nick themselves on the blades, but that was another job I'd put off. I'd been going through a real lack of will with magic these past few weeks. I determined that I would fix my problem once I'd dealt with my grandmother and the vamps and all the rest of the junk Wayland City would throw at me in the next little while. Eventually, eventually I would deal with my procrastination.

"They merged two circles, things proceeded well, then they tried to add a third." Josie gave a sheepish grin.

"And you didn't warn them why?"

"They wouldn't listen. They thought they knew better than me," she replied with a huff.

"Eyebrows gone?"

"A few, but they're micro-bladed anyway so they can draw them back on."

"How's the salon going?"

Some of Josie's witches had started their own salon, making all the products themselves. It was a hit with the nouveau riche who were trying hard to become known in the city. Josie's Café was run by Benji's girlfriend Sarah, as Josie didn't have time to keep up with everything.

"It's taking off. We even had some shifter teens come in this week, so things are looking up." The chair squeaked as she sat next to me.

I drained the cup and stood up, my knees creaking along with my back as I did so.

"Got little sleep?" she asked.

"The bags under my eyes have their own set of luggage, don't they?"

She squinted as if trying to see better. "Let's say Cole made me promise we'd let you get at least five hours."

"Well, I got some sleep. I guess that's the best I can do right now. How bad is downstairs?" I took my cup back to the sink in the kitchen.

"It smells of singed hair, but not bad," she replied.

It was hard trudging down the stairs. My legs were wobbly and my brain was still fuzzy from sleep. The floor had two nicely drawn magic circles, but the third intersected at the wrong junction. Who taught these kids? Circle theorem was easy. This should be first year apprentice magic. I turned and noted that Josie had a grin on her face.

"Told you they wouldn't listen," she replied. "I should get my teacher to come deal with them. She wouldn't put up with this rubbish."

"You had a teacher?" I'd forgotten that Josie had grown up a white witch and that there were schools where young witches studied how to work with their magic.

"Yep, tough old broad, if you didn't get it right you didn't leave the room until you did. Mistress Kable scared the life out of many of my peers." Josie's tone was full of glee.

"But not you?"

"Nope, I was her favourite. Circle magic is math and math is the easiest thing in the world," she replied.

I threw her the nastiest stare I could. "Math is easy? This coming from you?"

"Well applied math, all the multiplication and stuff sucks, but circle theorem is easy. It's so simple, I can't believe these girls don't get it."

"You'd better send for Mistress Kable then, because I'm losing my patience with your charges. Besides, some things have come up. I won't have time to help." I sighed at the knowledge that I didn't have time to get everything done that I need to.

Josie arched a perfectly bladed eyebrow and waited for me to continue. Never try to out-stare a white witch. They've spent years perfecting standing still over their kitchen pots, waiting for the chemicals to react. They will outlast anyone in a one-on-one staring match even against wolves.

I let out a huff and continued. "My grandmother is here. She's killed some vamps and has harvested all the ghosts in the area."

Colour drained from Josies' face. "She's here? My girls aren't ready."

I ran my hand over the bottom of my neck. "I never meant for you to get involved in this. If I could, I'd run and fight her where no one could get hurt."

"That's nonsense. We're here with you. Don't you go doing stupid things. Look where that got us last time," she replied.

She was right. I had tried fighting on my own before and that had led to too many getting hurt. When I accepted help, things became easier.

"I can see what you're thinking." Her tone held a warning note, she knew me and what I was willing to do to keep everyone safe.

"What? I'm not thinking anything."

"You're going to confront the old woman head on in a one on one and try not to include any of us to help you. Then you're going to get yourself killed in the process and the wicked Blood Witch will come and slaughter us. It's better if we all work together to take her down. As powerful as she is, she can't stop all of us."

"I know you're right. It goes against everything I've tried to do. I don't want anyone getting hurt because of me. I should have left years ago," I muttered.

"And done what? Run for the rest of your or her life? What a shitty life that would have been."

I ran both hands through my hair. I had tangles on tangles and it was good pulling at them when I didn't want to think of a way to stop Josie from interfering in my fight. "I can't guarantee that you will survive. She's the most powerful of our clan in four hundred years. She's spent her long-life perfecting taking energy from others. She drained five vampires before they could even respond. I don't know how she's doing it."

Josie slung her arm over my shoulder and steered me towards the bathroom. "We will work it out. Right now, you need to go have a shower. We'll work it out afterwards."

"You're saying I stink?" I put extra emphasis on the word stink.

"Yep. You must be exhausted if you can't smell yourself. Go bathe, we'll figure something out. I'm going to call Mistress Kable. She's my best bet at stopping these girls from blowing themselves up. Your best bet is to use the heavy detangle shampoo and conditioner the girls brewed up last week." Josie lifted a strand of my hair with her fingers. There were knots in my knots.

"Fine," I replied with a huff.

Josie was right. I felt a lot better after having a long shower. Several strands of hair had been sacrificed when trying to brush out the knots. Even the detangle solution couldn't work miracles.

Benji and Sarah were sitting in the kitchen when I came out. Both had huge grins on their faces and the other witches were gathered around, whispering excitedly to each other.

"Finally," Benji said. "Thought you were going to drown yourself in there."

"Nope, I tried, but it didn't work. What are you looking so happy for? Did you score free doughnuts again?"

Benji was once the head of the gang that hung around my old apartment. He was caught doing something and his grandma made him straighten up. So, he became my trainee at Swift Security and had passed with flying colours. He now had taken up his own route and I think Marg was training him to take over the business. She'd mentioned it to me once in passing. I almost choked on my tea when she had suggested it. For all his faults, Benji was a stand-up guy. You could count on him when things went wrong.

He was also deeply in love with Sarah, a white witch who ran Josie's Café. They both had enormous grins on their faces.

"Nope, better than that," Benji said as a blush rolled across his cheeks.

Sarah extended her left hand and, sitting prettily on her ring finger, was a tiny diamond.

"Congratulations," I said automatically. "When's the big day?"

Benji shrugged. "I got to this part. We haven't set a date yet."

"How's grandma taking it?"

Sarah stepped forward. "She is thrilled. I think she wants him married off before she goes."

Pain rolled across Benji's face.

"Is your grandmother not well?" I asked Benji.

"She's got cancer. Nothing we've done is helping. Doctors say it's time. She's in her eighties, but you wouldn't know it," he said.

"So, you are going to have a fast wedding?"

"I want her there," Sarah said. "And all of you, we can't get married without my coven."

"That will be nice." My gaze was still glued to Benji. He was trying hard to keep it together.

"We want a traditional wedding; the equinox is in a week. It's going to take a lot of work to get ready," Sarah said.

"Can you book a church in that short time?"

My statement led to the entire coven bursting out laughing.

"What?"

Josie came to stand beside me. Her expression shut all the younger witches up, but they still kept the grins. "Traditional witch wedding, Lucy. Witch wedding."

"Oh, why didn't you say so? What's involved?"

"Lots of alcohol, nakedness and blood," one of the younger girls whispered.

"What?" I settled my gaze on the girl, she was one of the shyer witches who rarely spoke up.

"She's kidding. That's what people say. A witch wedding is a lurid affair-type stuff. Nope, it's good food, good drink, plenty of dancing and the happy couple celebrating with family and friends," Josie said. "Oh, we have so much to do. I can't wait to get started."

I sat at the table and listened to the girls start their plans. Benji came over and sat beside me.

"This is bigger than I thought," he whispered.

"Always is. You okay?"

He nodded. "Yeah. I am happy. I don't know how I'm going to afford it, though. Might have to get the gang to help me out."

I tapped him on the hand. "Silly, the coven has more than enough money to cover all the costs. Josie won't let any of the girls pay for things like this."

A relief spread across his face, working its way down to his shoulders, then he shook his head. "Nah, I'm supposed to help here."

"Nope, bride's family takes care of the wedding, you take care of the alcohol and honeymoon. There will be a honeymoon won't there?"

"We've got the café to run and my shifts. We'll go during the off season," he said matter-of-factly.

"That's responsible of you." I held back my smile. "Who would have guessed that Credz was going to be made a respectable man? Not me."

"Enough crazy dog lady," he replied.

"Crazy hot dog lady and don't you forget it."

"Aren't you supposed to be taking them for a run?" he asked.

"I've postponed the run today. There are some things I have to deal with. I might have to stop the business altogether."

The thought of not seeing my pack twisted in my guts. I have two jobs, used to have three. One is security guard at night, it pays the bills and is not strenuous. The second is my dog running business. I have a bunch of regular dogs who come with me for a run. I'm safe and they get to enjoy the outdoors. I call them my pack. They are great dogs who sometimes get a little over enthusiastic. A few months ago, we'd found a dead body together. They'd saved me from many things.

"Shame, you know TJ can run. If you need someone to take over for a while, until you sort stuff out, call him," Benji said.

"TJ? As in scared rabbit who won't say boo whenever I'm near you guys? That TJ?"

"Yeah, he can run fast. Probably beat even you," Benji replied.

"Maybe I do need someone to help. I'll keep him in mind. Would he work with me?"

"Lady it's a job, he'll do it," Benji replied. "Or his mama will smack him over the head. Done that once or twice."

"Thanks, I'll think it over," I said as Sarah came back over from the coven huddle to put her arm around Benji. "Uh oh Benji, you'd better run. I've seen that look before."

"Hush," Sarah said. "Don't spoil it."

Benji gawped at her with devotion. "What can I do?"

"We've decided most things. Just need you to work out who's coming from your side and we're set," she replied.

"Told you," I whispered as I stood up. "You're done for now Credz."

"You know this respectable thing isn't half bad." He wrapped his arm around Sarah's waist and pulling her down into his lap.

"Eww, get a room you two." I made my way down to the training room. It was quieter here.

The witches had cleaned up their chalk drawings, leaving only the original pentagonal painted on the floor. I grabbed some chalk and strolled to the centre of the room and sat down. It had been a few days since I'd meditated. I needed to focus on finding my grandmother and working out how to stop her. She would stop at nothing to get me. I knew her goal was to use me to open a portal to the Fae realm where she would get immortality.

It was a pipe dream. There was no immortality, it was a lie given by a bunch of parasites willing to do anything to suck the power out of unsuspecting victims. I'd never thought of my grandmother as stupid before, but she was. She'd believed the words of beings that had infected our world centuries before. They'd been eradicated from this world, with a few exceptions and she'd clung to the belief that if she brought them back, she'd be rewarded with eternal life.

I let the thought go and dropped my thoughts deep into myself. The good thing about the training room was that it was soundproof to a degree. I couldn't hear any of the chatter from above and they couldn't hear anything I did down here unless I made things go boom. I drew in my magic and stepped out of myself. The netherworld is all around us, but humans don't see it. It operates at a different frequency than the mortal realm and only those who are attuned can see both. Jessie now could, after I'd brought her back from death. Some psychics could and most cats definitely could. That's why sometimes they get the zoomies at 2am, it's them fighting the ghosts in their houses. I didn't keep pets; I prefer to hand them back after I've had fun running with my pack. I am a dog person, really. Josie loved cats but lucky for me a few of the witches were allergic otherwise Coven House would crawl with the suckers. Vamps didn't like any pets. Shifters felt that keeping a pet was enslavement.

"I'm here. Can you talk?" I asked of the netherworld.

A mild susurration drew near. Like someone was sending tiny electrical sparks into my skin as it approached. I ignored the zaps and waited for my parent to materialise.

"What do you need?" Death asked. It had appeared again as an androgynous human with long silver hair and dark eyes with almost black irises.

"Can't we talk?"

"No," it replied.

"My mortal grandmother is here in Wayland City. She will kill everyone I love in order for me to open the portal to the Fae. How do I stop her?" If Death wanted to be precise in our dealings, I'd give it precise.

"She has gained power, drained many. She is searching for the portal," Death replied.

"It's hidden."

"She will find it. What will you do then?"

"Stop her."

"That is why you are here," Death turned and reached out into the nether, pulling back a strange-looking scroll.

"Is that what I need to stop her?"

"No, this is a prop. I thought you might need a little reassurance," Death replied.

Anger churned in my non-existent stomach. "Don't do that. If you know how to stop her tell me, I'll do what you say and we'll be done."

A wry smile twitched at the sides of Death's mouth. "We are never done Lucinda. We have many things to do, some soon. You already know how to stop her. You must destroy the portal from both sides otherwise it'll reopen one day."

"Both sides? How? That means I have to open it first and then close it? How can I be in both places at once?" I threw my hands up.

"To open it, you need a lot of energy, to close it the same. One opens, the other closes."

"You are no help at all."

"I think you'll work it out once you observe it for a while," Death replied.

"It's an interdimensional rift. The power to open it would be phenomenal. To close it from both sides? I can't do both. I can do one side, truly I can. Someone would have to go through and blast it from the other. Who'd do that?" I scratched at my eyebrow.

"That is the way it must be done, or it will open fully. We cannot have that," Death said.

"Yep, no shit Sherlock. I don't know how I can do both. Can't you give me a hint?"

"I am not Sherlock and no, I cannot."

"Thanks for nothing." My words bristling with condescension, which seemed to fly right over Death's head. Why couldn't they just tell me what to do and I would do it?

"You are angry. Once you calm down, you will see what you need to do." Death dematerialised before I could retort.

"Calm down? I'll show it calm down," I muttered as I stood up. My knees creaked and I was light-headed as I did so. "Stupid Death."

"Are you muttering to yourself again?" Josie asked from the stairs.

"Death told me to calm down. Can you believe that? Calm down. Who does it think it is?"

"Death?" Josie's tone was one of helpful, trying not to burst into laughter.

I grunted and shoved past her. "Not helping."

"I'll never get over the fact that you talk to Death, as if it's a person. It is mindboggling."

I turned on the stairs and huffed out another short breath. "Death is as annoying as any parent can be, so freakin' cryptic and doesn't offer any answers, more frequent rantings like 'you'll know how' and 'shut the portal from both sides' type garbage."

"Both sides? That's impossible."

"I know, right? See? Both sides! How?" I stomped up the rest of the stairs.

"We'll figure it out. We always do," Josie said behind me.

"But what if I don't?" Guilt and worry slammed into my stomach like a sucker punch. What if I didn't? How many people would die because I had no clue how to shut a portal from both sides?

6

It was early evening before I could escape the bustle of Coven House. I relished the quiet hush of traffic heading out of the city as I rode the bus to Rory's nightclub. I needed to talk to Raoul and not raise suspicion and hoped that Rory would be too busy to recognise I was in his club. Of course, I knew I was kidding myself. Rory knew every heartbeat that entered his establishment. Whether he would deign to speak to me was another thing altogether. I'd upset him the last time we spoke. I'd accused him of selfishness over a small matter and he'd taken it to heart. I hadn't apologised and he hadn't forgiven me. So, we were in the 'let's see who breaks' part of friendship, I guess. Not friendship, really. You couldn't truly be friends with a thousand-year-old vampire who'd rip your throat open at a whim. Rather, we were at an impasse and I was betting he'd break before me.

"Joseph." I hugged the mountain of a bouncer as I strolled into the club. I'd dressed conservatively, boots, black pants, black shirt. My hair was tied in a side braid with tiny little slivers of silver stuck throughout.

Joseph gave me a friendly pat on the shoulders and stepped back. "He's in a mood today. Best not rile him up."

I shook my head. "I'm not here to see him. Just wanted to get a good drink. Is Raoul serving at the bar?"

Joseph nodded, then leaned down to whisper in my ear. "Don't let on you know. His Kingship found out and is ready for heads to roll."

I reached up and patted him on the cheek. "I need a good drink. Raoul is the best bartender."

Joseph stepped back and let me through to the quiet bar the more discerning customers of the club used. The walls were a conglomeration of plants and mirrors. Dark green and teal chairs lined the walls underneath the greenery. The bar was old oak or mahogany. I hadn't tested it to work out which. Raoul was working seamlessly behind the bar. I offered a smile and indicated that I'd like a drink.

That was the good thing about being friendly with the bartender. They never got your order wrong. Raoul stepped towards me with my drink and refused my money again. It was a running joke. I'd offer to pay and every worker in the club knew to refuse. I'd helped the vamps out a few times and one way they showed gratitude was to never charge me for any drinks or food I ordered in the club. I could get drunk as a skunk on the most expensive wine there and Rory would pay for it.

I didn't abuse the offer, though. The last thing Wayland City needed was me drunk, waving my powers around. I tended towards friendly gestures when I drank and tried to fix people's problems. My powers were easy to control when sober, but drunk me had recently discovered that my magic got drunk as well and didn't cooperate easily when sloshed in gin. That had been a wild night. Josie and Cole both had stepped in and stopped me trying to show how you can make hellfire if you use the right spirits. Luckily Rory hadn't been in attendance that night. He would have called my bluff to see what type of chaos I could release.

Josie had told the drunk chicks around me that it was a new cocktail. Cole had thrown me over his muscular shoulder and carried me out of the bar to the cheers of the drunk hen's night girls yelling 'get some lumberjack for us baby!' and 'I'd mount that in a heartbeat.'

Cole had ignored them and Josie had been given a few phone numbers of her own. I hadn't come back until tonight. Embarrassed that I'd made such a spectacle of myself. Raoul had warned me that the spirits I'd been drinking that night were aged. He didn't tell me they gained potency with age. So, he was partially to blame.

"Good drink." I took another sip.

"We are good here," Raoul said.

"That's great." I turned my seat so I could see the rest of the bar. "How's his majesty?"

Raoul rolled his eyes and then his shoulders slumped as if a weight was added. "He's upset. He's at a council meeting right now."

"Oh, I forgot that was tonight." I lied through my teeth.

"Of course," Raoul replied.

"You might want to make sure all your businesses are secure. Talk to Coven House. They'll re-ward them to my standards. That will help, but it's best not to go out much right now. I'm still working on it."

A darkness rolled over Raoul's face before he controlled his features and settled back into his role as chief bartender. "The King has ordered that already. There will be a few changes in how we operate over the next little while. We'll be shutting the bar down for renovations."

"Ah, I like the colour scheme. Try not to touch that and the plants. They're lovely."

Raoul sighed with his usual dramatic flair. He then shut down like a robot without a battery when Joseph loomed large behind me. I looked up into Joseph's face and noted the red sheen in his eyes. Either he was ravenous or something very, very bad had happened.

"Is he back?" I hopped off my stool.

Joseph motioned towards the stairs to the upstairs office. The silent treatment was not a good sign. I drained my cup and placed it gently on the bar, then threw my braid back over my shoulder and pushed past the vamp. "Let's get this over with."

Rory's office was dimly lit when I entered. Joseph shut the door behind me and the sounds of the club were immediately cut off.

"Spill your guts Rory, how bad is it?" I flopped onto the couch that sat along one wall.

"It seems the northern chapter of the Witch Hunters was decimated. No hunter survived a slaughter between themselves and a group of Blood Witches." Rory gave a strained cough.

I straightened at his words. "Where?"

"In Meridian, the small town on the state border. The town folk had been warned to leave, those that stayed didn't survive either. I think they were caught up in the crossfire." Rory poured himself a drink and sat opposite me.

"She's here already. She's the one attacking your premises."

He nodded. "The Council have decided that Blood Witches must be taken care of permanently."

"Wayland City Council has that much power?"

Rory stopped his glass half way to his mouth and frowned at me as if I had said something astonishing. "Not Wayland City. The Vampire Council."

"Oh, them. Well, that's good of them then."

With a shake of his head, he sculled the rest of his drink and placed it on the coffee table between us.

"The Vampire Council is worldwide. For this to come to their attention, it has to be important. They would normally let these groups wipe themselves out. There are rumours of a cure," Rory said.

"Ah." I leaned back.

Rory uncharacteristically scratched at the stubble on his chin. "I am out of options."

"So, let me guess. You've been told that you are to buy the cure at all costs, wipe out the Blood Witches before they can find it and destroy it, or you will be eliminated and someone much nastier and meaner will come in to do the job for you?"

"When you say it like that..." Rory's words were strongly tinged with his original Irish lilt. He had lived a long time and often I forgot his origins as he kept his accent hidden until times like this when stress overrode his usual calm demeanour.

"It's simple. We will defeat the Blood Witch, of which I know there's only one left. Then we'll get rid of the vampire council, so you can go back to being normal annoying Rory and we'll be fine." I offered him a pre-emptive smile.

"Ah youth, I remember my arrogant days well." Rory didn't return my smile, in fact his face took on a haunted look. "The Council have been around for millennia. There are few that old, but they've survived because they're very, very hard to kill."

"What if we shot them with the cure, turn them mortal and then take them out? Would that help?"

"There is no cure Lucy, you and I know it. What you did for Raoul worked once. I had your blood and I was not affected," he replied.

I didn't know if it was jealousy or regret that tinged his words. Rory knew my secrets, I knew some of his. We worked together to save the city twice.

"Up until this morning, I didn't know it could." Honesty was the best policy. "I can give you some and we'll see how you go?"

Rory froze, his eyes wide. I counted three of my breaths before he regained humanity.

"Never. Offer. Your. Blood. Lucy." Rory's accent roaring to life in his words as he struggled to speak.

"Sorry."

"You don't know how tempting you are." He closed his eyes as his fists stayed balled beside his hips.

"So, are these vampires on their way here?"

"No. They have given me no timeline. I'm sure they will start infiltrating our city soon enough, but at present they are keeping their distance."

"How do they know about the cure?"

"They note everything that goes on in my realm." He let out a drawn-out sigh. "I am a thorn in their side, have been for a long time."

"Well, you are annoying. I can understand that."

His lips thinned as if he was about to say something that might be too truthful. He blinked and then old Rory was back. "Touché. That I was born to rule a kingdom and most of them were sewer dwellers is one reason, the other is the fact that I give my people freedoms that others do not enjoy. I am too progressive for the Council. They've made it known that they would replace me in an instant if they could."

"No one takes my annoying vamp away from me. We'll deal with them when they get here."

A smile tugged at his corner of lips. "You always are refreshing Lucy. But we do need to deal with the Blood Witch for now. She's taken a lot of my people, which I just recently found out."

"Don't get upset with them. They were looking out for you. They thought they could deal with it, so you weren't under any more pressure." My hackles raised at the thought of Raoul or Joseph being in trouble.

"They thought they could do my job better than me?" He looped an arm over the back of his chair and crossed his legs.

"No, they thought that it was a small matter and didn't want to burden you. As you said you've had bigger things to deal with. You've taught them to be self-managing and they were. They didn't realise this was bigger than they thought," I replied. "Do not harm them or you'll answer to me."

A spark of mirth ignited in his demeanour, the old Rory was definitely back toying with me. "And what would you do?"

I leaned forward, coiling death magic in my hands, its dark tendrils caressing my skin as I sent a tiny branch out towards him. Rory stopped smiling and reverted to robot still.

"I would show you eternity."

He continued staring at my hand and the magic softly billowing around my fingers. "Now that is tempting. I have often wondered what happens next to creatures like me. Though I somewhat dread the judgement, I will receive for the life that I have led."

"I can tell you one secret if you'd like, as a taster." I pulled my magic back inside myself.

"Go on," Rory said as a brief appearance of longing swept across his features.

"There is no judgement. Death separates us from the living. But judgement is not on the table. Does that help?"

Rory was on his feet in a blink, stomping behind his chair. "No. Damn it. You can't tell a monster like me that we won't be judged for our sins. That's all that stops us from rampaging through the world slaughtering masses. The thought of being judged in the afterlife keeps us in check. Don't tell a soul."

"You deserve to know that the things you've done in your life are yours to remember always, but there is no judge. There is eternity. I could ask Death to arrange someone to spank you as you depart. Would that help?" I tried to keep the cheekiness out of my voice and failed.

Rory again stopped mid movement and then tilted his head towards me. "A spanking?"

"I thought, well, you're over sexed. It might help?"

He burst out laughing at my statement, and doubled over trying to get a breath in.

I raised an eyebrow at his antics. "Vampires are so dramatic."

"Okay, brilliant way to pull me back from a psychotic episode Lucy, but please in future I might not control myself if you offer. For my sake, don't." He poured another drink.

"I'll make sure I don't. Now, can we talk about more important things?"

Rory was about to answer when Detective Pearce burst through the door dragging Joseph behind her like a rag doll.

"Pearce, put Joseph down." I modulated my tone with all the authority I could muster.

"Fuck off Lucy, this is vamp business," Pearce said, squaring up to Rory. "You should have told me."

"He didn't know. Think. Think carefully, before you accuse him of stuff. He didn't know." I stepped between Pearce and Rory, my arms raised against both. "I can explain. But let go of the Slayer, we don't want him going off."

Joseph pulled his arm from Pearce's grip. I was both impressed and a little frightened that he'd not turned into instant slayer mode when she tried to manhandle him.

Pearce turned her red-blooded gaze to me. "This better be good."

"As you know my grandmother is the head of the Blood Witches. She's sort of the Queen, if you will. She's decided its time to come to Wayland City and kill everything in her wake so she can open a portal to the Fae Realm and bring about the destruction of Planet Earth and all we hold dear."

"Lucy." Pearce's resting bitch face was slowly returning. Her fiery ready to kill face was quite scary. I wouldn't want to meet her in a dark alley when she was in that mood. Relief slid through me as Bitchy Pearce stepped back into action.

"Trust me. I know it sounds a bit soap opera-ish. My family are nasty witches who don't care about anything or anyone except getting as much power as they can."

"Sounds familiar," Pearce said.

"Except she can. My grandmother kills indiscriminately and she's coming to get me."

"Did they tell you how many vamps are dead?" Pearce asked.

"I guessed a lot. Rory only found out. The others kept it from him and I was negotiating that he not kill them all for their insolence before you barged in here like a hell cat ready to kick arse. It was impressive, but I had things under control."

"They should have told me." Her voice dropping an octave. Pearce's frustration rising like kettle about to boil over. There was no whistle to warn those around us of the impending explosion of emotions she was about to unleash.

I held my hand up hoping a simple gesture might stave off the furiousness of the vampire. "Yep, but they're stupid men who've had centuries of misogyny drilled into them. I don't believe they even know that women can actually think for themselves yet."

Pearce stood quiet, as if in contemplation of my words. Joseph had drawn back and was looking between her and his King, probably wondering which one would attack him first.

"Are you done yet?" Rory asked Pearce as he clenched his fist, cracking a knuckle. The sound travelled through the room and the collected vampires flinched.

"I find killers. That's what I do. They should have come to me and I could have prevented the other deaths." She was somewhat mollified at my words.

Her eyes had reduced from blazing red to a pink blush. She wouldn't let this rest, but she'd realised that Rory was on the verge of showing us the reason he'd stayed a king for so many centuries and it wasn't because of moderate policies or fair-trade marketing.

"Yes, they should have and they should have told me and not kept this from me for two weeks." Rory stared over my head at Joseph looming to the side.

"Okay, we've gone over this already. They were wrong, they're sorry. Nothing's going to bring the people back, but we can stop the attacks." I waved one hand in the air as if I was dictating a boring letter to a scribe.

"Okay little miss sunshine, how do you plan on doing that?" Pearce growled her best at me.

"There are wards we can use to stop her entering your businesses. It might not stop an attack on the street, but you won't die in your houses."

"And you know how to make these?" Pearce asked.

"I will need help, but yes. It will work for her. I don't know about anyone helping her, though. By now she will have helpers somewhere in the city."

"I have put my people on notice." Rory had remained silent but as he spoke I could feel rather than hear his utter determination not to lose control. "How fast can you ward our places?"

"I don't know. I'll talk to Josie and the Coven. They'll charge you a fortune, but they'll get it done."

Rory gave a small pause before answering, the stillness of the room was unnerving. "Obviously, they're witches. They overprice everything they do."

"You two can sort that out. I'll teach them the wards and they'll go to your places and fix them. But they'll only last for about a week, then they need to be reapplied."

Pearce crossed her arms and paced. "That still doesn't change the fact that there is a homicidal Blood Witch in my city and you're letting her get away with murder."

I slowly turned to face her, trying desperately to control the rage that was churning in my chest. My face was heating as I let out a long breath. "I only found out. I'm trying my best. I don't have any resources to track her down and I have stopped Rory here from killing his friends. When I get a chance, I'll track her down and kill her."

Pearce chewed on her bottom lip as if mulling over a retort. She let out a sigh and turned back to Rory. "I'm off Lucy watch and I'm going to find this bitch."

"You are still on Lucy duty," Rory replied.

"Hey, no one needs to be on Lucy watch-duty-whatever. I'm good. I can take care of myself."

All three vampires chuckled at once, as if I'd said the most hilarious thing any of them had heard in the last few centuries.

"It's true. You don't need to follow me around like stalkers, watching me in my sleep." I bunched my fists on my hips.

"You are an idiot," Pearce said.

"Pardon?"

"I've already told you how many attempts on your life I've stopped these past few weeks. Joseph's tally is bigger than mine. I think the wolf is at the same score. His majesty here's been too busy with continental vamps to join in the fun. Raoul has less than me. There's a whole betting industry seen who'll win." Pearce pointed her thumb out the door indicating the many vampires downstairs I couldn't see.

"Surely there can't be that many."

They all nodded and waited for the penny to drop in my brain. I refused to let it drop.

"Why would anyone come after me?"

Pearce held up her hand and tapped a finger. "You killed a Blood Witch. You killed a Witch Hunter. You're exasperating and annoying. Hell, I'd kill you to stop you being a pain in the arse, but his majesty here thinks we need you. He's become attached."

Joseph stood silent and shook his head. Rory's glance told me plainly I was in over my head.

"How many all up?"

"Thirty-seven," Joseph replied in his baritone voice.

"That's not that many. I could have taken them."

"Once word gets out that you're responsible for the cure, there will be a hell of a lot more after you. Right now, people want to kidnap or kill you because you pissed them off. If the vamps find out that you're this secret cure to vampirism you're fucked," Pearce replied.

"Thanks Detective, I'm so happy you give it to me plain."

"She's not wrong. There are vampires who would imprison you and siphon your blood for years. Others who would do untold things to you and keep you barely alive. Others will kill you outright." Rory's harsh tone was punctuated by his frown.

I crossed my arms and thought for a moment. "Then I'll have to disappear. No one will find me."

Rory shook his head, dark bags under his eyes made him appear older than his death age. "I don't think there's anywhere on this planet you could hide."

I stood taller, cracking my neck as I did so. Instantly the vamps full attention was on me. I forgot what that sound does to the undead. I gave the group a little smile.

"Then I'll have to fight them all."

7

After my resolution, I had gone home and slept again. Coven House was full of noise as the girls all scrambled to come up with ideas for Benji and Sarah's wedding. I had grabbed a snack from the fridge and hidden in my room. The minute my head hit my pillow I was out. I was up early the next morning to take my pups for a run. I'd missed them and by the barking and wagging of tails that met me when I picked them up, they definitely had missed me.

I have a planned route every run, trying to keep it fresh so the dogs don't get bored with the scenery. Josie had told me that dogs wouldn't care if you ran to the park and back a thousand times. They'd still love it. I liked to change routine. You never knew when a stalker would pick up your pattern like a crocodile and lie in wait to attack. Heaven help the stalker that tried to get to me through the dogs, though. Usually, Wolf would come along for a run to stretch his legs out, but today he was a no show. A small part of me was disappointed, but knowing what was going on I didn't blame him.

My dogs comprised a couple of Shepherds, Kelpies, a Great Dane who feared pigeons, don't ask and a Poodle with psychopathic tendencies. Shyla, a Kelpie, was turning one and his parents were excited for this run. They were busy planning his birthday party while we were away. I had shrugged and promised them he'd get a good run, meaning I'd take some of the hyperactive edge off him so they could have a fairly normal dog birthday party.

We ran down by the bay, a quick turn then ended up meandering through the wealthier suburbs which had lots of trees to inspect and a couple of cats to threaten with a bark or two before we made our way to the dog park to let them off for fun time. I had hidden two balls in my hip pack and threw them in different directions for my crew. It was chaos, but they loved it. I sat on the bench and let my muscles relax while the dogs chased scents in the cold morning light.

"I see you're out with your pack again." Brad, the shifter alpha, closed the gate behind him.

"Yep, they needed a good run and a play." I watched the dogs scurrying around. I turned my head to him and asked, "is it your turn to tail me?"

"No, that's been taken care of." Brad's rumbling voice was quiet against the noise of the dogs playing. He was a large man and the bench dipped slightly when he sat.

"They were good. I didn't pick up until we hit High street that they were there."

Brad shrugged one shoulder. "He'll be happy to know. We test all our operatives on you now. If they can go more than an hour trailing you without getting caught, they're cleared for duty."

"Glad I could be of help." I threw the ball again for Shyla. He was ball crazy.

"Cole let me know about the vampire situation," Brad said.

"Has anything happened to any of your pack?"

He shook his head. "No, we've re-warded our places, as Cole reminded us to do. But that's not why I'm here."

"Jessie's not doing well?"

"She's very upset. She's talking about taking on this Blood Witch herself. I need you to talk to her. Her mother and I make her angrier." Brads shoulders slumped as if in defeat.

"She's lost her friends to a monster. It's only right she would want to hunt them down and put an end to it. I've got to get my pack back to their parents in a minute. Do you want me to come to your house or meet somewhere?"

"I'm taking her to the museum at eleven. Can you meet us there?" Brad was the alpha of the shifters in Wayland City and surrounds. He was used to giving orders and for them being obeyed. Having to ask me for help must have taken a lot out of him.

"I'll be there. Do you want me as good cop or bad?"

"Just speak sense to her. I don't want her wandering off. If she got caught..."

I nodded. I knew exactly what my grandmother would do with a shadow walker. The amount of power Jessie had would be a gold mine for a Blood Witch to harvest. She'd take her time and it would be excruciatingly painful right up until the last moment for Jessie. A shiver rolled through my body. That wouldn't happen. I'd make sure of it.

Brad left and I put the dogs back on their leashes. Thoughts of Jessie falling into my grandmother's hands kept me hypervigilant as I ran the dogs back to their parents. I caught the bus back to Coven House to get changed and grab some food. As I stepped off the bus at the corner of our street, I could see a new string of multivariate pothos had grown around the columns of the front porch. The witches had been practicing again. It was the middle of winter and they were draping tropical vines over the walls, using magic to keep them from freezing. Our house would turn into a jungle pretty soon. I liked plants but couldn't keep one alive if I tried. Josie was a green thumb. She'd rescued more plants from my old place than I care to remember. I guess it was good advertising, magic certainly in abundance at our house.

As I entered the kitchen, I was greeted by a sturdy older witch who instantly gave me 'sit up straight and pay attention' vibes.

"You must be Mistress Kable." I tried to keep an even smile on my face.

I had faced down many a teaching witch before. Although mine could dole out whippings if I didn't get my lessons completed. This lady, with her purple hair, sandals and t-shirt that read "Circle Theorem 4 Lyfe", certainly didn't look the part of teacher. Unless you attended a hippy white witch school, then I guessed she fit the bill perfectly. Her facial expressions though could have given my teachers a run for their money.

"You are Josie's friend, Lucinda Driver," Mistress Kable said.

There was no emotion in her tone, she exuded a no-nonsense, we're busy here vibe.

"Yes. I'm sorry I wasn't here to greet you when you arrived," I replied. I was actually a little shocked that Josie had brought her to our Coven so fast. I stopped my thoughts for a moment and realised I'd referred to the girls as 'our' coven. I don't know when I'd decided that these women were a part of my inner circle.

"The girls are an excitable bunch." She sat at the table perched on her chair like a small hawk ready to take off.

I winced. She wasn't wrong. "Did they tell you what they tried to do with circles?"

She closed her eyes and shook her head. "They tried to show it to me. I put a stop to that. Circles are dangerous at the best of times. They were trying to wing their way through it without the basic mastery. You should never have allowed it."

"I don't have any say." Shock had quickly registered on my face before I tried to school myself into remaining calm.

"Your aura tells me you are more than competent in circle theorem and more. It's your duty not to let them blow themselves up with simple witch math." Kable's condescending tone rankled my pride.

She was right, but I had no idea they were playing with magic while I was sleeping. I readied myself to reply when Josie stepped back into the room with a big smile.

"Ah, I see you've met Lucy," Josie said to Kable and then pivoted and showed me an even bigger smile. "Lucy, this is my teacher

Mistress Kable. She is the BEST witch at circle theorems I've ever encountered."

I nodded with a fake smile. "Yes, she was telling me."

Josie sighed and then plunked herself at the table. "The girls are using the chalk tablets to work on their designs. I think a few are promising. Lucy are you able to stay and help today?"

I shook my head. "No, I have to go see the Alpha at eleven."

A shudder rolled down Kable's back. "Witches working with shifters. Who ever heard of it?"

"I do. I work with shifters, vampires, humans, the lot. Wayland City doesn't hold to segregation. We've found bad things happen when we don't help each other."

Kable waved her fingers dismissively. "Can they use magic?"

"Yes, there are a few that can, so I'm helping them control it."

Josie frowned at me.

"Then bring them here and we'll teach them properly to keep them safe from disaster," Kable said.

It was my turn to frown. Witches hated shifters and more especially vampires. Here was an older witch willing to teach them? It was unheard of. Perhaps I'd judged her wrong.

"I will ask. I don't know if they will agree. They seem to have the same attitude towards witches as you do against them."

Kable shook her head. "Nothing should impede education. If we educate young, then we can stop a lot of foolishness later on."

"I can agree on that." I focused my attention to Josie. "I'll get changed and head off. Good luck with the girls."

Josie nodded to me as I headed to my room. I showered and changed quickly. It was a cold day so I chose boots and jeans and my new thick jacket. A few months ago, I had a threadbare jacket and a couple of pairs of jeans to my name. Now, thanks to Josie's constant shopping I had a closet full of temperature appropriate clothing. She claimed that she did it so I would stop stealing her clothes, but I think she was using me to enable her shopping addiction.

The bus ride to the museum was uneventful. The usual characters were on board. One old guy had a six-foot crucifix on a wheel that he tried to bring aboard. The bus driver told him no. So, he flipped a few latches and the crucifix folded down into a two-foot structure. The driver nodded and let him in. I admired the commitment to his faith, but hoped he wouldn't sit anywhere near me. I was relieved when he wheeled the creation up the aisle and sat next to the door seat.

The museum wasn't busy today. Most schools were in the middle of testing season, so no school trips. I ambled through the gift shop and into the museum proper. I knew where I'd find Jessie and her Dad. The museum was having an Egyptian phase, bringing in mummies and sarcophaguses. Jessie loved all things death related now, since I'd brought her back from the dead, I mean. She would be somewhere in the exhibit with her long-suffering father trailing behind. I thought I caught a few other shifters in the outer regions of the museum. I wouldn't be surprised if most of the pack were around somewhere.

"Jessie, did you see the gold Anubis statue?" I walked up to them as casually as I could. It wasn't good to startle a shifter, no matter how old they were.

"He's roped you in to 'talk' to me, hasn't he?" Jessie's accusatory tone rippled through her words.

"He's worried that someone terrible will try to hurt you."

"I've dealt with bad before."

"I know. And your dad was there to help you." I nodded as we ambled forward through the exhibition. "Seems that if it was me, I'd want my dad to help me every chance he could."

Jessie gazed up at me, biting her lip, after a moments' hesitation she asked, "where is your dad?"

I waved my arm. "My 'dad' is in the netherworld."

"Oh, I'm sorry, I didn't know he died." Worry etched her brows closer together.

"Did you want to meet him?" I blurted the words out before I could think. I wondered what Brad would think of me introducing his only child to Death. Yeah, that will go down well in the shifter community.

"Yep, let's do it." Jessie gave me a sympathetic smile.

"Hold my hand, I'll tell your dad what we're doing and then we'll take two steps. Hopefully, we'll meet him, but I can't guarantee it."

Jessie nodded and waited as I waved Brad over with my free hand.

"I'm going to have to take Jessie into the netherworld for a moment. She has to see something. We'll be right here, but I need you to keep your shifters close in case someone tries to interfere. We'll be vulnerable."

Worry creased Brad's face, aging him twenty years in an instant. He closed his eyes as if communicating with his pack and then from deep in the shadows of the exhibit, at least eight shifters emerged.

"Oh, they did well. I didn't see all of them. Well done you guys." Shifters could hear very well. One of the younger ones smiled and then shut his emotions down to serious shifter face when he thought he'd been caught.

"Okay Jessie, let's sit on this bench, close your eyes, pull inward. You know how you do before you walk. Keep a hold of my hand. Let's step on the count of three, one, three."

Jessie opened her eyes in the netherworld. "You forgot two."

"I did. Good of you to notice."

"I've been here before," Jessie's hushed tone changed as she glanced around the area. "This is where I went."

"Yep, you were travelling and I stopped you." I couldn't keep the note of worry that she might get upset at me for bringing it up out of my voice.

"Yeah, I'll travel it later. My parents need me for now."

I nodded. "I'm going to invite my parent here. Don't get scared."

Jessie scoffed. "Your dad can't be that bad."

"Nope, but some people fear him."

Jessie held my hand tighter as I reached out my magic. "That tickles."

"I know, right? Look how pretty it is."

In the mortal realm, my death magic appeared black, dull, but here in the netherworld it glowed with so many colours. As if all the energy from life had been twisted into it.

The usual susurration came flooding towards me as my parent emerged from the nether. Jessie tensed, though her face showed she was more curious than scared.

"Lucinda, you called." Death appeared and had taken on the kindly Elven prince demeanour for our meeting. I preferred it to be in nebulous true form, but I guess this was what it preferred.

"Parent, I want you to meet Jessie. I brought her back from your realm and accidentally changed her."

"You want me to take my gift back from her?" Death asked.

"Don't you dare," Jessie hissed letting go of my hand and stretching her fingers out like claws ready to attack if he came near.

"No, we know that she needs to meet you to understand where her powers come from. Why we should be cautious using them." I lowered Jessie's hands with my own.

Death glided towards Jessie who pulled away from me. She tilted her head in contemplation for a moment and then extended her hand.

"Nice to meet you," she said.

Death shook her hand and presented her with a smile. "You are not scared of me?"

"Why should I be? You are energy and energy isn't to be feared. Dad says you have to learn to use energy whatever type it is."

"Good. You can talk to those who have departed mortality and walk my halls," Death said, turning her hand over.

"Yes, she can, there is more she might do but I wanted her to know that there are dangers in the magic as well." I strained my voice to emphasise the danger part in case Death didn't get it.

"Nothing here can harm the living. It's the living that harm them," Death said. "But you mustn't spend much time here. It can drain you of your will to go back."

Jessie nodded.

"Jessie wants to kill the Blood Witch who took the dead from her."

Jessie's annoyance was clear in her stare and clenched fists.

"She has taken from me. It is right that she should be stopped," Death said.

Jessie poked her tongue out at me and then shot Death a smile.

"That's my job. That's why you had me. To stop her. Jessie is young and I know she wants to help, but the Blood Witch has gained vast power. I don't want Jessie getting hurt." I ignored Jessie staring daggers at me.

Death finally clued in and its face changed to grave and concerned. It kneeled down next to Jessie, so she was eye level. "You have greater things that you will do with your life. We will need you later. Right now, you need to learn, to grow stronger so that when I call for you, you will be ready."

Jessie's ego deflated. Even Death was trying to stop her from killing the witch who took her friends.

"How do I get them back?" she asked Death.

"I have one who has been sent to me, the alpha. The others will come when Lucy stops the witch," Death replied.

"But what if she can't?"

Great, thanks for the vote of confidence. "I will. It's what I was put on Earth to do."

"You can help her," Death said.

Jessie's face brightened at the words.

"But you are weak. You must train. Lucy will need all the help she can get," Death replied.

Jessie sighed at his words. "Fine."

"Thank you." I almost rolled my eyes at my parent's ability to make things worse. "My grandmother has killed witch hunters and her coven. She's drained the city of the departed. How do I stop her with that much power?"

Death stared at me, then smiled. "You are more than capable."

"So, you can't give me a hint?"

Death smiled and faded.

"Shit."

Jessie giggled.

"Sorry. Death makes me so mad."

"My dad never tells me anything, either." Jessie patted my hand.

"Time to go back?"

She nodded and took my hand. In a blink, we were back sitting on the bench. Cold seeped around us and the shifters were looking terrified as we opened our eyes.

Brad sunk to his knees, grabbing Jessie and pressing him to her. "Never do that again."

"It's okay Dad, I learned things," Jessie replied.

Brad growled low into her neck as he kept squeezing her. I stood and moved away to give them time to settle. The shifters all pulled back from me as if scared. I was used to people not understanding my magic, so I left them alone and walked towards the fake portal to the Fae realm. It was a good likeness. The inscription was off, as if whoever had made it hadn't read the words right. Or had no idea what the Fae runes actually were. I had tried and failed to make a real one. This replica was the best mortal man could get at the magic used.

I turned back to see Brad and Jessie walking towards me.

"Jessie told me she has to learn how to control her magic." Brad's face still appeared unconvinced.

"The witches have brought in an expert. She's a snarky lady who knows her stuff. She has said she will teach Jessie if you allow it," I replied.

Brad shook his head. "Working with witches. I will never hear the end of this."

"If it makes it any better, she was not happy about it at first, but education is more important than nature. Jessie's magic can do a lot of harm. She needs to control it and be safe." I didn't meet his gaze as that would be a challenge to his authority and he was liable to burst at that moment.

"We've never done this," Brad said.

"I know, but there's never been a Shadow Walker before."

Jessie appeared as if she was holding her breath.

"I will have to clear it with her mother." Brad wiped his face as if considering a dangerous thought. "She's going to kill me."

"She will know that Jessie needs training and seeing as though there's a qualified teacher in town to do it. I'm sure she'll be fine," I said. "Besides, she can come and supervise if she wants."

Both Jessie and Brad's breath hitched at my words, then they side eyed each other and shook their heads.

"No, we won't be doing that," Brad said.

"She can start tomorrow morning if you want. I'll let the teacher and Josie know Jessie's coming."

Brad nodded, hugging Jessie to his side. "Let's face your mother."

8

— · —

I was sitting at the Sugar Shack, enjoying a burger during my night break for my security shift when Detective Pearce plunked herself down in the booth opposite me. She stared at my plate with longing.

"I miss these burgers." She swiped a chip from my plate.

"Hey, that's going to hurt." I frowned at her audacity, I was saving that chip for later.

"I can sniff it. I miss the oil. This is a shitty gig." She held the chip up to her nose and closing her eyes.

"It tastes good. The meat and the barbeque sauce and fried onions dripping down. Mhhmm, mhmmm." I held the burger up to my mouth and took a big bite. The savoury spices Marty used in his cooking was more addictive than MSG. I needed the calories, I needed the taste, I needed the feeling of home his cooking gave me. His food gave me a sense of belonging when I felt off kilter.

"You're a bitch." Her words held no heat.

"I can't hear you. I'm chewing on a deluxe stack burger. Awesome." I spoke even though I had a mouthful of food and a couple of stray bits flew out of my mouth onto the counter.

"That's gross. You've got no manners." She stared at the offending splatters.

I took my serviette and wiped the table down. "Says the woman who stole my chip."

"You want it back?" She held the chip out to me, waving it in my face.

"Eww, nope, you can sniff it all you want. I've got food to eat." I took another bite.

"Some nights I want to bite you," she snarled still clutching the chip.

"Later I'm going to have a deluxe doughnut with salted caramel and chocolate topping." I gave her my shit-kicking.

"Fuck you."

"What do you want? I'm taking it you normally don't have time to sit and chat with me, so something's up."

She placed the chip onto the table with reverence and then shook her head. "There's been a fire."

"Where? I've only been here ten minutes." My security shift took in the industrial side of Wayland City, which also included the Sugar Shack, my favourite place to eat.

Emerald came over. She had worked at the Sugar Shack for years and took the early night shift often. "Detective Pearce, we've not seen you for a bit. You on a diet?"

"Nah, trying to keep a low profile. I upset some powers that be and they've had me on the shitty shifts," Pearce replied.

"You punched the captain in the face yet?" Emerald asked her eyes lighting up with mirth.

"Don't tempt me," Pearce .

"You want anything?" Emerald asked.

"Nah, have to drag this sack of shit's sorry arse out for a bit," Pearce pointed at me.

"What did I do?" I shoved the last of my burger into my mouth and put my hand over my remaining fries in case the chip thief tried to strike again.

"Nothing, but you do need to come to the precinct."

"Oh, you're in trouble now Luce, the cops are on to you," Emerald said. "You want your doughnuts to go?"

I nodded and bit down on a couple of cold chips. "Let's go then."

"You're driving." Pearce stood with that unearthly speed vampires have.

"Slow down, your inhumanity is showing," I whispered.

She nodded and slid out of the booth at a more appropriate speed. "After you."

I had to radio in to Marg that I was going to the precinct. Marg let me know that she'd get Benji to do the final run for me.

"Am I in trouble?" I turned the car towards the precinct.

"The captain would like a word."

"Oh, so why send you and not officers in uniform?"

"I was on Lucy duty anyway and volunteered when I heard the message. The captain was not happy, but he couldn't say no in front of the other officers there." Pearce had a snarl in her tone.

"Well, there's nothing I know that could help him. I've been at work and my movements are logged."

Pearce let out a short snort. "Your fingerprints were found at the scene."

"Where?"

"A chop shop."

"Oh, well that explains it." I cursed myself silently for touching Raoul's desk. "Are the vamps okay?"

"Well, they deny any involvement, but forgot to mesmerise the young forensic scientist who took prints from all over the scene. Hence your fingerprints were found."

"Damn," I replied.

"You got a story?"

"It's on my route. I have checked the security of buildings before." My excuse was a shamble and we both knew it. Marg would back me up on anything I said. However, not even her quick wit could save me if I stuffed up the delivery.

"I'm having Cole's team fix your logs as we speak. They'll show that two nights ago you were called to the area on an alarm. You went in, found nothing, reset the alarm and logged it in. Hopefully, he'll buy that. If not, you're in for a rough night," Pearce replied.

"I've stayed off the radar for years, now it seems I'm surrounded by cops." I drove into the precinct carpark.

"Ha, if we wanted to find you, we would have." Pearce unbuckled her seatbelt.

"I wish I could go back to hiding."

"Too late. All the supes know who you are. It's lucky they don't know what you are. Hopefully, we can keep it that way." Pearce swaggered through the doors.

Several younger cops saw her and froze. She had that effect on people. For a short woman, she had some clout. I didn't want to get in a fight with her. She was like a Jack Russell Terrier. She'd bite in and not let go. Even if the odds were completely against her, she'd hold on until the bitter end. It was a good trait in someone who was on your side, but I would hate to be on her bad side.

"Sergeant is the captain in?" Pearce asked over the desk.

I smiled when I realised the police officer was Sergeant Hazel Offord. She'd helped me a few months ago when I'd suspected Pearce was a killer. Luckily for me, it had turned out it was her partner that was the witch hunter, not Pearce. It was the same partner that killed Pearce and forced Rory to turn her. I don't know if forced is appropriate for the situation. Rory changed her, even though she was officially dead. When Pearce came back, she was livid. She still hadn't let Rory live it down that she hadn't consented to becoming the living dead.

"Lucy, it's good to see you," Sergeant Offord said. "He's in his office, in one of his moods. The mayor has been in."

"Fuck," Pearce muttered under her breath, then eyeballed me. "Let's go find out the bad news."

I followed behind. The sounds of the police station flowed around me as I concentrated on getting my story straight. I could throw my magic at him and wipe his memory, but someone was bound to be recording everything I say so I'd have to stick to the story.

Pearce knocked once, then opened the door to a rather cluttered office. There were citations and merits hung proudly on the wall, next to pictures of the captain beside several big wigs that I couldn't name if you prompted me.

"Pearce, Miss Driver, please have a seat." The captain was sitting in his large brown leather chair.

The chairs he directed us to were shorter than the desk and made me feel like I was in the principal's office waiting for punishment.

"Sir, I can take Miss Driver's statement and get that organised for you." Pearce's tone was dull, as if she was bored already with his presence.

If I could, I would have kicked her. I didn't need her getting on the captain's nerves, that wouldn't do well for me or her. I guess as an immortal now she didn't need to work, but Pearce was a damn good cop and I think her pride wouldn't let her stop.

"No, no need for that. The mayor has insisted that this get cleared up as soon as possible." He refused to meet her gaze.

I noted that he had a small crucifix on a chain around his neck that had got caught on his tie knot. I didn't know if he knew she'd changed or if he'd always avoided her. It could be a combination of both. Pearce was hard to read and now she was a vampire she was even more prone to strange looks and sudden stillness. I tapped her foot with mine slightly, reminding her to pretend to breathe, maintain humanity.

"Yes sir." Pearce offered him a tiny smile. One that a kid would give his estranged aunt at a family reunion.

"Miss Driver, can you tell me why your prints were found at an illegal chop shop?" The captain had turned on his recording device and had leaned back from his desk as if he was casually chatting with an employee and not a potential felon.

"I was on my nightly rounds for Swift Security when an alarm went off. I had to investigate, saw that no one was in the building and so I radioed the action in, locked the gates back up and continued on my route." I crossed my toes in my shoes, hoping he would buy my lie.

"This area isn't your usual route, though. Why did you attend it?" The captain kept his face blank, but I could tell he thought he would catch me out soon.

"The other security guard who normally does that route was off ill with this pandemic thing that's going around. Benji and I, another security guard, had split the route and mixed it in with ours to cover John while he's ill. We are down staff and can't get any replacements."

The captain nodded his head. Everywhere was feeling the pinch. The police weren't any better.

"So, you're saying you went into this building where there were dozens of illegally seized cars being cut apart and you didn't report it?" he asked.

"Sorry, I don't have a car of my own. I drive the security car only at night, so I don't know what an illegally seized car looks like. On paper, it's a mechanics shop that I was called to check out because an alarm had triggered. It's not my normal route, but I had to fill in while John was ill. I went to the place, couldn't see anyone, lights were on, but there wasn't anyone there. I figured they'd forgotten to turn off the lights. It happens sometimes. That's why Swift

Security is here. We help those who need security." I offered a smile. Marg had drummed that line into me from my first day. Swift Security knows how to secure a building.

"I see from the records we've got from your supervisor that you are telling the truth," the captain said.

I shrugged. Pearce gave a small cough, gaining his attention.

"Sir, if the records check out, why is Miss Driver here?" She kept her voice even and put in a few breaths to maintain normalcy. I thought I needed to remind her to blink but as I was about to say something she did. It must be hard not being human anymore.

"The mayor was the one who asked me to talk with Miss Driver. He seems to think she might know more than she's letting on," he replied.

I frowned. When had I come on to the mayor's radar?

"No sir, she's a stupid doughnut cowboy following her routine. I don't think she has enough sense to come up with any hair-brained schemes that would get her on our radar." Pearce threw a bucket load of derision in her tone.

Before I could reply with a 'thanks, bitch', the captain cleared his throat. He obviously thought her words might have been a little harsh, but he didn't counter them.

"Be that as it may, Miss Driver was the one that discovered the Witch Hunter's lair recently and she had come across the body by the bay. Her name seems to be coming up frequently." He spoke over me to Pearce as if I wasn't even there.

"She was at the wrong place at the wrong time. She called it in like any doughnut cowboy would. She isn't good enough to get on the force, sir, but she does her job and follows procedure. Mrs Swift reassured us she's had no problems with her," Pearce said.

"Can I say something?" Even though I had decided not to make myself any more of a target of derision than I already was, I couldn't stand being talked over as if I didn't matter. The Captain had managed to get under my skin.

The two of them turned and scanned me as if I was irrelevant to their conversation. I shivered at the glare Pearce levelled at me. She was not happy. I should have shut my mouth.

"Go ahead," the captain said after he caught Pearce's look.

"Sir, it's true I did find a body, but that was Rembrandt. He was such a good dog."

"He was, awful thing, him dying," the captain said with genuine emotion.

"And as for finding where the Witch Hunter had taken that little girl, that was a fluke. I was training for a half marathon and I saw something suspicious. I called Detective Pearce, then her and her partner came and well, poor Detective Moore." I let my words trail off.

"Yes, yes, that was a sad day. I note though he took you to the ball as his plus one," he replied.

"Yes, he was my neighbour and didn't have anyone to go with. I owed him a favour so I went along. I'd never been to anything so fancy. It was awkward, but he was a good guy and made the night fun. There was nothing untoward going on."

Truth be known, Ethan Moore was a crazed witch killer who had tried to kill me and many others before I killed him. Rory had covered it up by bringing the roof of the cave down on him, so his body was never recovered. I'd saved Jessie but not Harrold the hobo who had stalked me for years for free doughnuts.

The captain waved his hand in the air. "The mayor and I were under a great deal of pressure after that event, especially from Detective Moore's folks and his former precinct. Had to talk them out of coming in here to do their own investigation."

My heart sank. Ethan's folks were Witch Hunters, generations of them and if they came to Wayland City, then there would be hell to pay. They'd work out what happened fairly fast and then I would be in big trouble.

"What's happening?" I asked.

"The mayor told them the official story. He died a hero, blah, blah, blah and then made a rather large donation to a charity in Moore's home town. He's now out to blame someone for the mess this city has been in lately and I think he might try to pin it on you." The captain pointed his arthritic finger at me.

"I'm a security guard. I don't know how I can be to blame. I have eaten a lot of doughnuts lately, but that's stress eating. Doing double shifts does that to you." I shrunk into myself.

The captain reached over and turned off his recording device, then leaned back in his chair. "Well, I can tell you have nothing to do with this. We have to convince the mayor of that. I blame that dickhead of a son he has, trying to stir up trouble when there's none."

I frowned and held my tongue. Pearce remembered to shuffle her feet and then scratched under her chin trying to feign humanity.

Pearce sighed, as if she was done for the day and had been kept back for an unscheduled useless meeting. "His name's Tucker, thinks he's god's gift to the world, hasn't held down a job, been kicked out of several universities for things that the mayor has had to buy him out of."

"Yes, we know he's a dog short of a flea circus. But he's the only child," the captain said and then focused his attention on me. "I'm sorry we've wasted your time Miss Driver."

"Do you want me to do up the report, Sir?" Pearce asked.

"No, I've got this. The man's trying to cover his arse, but I'll not let him blame us for his inability to govern this city."

We left the room and Pearce shook her head at me to not talk until we were out of the precinct. I sighed and followed her. For a short woman, she could walk quick. I waved to Sergeant Offord as we exited the building.

"What the hell does that douche canoe Tucker have to do with anything?" I opened up my car door.

"He's had many convictions squashed and hushed over by his father. I think he's got it in for you," Pearce said.

"I should have shot the turd when I had a chance."

"His father has ties with the Witch Hunters. Moore vouched for you that you weren't a witch, but Tucker's been in his ear," Pearce's vampire hearing meant I couldn't mutter without every word being heard.

"Can I drop you somewhere?"

"I'm on Lucy duty, so I'll follow you home before clocking off," she replied.

"Are you mad at me?"

Pearce squinted at me as if I'd grown an extra appendage on my head. "What for?"

"For not stopping Rory from turning you. I could have, you know, stopped him I mean."

She stilled and then let out a long, drawn-out breath. "No. I didn't want to die. Moore can go to the seven hells and back, but I had a lot of prejudices before that I now see are wrong. I'm glad I'm still here. If only to give you crap for the rest of your mortal life and to give Rory hell for the rest of his immortal one."

"I'm not mortal." My voice was barely a whisper.

"Yeah, I can see that. You get out of scrapes that would kill most people. I figured something was going on," she replied.

"Wow Pearce, you sound almost like a normal person."

"Fuck off Driver, I'm better than that." She focused on the darkened streets as we drove back to Swift Security not deigning to look my way.

"Of course, you are." I threw as much sarcasm as I could muster into my answer.

"People need to recognise it. I might have to hit them over the head a few times before that happens, but they'll get there."

"I can see why you piss Rory off so much."

Pearce tapped the door handed as if she was slapping a desk. "Ha, I've got nothing on you. You drive him crazy. He's beside himself, trying to stop the old vamps from coming here and discovering you."

"Well, that's not my fault. I didn't want any of this. I wanted to lie low and work my way through life. I was doing fine with none of this."

"Driver, I saw your living accommodations. You were not doing well," she said with a laugh.

"It was enough." A sulky twinge tainted my tone.

"Now you've got a vampire king at your command and a sigma wolf who is desperately trying to woo you. Now the mayor's douche nozzle of a son is trying to frame you for murder. Good times." She gave another grunt.

"Fuck you Pearce."

"Fuck you too."

9

I'd had to explain the whole situation to Marg, the company owner, who was ropable when I got back. Pearce backed up everything I said and added a few observations of her own.

"So, what are we going to do with the dickhead?" Marg asked when Pearce had finished.

"I think he'll get what's coming to him, sooner rather than later," Pearce replied.

"If it's all the same to you, I'm going to head home. I've got another teaching morning ahead of me." I handed the keys over to Marg.

"You aren't getting enough sleep Lucy, look at the bags under your eyes," Marg said. "Are you eating enough?"

"Marg, I promise the witches have plenty of food. It's not all vegan."

"She was stuffing her face at the Sugar Shack when I picked her up," Pearce added.

"Thank you. It was good food, too. You could have had a burger." I pointed at her.

"Some of us take care of ourselves Driver," Pearce said.

"Yeah, yeah, thanks mum."

Pearce shook her head but didn't reply. An uncanny stillness settled on her as she turned on full alert. One second later Rory strode through the doors, his coat smattered with rain.

"Oh, hello, we haven't had this type of sexy in here for years. What do you want your kingship?" Marg gave Rory a long stare, which made me wonder if they'd had some sort of relationship back in the day.

"Mrs Swift, it has been a while." Rory genuinely smiled as she got near.

"You need security?" Marg asked.

"We have enough for now. I was hoping to give Lucy a lift home. There's been some trouble with the local bus service," Rory replied.

"What happened?" I asked.

"Someone blew up a bus," Rory said.

"Fuck me." Pearce took her phone out of her pocket. She seemed to fly through her messages. "I have to go. You've got duty, Rory."

"Obviously." He bared a bit of teeth to her.

Storming out of the room, Pearce was ready to kick some arse and maybe take names. She shot a look over her shoulder at Rory. "Keep her safe or else."

Rory viewed the closing door, dumbfounded then spun to face Marg and I. "She does know who I am, doesn't she?"

I patted his arm. "She does. She doesn't give a shit."

"Good on her." A twinge of viciousness swirled in Marg's tone.

Ah, there had been something there. Marg was only ever the soul of courtesy to customers.

Rory focused his extraordinary attention back on me and extended his arm. "Shall we?"

I offered a tight smile and then let out a breath. "I guess we'd better."

Raoul was designated driver. He opened my door as Rory walked around the vehicle.

"How many people are hurt?"

"The passengers got off. There were only a few. The driver was hurt, but he was a shifter, so he has healed. Your boyfriend is raging," Rory replied.

"Was it my route?" I knew the answer before I even asked.

Rory nodded.

"So, if I hadn't gone to speak with the police I would have been on time. They didn't count on that." I chewed at my thumbnail.

"Don't do that," Rory said.

"What?"

"Chew your nails, it's unsightly," he replied.

I sighed and then sat on my hand so I wouldn't be tempted to get the other nails as well. "Do you think this was my grandmother or someone else in play?"

"The fire was not magical in origin," he said.

"Any trace of hunter?"

"No, but the shifter is on that. My job is to keep you safe," Rory replied.

"You know, you haven't told me about the vamps that are looking for the cure." I flicked my hair away from my shoulder trying to distract myself.

"What's to tell? They're old, they don't adapt to modern ways. They are doomed." He gave an uncharacteristic snarl which curled around his words. He was a predator and every now and again it escaped his urbane demeanour.

"That might be true, but are they going to come here to find this thing or send lackeys?"

Rory shrugged. "They are direct. But it is a long way to travel and I don't know if any of them have the commitment to do so."

"We don't have to worry about them yet?"

"No, we have more pressing things to deal with."

I picked at my other thumbnail but didn't bring it to my mouth. "She is trying to open the portal to the Fae realm. She needs great power and then she needs the key. I think she's been to the museum and realised the one there is a fake."

Rory nodded. "The real one is safe."

Dread sunk deep into my guts. "How do you know?"

"I am the only one that knows the exact whereabouts," he replied.

"That you know of."

Rory frowned. "No one else has been there. Those that helped me died a long time ago."

"Did they depart?"

"What?"

"Your helpers died, like real death and were you sure they departed, or did one of them have an insane loyalty to you and decided they needed to watch over the portal?" The dread feeling spread across my stomach and into my spine. I knew the answer already.

"Lyle would have," Raoul said in a whisper.

Grief flittered across Rory's features before worry replaced it. "It was centuries ago."

"He would have stayed and guarded it," Raoul said.

"Damn it," Rory replied.

"She has been pulling all the ghosts in to her and syphoning off the energy. When she does that, she can sometimes gather information as well."

"Bugger." Rory bit his thumbnail.

I absently pulled his hand away from his mouth. "Unsightly habit."

"I'm sorry Lucy, I'm going to have to cut our night short. I have some things I have to look in to," Rory replied.

"Don't go there."

He stilled in his seat. "What?"

"She's waiting for you to panic. It's what I'd do. I'd set you up so you would go check on the portal and then while you're there I'd drain you of your energy, kill you and take the portal."

"You're saying it's safe if I don't go near it?" His face took on a desperation that I'd never seen from him before. He always affected a casual nonchalance or a sleazy grin when I was around. This was pure worry, as if his soul was on the line.

"For now. Trust me. I know how she thinks. She's getting desperate. Something must have pushed her over the edge to do this now," I said. "Don't go near it."

"You don't know what it was like when the Fae walked the earth." His voice dropped to almost a whisper.

"No. But if you go near the portal, she's one step closer to unleashing them. It's safe for now. I don't know why I'm telling you that, but it is."

With a dramatic sigh, Rory leaned back in his seat. "I wonder if all this is worth it."

"All this?"

"Life. I should have been long gone, but I'm still here, clinging to a semblance of humanity."

"Raoul?"

"Yes, Lucy?" Raoul glanced over his shoulder at me from the front seat. Tension still clear in the way he set his jaw and the tightness to his eyes.

"Don't let him get drunk."

"We can't. That's the problem," Rory replied. "Unless we drink from someone very drunk, it won't affect us."

"Well, do nothing stupid until I have time to work out what we're going to do." I scrunched my mouth holding in what I would really like to say as we pulled up to Coven House.

"Yes, my queen," Rory replied.

"Give it up Rhuairigh, I'm not going to be queen of anything."

"One day. I have hopes," he said half-heartedly.

"You keep dreaming buddy, keep dreaming." Raoul opened my door for me.

"Be careful," Raoul said.

"I always am." I tapped his shoulder and then touched the wards guarding my home. There were no disturbances to the invisible barrier that kept nasties out of my house, so I walked up the driveway. Rory's car left as soon as I opened the front door. Such a gentleman.

As soon as I opened the door, I was assailed with laughter and the aroma of freshly baked cakes. My stomach growled in response.

"Lucy, good, you need to taste this." Josie jumped up and ran to the kitchen.

"Okay," I replied, shutting the door. I bent down to take off my boots. They were filthy from the slush and I didn't want to have to ask the witches to clean my footprints again.

I then followed Josie to the kitchen and was surprised to see several types of cake lined up on the bench.

"You girls have been busy." I eyed off every cake with equal longing.

"Shush, you need to try these. We were going to blindfold you and get you to choose because we can't right now," she replied. "But take a bite from each of them. Tell me which one we should go with."

"You're expecting me to choose the bridal cake? Why me?" I turned around as the other witches gathered behind me.

"If your guts like it, everyone will like it." Josie had a sing-song tone in her voice like a little child in a chocolate store.

The excitement was contagious. I couldn't help but smile. "Josie, I'm so starved right now. I will like everything."

"Shut up and eat." She held out a small fork and a plate.

I tried the first one, chocolate mud. My tastebuds danced with delight. "This is good."

Josie shook her head and pointed to the next one with an impervious wave of her finger.

I swallowed the next bite. "Red velvet, nice."

This continued as I worked my way down the bench. There were six cakes in all. My stomach was most appreciative of all of them.

"I can't choose." I belched quietly at the end. "Why not have all of them?"

The girls gawked at each other and then stared at me.

"What? You can have layers on a cake. Stack them up and everyone can have a bit."

Josie slapped herself on the forehead. "Why didn't I think of that?"

"Because you like uniformity and I'm not a perfectionist. They all taste divine, so why limit ourselves to one?" I used my fork to dig a little more of the white chocolate raspberry cake. Truth be told it was my favourite, but I wouldn't let them know that. I wanted them all.

"Well, there hasn't been a wedding here for decades, so I guess a big cake is needed," Josie said.

"If you put all the layers together in one of those topsy-turvy type cakes, that would be cool."

"No, topsy-turvy is out. We have to have class," Josie said.

I scanned the room for Sarah who was conspicuously absent from the decision-making table. "Sarah?"

"She's busy being fitted." Josie waved off my concern with a tinkling of the bangles on her wrist. "The theme is dark green. This could work. Large layers going up into smaller. Girls, put these in line biggest to smallest."

I shrugged and was about to walk away. "I think I need a shower. I'll leave you to it."

"Lucy."

"Yep?" I tried not to appear distracted. The last thing I needed was Josie going into over thinking mode.

"Why did the vampires drop you home?"

I gave her a half-hearted smile. "Someone blew up my bus."

"What?" Josie's fork clattered to her plate.

"I wasn't on it. I was at the precinct answering questions."

Josie's bangles tangled in her hair as she pushed her hand through her curls. "What?"

"Don't get your knickers in a knot."

"I don't wear knickers," Josie countered shaking her arm to dislodge the metal from her hair.

I put both hands up. "Hey too much info right there. I was called in to answer some questions over a building I had to check out for work. Someone tried to burn it down and my fingerprints were there from the night before."

"And they suspected you?"

"Nope, the mayor is trying to blame someone for all the shit that's been going down recently and his dickhead of a son has it in for me so I got hauled in for questioning." Thinking about Tucker left an unpleasant taste in my mouth.

"Do you want me to hex him?" Josie asked.

"I wish. No, the douchebag would enjoy the attention."

"I could make his dick shrivel. I read some of old Mistress Hegarty's books." A wicked grin teased on her lips. She could do it and she knew she could. Confidence did something to a witch.

"No dick shrinking needed. I don't think it's that big to begin with."

"No, then your bus blows up but you're not on it." Josie waved her finger in a circling motion, trying to get our conversation back on track.

"Yep, no one was hurt, but the mayor is now down one bus."

The city needed to invest in newer models anyway, but still the thought of what could have happened to the passengers sent a shiver through me.

"What are we going to do about this?" Josie asked.

"I'm going to bed. Jessie will be here in the morning to train with Mistress Kable."

Josie's mouth hung open for a moment. "You convinced the shifters to send the Alpha's daughter to us for training? How in hell does that happen?"

"I'm that good, remember?"

"I'll see you in the morning," Josie said.

"Please leave me some of the cake." I batted my eyelids at her.

"There's plenty. This was the second batch we made tonight," she replied.

"You're stress baking again."

She clenched her fists and then flexed her hands. "I know. You know it. I don't know how we're going to pull this off in one week."

"Does it have to be big?"

"No, but there are things we have to have, witch wise and well, I want it perfect," Josie replied.

"Benji and Sarah wouldn't care if they had their reception at the Sugar Shack, they are in love, they want to be together. This isn't about you." I bopped her on the nose with the end of my finger.

"It's a show of my abilities as coven leader. I have to show the city that I am capable," she replied.

"Oh, they know you are. Did the vamps get in touch with you about re-warding buildings?"

"Yes. I guessed that was you. I could use the money right now."

My eyebrows shot up and I was about to say something when she waved her hand in front of me.

"No, we've got plenty, but it's good to get some steady income coming in, in case," she replied.

"I can help."

"Nope, you do enough. I don't pay you for tuition as it is, so I'm still in your debt."

"You let me stay here rent free. I eat a lot and use a lot of hot water," I replied.

"And you train the girls in a magic no one else can. People would pay big bucks to gain that knowledge and you have warded our house with the best wards I've ever come across. I don't think I could do them. And you bring in money from the vamps and shifters." She ticked the list off her fingers one at a time as she spoke.

"Still." I held my arms up in a questioning manner.

"If I need help, I'll ask. Go to bed, you look like crap." She turned from me.

I waved my hand and shut the door. It seemed all I was doing lately was crashing in bed, waking up and then crashing in bed again. Every day and night filled with people wanting me to do things, one disaster issue after another. I missed the days when I could plod along and only have to worry about hiding out.

I wasn't as lonely now, but sometimes I did long for solitude. My own place where I could hide from the world. I stretched my back and heard a long series of cracks. I hadn't worked out in a while, except for running. If I mentioned it to Josie, she would bring out the Yoga mats in a heartbeat. The last thing I needed was to be reminded that I was as coordinated as a drunk penguin in yoga poses. I kept having to hold in farts and then I got the giggles and Josie would be furious at me for not taking it seriously. Good times.

10

— · —

"Stop pacing or you'll wear a hole in the floor." Josie packed the dishwasher loudly.

"This is a big step," I said. "If her mother gets her nose out of joint, that'll be the end for Jessie. She needs this."

"I'm sure everything will go okay. Mistress Kable is already working with the other girls downstairs. It'll be fine," she replied.

"Don't say another word."

"What?"

I held a finger up. "You were going to add 'what could go wrong'. The minute you do that, you know the universe will conspire to prove to you exactly what it might do."

She chucked a tea-towel at me. "You're a pessimist."

"Realist, I'm a realist." I slung the towel over my shoulder.

There was a knock on the front door and I raced to open it. Brad's dishevelled demeanour was in stark contrast to his usual alpha stoic statue that he exuded. He must have had a rough night trying to convince his wife to allow Jessie to come over and be taught. He certainly was a brave man.

"Alpha, please come in." I pointed at the entryway.

"Come on Dad, don't stand there looking like you're afraid of some little girls." Jessie bounced past him into the house as if she belonged.

Brad coughed apologetically and stepped into Coven House. He'd been here before, but only under dire circumstances. There was an uneasy truce between the witches and shifters in Wayland City now that Josie was Coven leader. The last leader had been an egomaniac who had gotten most of her coven killed. Josie was rebuilding the witching clan, hence the need for teachers.

Brad followed Jessie into the house. "Thank you."

I couldn't see any sweat on the man's brow, but his body language screamed worried. I gave him a tight-lipped smile and shut the door behind me. He jumped a little as the sound carried over to him. I didn't know what stories he'd been brought up with, but the inner child in him seemed genuinely scared to be in the witch's house.

"You must be Jessie." Josie's red hair flamed behind her. Josie was wearing a green maxi skirt with small coins embroidered at the hem. She jingled as she walked, sounding sort of like a Christmas fairy without all the tinsel.

"You're going to teach me?" Jessie asked hopefully.

"Mistress Kable will. She was my teacher," Josie replied.

Jessie screwed up her nose.

"She's tough but fair." Josie winked.

As if she'd been summoned from the depths, Mistress Kable emerged from the training room. Her purple hair had escaped her neatly placed bun and she appeared a little frazzled. I hoped the girls had blown nothing up. Brad's muscles twitched like he was ready to bolt at the first noise.

"Ah, I think I heard my name being taken in vain," Kable said.

"Mistress Kable I was telling young Jessie here that you like students who put some effort in," Josie replied, shooting another wink at Jessie.

"That's true. You do your best and I'll help as much as I can. You don't pull your weight, I'm going to sit back and watch you drown," Kable replied.

I held my hand up to Brad and whispered, "She's joking, I promise."

"Ah, the Alpha. Nice to meet you finally, been a few years." Kable held out her hand.

Brad took it automatically and winced as she squeezed it tight. "A pleasure, I'm sure."

"This is Jessie." Josie indicated Jessie standing beside her.

"Jessie, well, there's no time to be wasting. Let's see what you can do," Kable said.

Jessie glanced at me and then her father, then back to me. "Should I?"

I raised an eyebrow and glanced around the room. "I'll keep a look out."

She closed her eyes and walked. One moment she was in the kitchen, then next she was in the lounge room, a darkened glow flowing around her.

"Samhain on a motorbike, I never thought I'd see the day!" Excitement lit up Kable's face as she shuffled on the spot in what I thought might be a tiny dance move.

"I can do other stuff too," Jessie said tentatively.

"Yes, yes, come on, downstairs we go. This is exciting. The training room will keep you safe," Kable said, grabbing Jessie by the hand and hustling her off.

"Um, I guess that was exciting."

"Do I stay here?" Brad's face was a mix of bewilderment and worry.

"The witches are in the middle of organising a wedding. You can stay if you are willing to be a guinea pig for some of their wilder ideas." I gave him an expectant smile.

Brad's Adam's apple bobbed in his throat as the thought hit home, he grabbed his keys from his pocket, holding them like an exorcist holds a crucifix when being attack by a demon. "I'll come back."

"Good choice." I heard a loud laugh of excitement from Kable coming up the stairs and said, "I think I might watch Jessie learn."

"Keep her safe." From Brad's tone it wasn't a warning but more a plea.

"Always."

I escorted him out of Coven House and saw his shoulders relax as he stepped onto the front stairs. I turned and then went back to find Jessie. I took the stairs quietly and watched Jessie sitting crossed legged in the middle of the room. Other witches were showing her how they drew fire and made little butterflies that sparkled. They were perfecting their magic tricks for the wedding. It wouldn't do much in a fight, but it was pretty to look at. Jessie beamed encouragingly as Mistress Kable pulled out a chalkboard from somewhere in the back of the room.

"Okay, we're going to learn how to mess with shadows. Now we've got Jessie here to work with us. This is your lucky day ladies. Once in a lifetime do we get someone who can do this?" Kable clucked as she sorted out her coloured chalks ready for the lecture.

Jessie was about to say something when she noticed me on the stairs. I tilted my head and arched a brown at her, hoping she would understand what I meant. No one needed to know what I could do, especially a witch I didn't know. Jessie sent me a knowing nod and turned back to concentrate on Kable's talk. I settled on the stairs, listening to the sounds of chalk tapping on the board.

"Lucy," Josie shook my shoulder and I came awake with a start.

"What? What?" I scanned the room, rubbing my eyes, my neck cracked as I took in where I was.

All the witches in the room were staring at me. Several hid smiles behind their hands. Others beamed outright at me.

"You were snoring, dear," Kable said over her half-moon glasses.

"I wasn't." The words came out automatically.

"Well, I'm sure the native forest you logged for us for the last half hour appreciates your candour. I had thought at first that my teaching was boring, but Jessie here tells me you've been doing a lot and not getting enough sleep. I would recommend your bed rather than the stairs in the future," Kable replied.

I stared at the drawings she had done on the board. They were a complicated mass of circles and mathematical formulas. A blush blazed over my face as I stood.

"My apologies."

"I was saying to Jessie that she shouldn't walk in the shadows until she knows how dangerous they can be," Kable said.

"She has experienced a little of that."

"Yes, but mathematically, she's folding space. That's how she goes from here to there in an instant. She could accidentally fold space to the other side of the universe into null space. It's dangerous."

I glanced down at Jessie. Her stubbornness had risen to the fore while I was napping. "Mistress Kable is telling the truth."

"I only walk where I've been," Jessie said.

"What if you get overtired like Lucy here, who apparently doesn't snore? You could make a wrong turn, use the magic slightly differently and end up flying into a black hole or worse." Kable's voice was soft but firm.

Jessie's shoulders slumped as she let out a sigh.

"I think we need to eat."

Mistress Kable appeared to consider saying something but then noting her charges had all perked up at the thought of a break she nodded.

"I've got pizza in the ovens," Josie said.

The witches filed past me on the steps, dragging Jessie with them.

"Lucy, may I have a word?" Mistress Kable asked before I could leave.

"Yes." I strolled down the stairs. My legs had pins and needles from my crouched sleeping position.

"Jessie is the daughter of the alpha, so by rights she's a shifter."

"Yes, the only child. I think there were some complications and they can't have any others."

Kable nodded and then tapped her glasses to her chin. "She can't have inherited these powers. They're a different sort of magic than I've ever seen."

"No, she was attacked by a Wraith. We pulled her back but she'd been changed." I measured my words out carefully. I didn't know this woman and no matter how much Josie vouched for her I didn't trust anyone with my secrets.

"I note a similar taint to Josie's magic. She had a run in with a Blood Witch and I'm wondering if the taint is from that," Kable wiped off the chalk from the board.

I crossed my arms as I watched her work. "There was a lot of magic during that battle. Josie was lucky to make it out alive."

"What I'm trying to say is, we can't let the witch council know of Jessie or Josie's magic. It's something we haven't seen before. They aren't the nicest at the best of times. They hate change and they could see them as a threat."

I rubbed the back of my neck. "I know."

"I've known Josie since she was smaller than Jessie. I heard about her parents. It's a scandal, but she's doing well for herself. She trusts you. We have to do everything we can to protect her. I'm not used to her new progressive ways, but I think if witchcraft is to survive, we need to change with the times."

I licked my bottom lip and thought for a moment before answering. "She is doing her best."

"Jessie having magic might have been from the Wraith, it could have transferred over. I take it you were the one that fought the thing?"

I nodded.

"And yet you don't seem to be tainted by the same darkness they are," Kable came closer to me, extending her hand.

"Don't do that. I'm not comfortable with people touching me." I held my hands up and stepped back from the witch.

She nodded and dropped her hand. "You winced when you looked at my formulas before. Why?"

I sighed. "You had the fourth circle crossed at the null point, thus any magic you tried to use would dissipate before you could power it up."

"Good, good. None of the others saw that. Josie told me about the explosions. I figured one or two of these girls will try to mimic my lessons and I'd rather they didn't go kaboom."

"There have been a few near misses." I winced remembering the other day's disaster.

Magic was hazardous at the best of times, but in the hands of novices who wanted to learn the showy things it was a disaster waiting to happen.

"And you knew about walking the shadows, yet you don't feel you have any serviceable magic at all. You're either talented at hiding or you are a null yourself. I'm still trying to work you out," Mistress Kable said.

"Something like that." I kept my hands and arms soft. I didn't want to confront her, but I would not let her try to hex me in my own house. Witches often tested each other to work out a pecking order. Sort of like chickens in a hen house. The more powerful the chicken, the higher they sat on the roost.

Kable went to speak and then shook her head. "I teach. I'm not interested in power for power's sake. I teach because I know what can go wrong if witches don't understand what they're doing. I've lost too many. Put your anger away."

"I'm not angry."

She stared at me. "Child, I've been teaching since before you were a mote in your mother's eye. You don't seem like you have magic, therefore I've found out that you are the most powerful magic user in this room. I may be older, but I'm not stupid. And my assumption would then be that you killed the wraiths with magic none of these girls have. You, therefore, were involved in the change in Jessie and Josie, which is remarkable. I've never seen the like. I hope that someday soon you'll let me see your magic, but not directed at me."

"I think the food is getting cold." My stomach growled in anticipation.

"Okay. When you're ready." She walked past me.

I stood in the middle of the room and kicked the piece of chalk she had dropped. There was a reason I didn't trust easily. Too many times I'd trusted and been proven wrong. Those I did trust had proven they could be. Cole, Josie, Benji, even Rory to some extent when he wasn't trying to sleaze his way into my pants. The thought struck me as odd. Rory had tried none of his sleazy routine on me when he dropped me home. Things must be dire for him not to resort to a crappy pick up line or two. My grandmother was coming to use me to rip open a portal into a parasite realm. The vampires were after me to cure them of vampirism or outright kill me, so I wasn't a threat to them. And if what Kable had said was true, the Witches would burn Jessie and Josie at the stake if they discovered their altered magic.

The only way through the muck was to keep walking. I wished it wasn't filled with such dire consequences if I got it wrong. Too many people I cared about would die if I didn't work out how to stop my bitch of a grandmother. Both sides. Death had said both sides. Both frigging sides indeed. Would I need someone on this side to shut it while I shut it from the other side and doomed myself to eternity in the Fae realm? My stomach again voiced its unhappiness about not being filled this instant. I picked up the chalk and placed it back on the ledge at the front of the board. When I touched the board, symbols flared into life, showing a complicated formula for folding space. At the end of the formula, a simple ankh sat like a signature.

Kable hadn't spelled this board, but I knew who the author was and Death needed to either tell me plainly what I needed to do or shut the hell up.

"Thanks Dad." I took my hand away from the board. As I did so, the formula flared once and faded. No trace of their symbols left on the blackened surface.

11

— · —

It was my night off from security shifts and I had planned to spend it with Cole, but he was busy with Wayland Council business until late. Brad had picked up a bouncing Jessie after lunch and he'd let me know that the mayor was having conniptions and had called the meeting. Cole had texted me soon after to apologise. We were going to go see the latest rom-com at the movies, but now I was left without a date. I didn't want to go on my own. It was Cole's suggestion. I'd rather watch horror or science fiction movies myself. The house was still bustling with the witches getting ready for the wedding, so I grabbed my coat and headed out.

Instead of taking the bus and endangering the commuters I walked into the back garden where the ceremony would take place and found a deep shadow underneath the oak tree which loomed large. With a huff, I stepped into the shadow and stepped out in an alleyway behind Rory's club. It was fairly early in the night, so it was empty of club goers throwing up or trying to hook up. I had been pretty sure I could walk undetected here. I shoved my hands in my pockets and scooted around to the entrance of the club.

"You looking for a good time?" Tiny, the doorman, asked me with a grin.

"Always Tiny, always. You offering?" I asked, smiling up at him sweetly.

"The King would rip my balls out and shove them down my throat before I could answer that question little girl," he replied, opening the curtain up for me.

"I'd fight him for you, if you want," I offered.

He shook his head. "Don't vex him too much. He's lost friends, he's liable to do something stupid."

I nodded and patted his huge forearm. There was a reason Tiny was on the door. He discouraged many who would be idiots from entering the premise. His beard made him appear to be of Viking descent. I hadn't got around to asking him his origins. In vampire law, it was an unsightly thing to do. Too many memories that a lot of the vamps had tried to suppress.

I was shocked to see Benji and a few of his gang hanging out at the bar. A low shout sped through the boys as they saw me approach.

"Dude, it's yer mum! Yer in trouble now!" Benji's best mate TJ had wobbly legs.

"Who let these children in here?" I shouted back at him.

"Ha, you wish. I'm man enough for you." TJ waved his glass around, suds spilled out the top splashing on the floor.

"Dude, give it a rest. This is the first stop and you're already a goner." Benji held out a beer to me.

I took the glass and raised it to him. "I didn't know you're having your bachelor party tonight."

"Nah, neither did I. Didn't want it, but dickhead here decided it was the night. Sarah's got me booked solid until the wedding." Benji watched TJ sidle his way towards the dance floor. The other gang members were busy checking out the talent in the room.

"Well, it'll be a short night the way your mate's going. He's liable to offend a vamp and then he'll be in trouble," I replied tilting my chin towards TJ and his antics.

"The big guy told me he'd keep an eye out." Benji pointed at Joseph patrolling the rooms.

"Unless he offends him, then TJ will have to face the Slayer." I took a sip and winced. It was awful. I put the cup down on the bench and swayed to the beat.

"You should go dance," Benji said.

"Nah, I'm not into it."

"Dude, you're dancing now. Come on. You scare the shit out of me and the boys, so let your hair down for once and dance. I've got to be better than you at something, so let's do this." He signalled his crew to hit the floor. They yelled back an affirmative and Benji swept me on to the dance floor.

I'd been in the nightclub many times but had never danced. I honestly couldn't remember the last time, other than dancing with Cole at the Shifters ball. A rocking beat came on and the gang went crazy, knocking and popping their way against the music.

"Come on Lucy, dance a little. Try to outdo this." Benji dropped into a head spin on the lighted floor.

"Can't beat that, but I can do this." I'd studied all sorts of dancing in my training to be the heir and the music called for a fusion of belly dancing and break dancing. I closed my eyes and started to flow with the music. It was good to let my limbs move of their own accord. I didn't care who was watching. It was early in the night. The dancefloor wasn't crowded and the boys were having a good time letting loose. I was invigorated, like the music was trying to seduce me, wrapping around me and letting the tension in my muscles go.

"Holy crap," TJ said.

I opened my eyes. All of Benji's friends were staring hard. I glanced briefly and turned my back to them. The music had caught me and I didn't care what anyone thought, I was free.

"Lucy, you'd better stop," Benji whispered close to my ear.

I glared.

"You're leaking magic. I can't see it, but the boys have definitely felt it. I think a few of them need cold showers," Benji replied.

I stopped then and leered. "Did I beat you?"

"In the fuckable dance routine, certainly. But you didn't do a '820 head spin', so nope. Points go to me." He pointed at his chest, beaming proudly at his accomplishment. He was slightly inebriated, I'd never known Benji to be so forthcoming. He usually skirted around looking me directly in the eye.

"Ah, that's a shame." I stopped what I was about to say as TJ hit the floor trying to head spin and ended up collapsing on himself. "I think it's time to get that boy home."

Benji shook his head and then ran his hand over his eyes. "Every bloody time. He's a one pot wonder."

"You need to fatten him up. The kid is sticks and bones." I yelled into his ear over the start of the next thumping song.

"Ha, he eats everything. I think I'm going to call him tapeworm." He bent down, lifted TJ by his armpits and dragged him off the floor.

I signalled to Joseph to take TJ for Benji. He nodded and lifted the kid up, threw him over his shoulder. "Get him home," I whispered.

Joseph tapped the side of his forehead in a salute as if he'd heard me over the crowd and left the room. I resumed dancing as Benji's gang stumbled back to the bar for the next round.

Rory slipped up beside me while Joseph was taking TJ out. "You should heed your friend's advice and not dance like this."

"I'm relaxing. Is there a problem?" I twisted my arms up into the air.

"Not from where I'm standing, but your boyfriend walked in and he's about to rip my skin off with his teeth." His sly chuckle accompanied a wink.

Rory trailed a hand over my ribs. I was wearing jeans, boots and a long-sleeved t-shirt but the touch of his fingertips sent little sparks on my skin. The cheeky vamp was trying to use magic on me. I glared at him, dropping my arms beside me.

"You are tempting." Rory stepped back as Cole strode through the crowd.

Cole stared at Rory. Rory stared back. I turned back to the music, swaying my arms. "Boys, go compare sizes somewhere else. I'm dancing here."

"Lucy, we need to talk," Cole's voice was husky and deep.

I let my hands fall by my side. The fun police always dropped in when I was enjoying myself. "There's always talk."

"He's right. You need to hear this," Rory said in my left ear.

"Fine." I headed toward the stairs to Rory's office.

Several guys tried to touch me as I pushed my way off the dancefloor. One look from Cole made them step back. The crowd parted before me like a biblical sea.

"Don't do the eye thing," I whispered.

"Not me, all him," Rory said behind me.

"Right."

I took the stairs two at a time and threw myself onto the couch its cushions squished at the movement. In the room's corner, near the fireplace was a statue of a grotesque figure in silver. I squinted to get a better look.

"Ah, I see you've brought my handy work out."

The statue was of Sciorsaidh, a Fae being who had killed Rory's mortal family and friends. I had eliminated her recently using science.

"I thought it added some ambiance to my abode." He gave me a toothy grin.

"It adds something," I looked once more over the reamins and then back at him. "What's going on?"

"There's been a fire bombing," Cole said.

"Of what now?"

"Sugar Shack," he replied.

I stood up. "Are Marty and Emerald okay?"

"They're fine. The shack is beyond repair. The firefighters were called while we were in the meeting. A few of the council decided that we needed to end for the night so the captain and fire crew could deal with it," Rory replied.

I sat back down. "Shit."

"The arsonists seem emboldened," Rory said.

"My grandmother will pay them a lot of money. It's what she does, comes in, causes a scene and while you're busy putting out fires she will wipe out those she sees as enemies or competition. She's predictable," I replied.

Cole let out a little cough. "We thought we had a track on her."

"Don't. You don't know how she operates. If someone spots her run the opposite way." I sat on the edge of the couch.

"That's not something we can do," Cole replied.

"I thought the wards around the shack were good," I muttered mainly to myself.

"It was done with accelerant, not magic."

"Humans." I spat the word.

"The police will let us know more when they find out. Pearce is there working the case," Rory replied.

"Pearce was homicide. Why is she there?"

Cole's eyes darkened. "Someone didn't make it out in time."

"Who?"

"Don't know, but I think it might have been the arsonist," he replied.

Rory leaned back against his desk. "What idiot sets himself on fire?"

Both men stared at me.

"One who's controlled by magic and has no choice than to burn with the evidence." I sighed, it was never going to end unless we took out my grandmother and doing that would take one hell of an effort and some if not all would get hurt or killed in the trying. "What can I do?"

"We need you to keep a low profile." Rory crossed his arms over his chest, his suit jacket pulled tighly across his arms. He had the guise of a CEO who'd just gained stock he shouldn't have and was trying to figure out how to get rid of it before the feds caught him in some kind of embezzlement scheme.

I raised my eyebrow at him. He needed to get a better poker face. "Ah, you had a chat before coming to talk to me?"

Their lack of denial spoke volumes.

"I lived a perfectly fine life without all this." I waved my hand at the two of them. "I helped you out and I'm dragged into this mess."

"We are sorry, Lucy," Rory said.

"She wants me. How about I go out into the middle of the city and call her out? Let's see what she does then." I ground my teeth.

Grandmother was not one for grandiose standoffs. She got in, killed without fanfare and left. I needed to be the same. I could hunt her, find where she is, kill her before she started the ritual to open the portal. But with vampires, witches and shifters getting in the middle of things there was no way I could do this without some of them getting hurt.

"I could bring the portal up," Rory said.

"Don't you dare."

Rory uncrossed his ankles and moved away from his desk. "You and I both know that it doesn't work. She won't be able to get it to work, but she thinks it will. As long as she thinks she's getting what she wants, she'll turn up."

"How will you do this?"

"There is a gala at the museum on Friday night. I can add it to the collection. It'll draw a crowd and get people talking," he said.

"Another gala. They never go well."

"I've been to a few that were relatively boring." Rory's answering sneer spoke volumes of his thoughts on the matter.

"You'd have to work out an exit strategy for when she attacks. People will get killed."

"Leave it to me," he said.

"You can't go near her. She'll drain you and make you into a Wraith. And you, she'd love to get her mitts on you." I poked Cole in the chest gently.

He placed his hand on mine, his warmth leaking through my skin. His eyes had turned a dark blue. "We've got you."

I moved my hand slightly. The touch wasn't unpleasant but it might lead to things I was not willing to cooperate with. "The wedding is this week."

"I've talked to the witches. They're holding off for another week," Rory replied.

"Really?"

"When I explained the situation, your lovely red-headed friend agreed it was too dangerous right now, besides it'll line up better with some moon plan fertility thing that they're doing," Rory replied.

"But Benji's grandmother doesn't have much time."

"I've taken care of that too." A smug expression settled over Rory.

"What did you do? Did you turn his grandmother? I'll kill you here and now if you did."

"So feisty, that's what I love about you Lucinda, always quick to defend. No, I've given her some of my blood that will help keep off the cancer for a little while," he said. "It's not a cure, there is none, but it'll make it easier for her to wait."

I stared at him, then at Cole, then back to him again. "How did you organise all this?"

Rory shrugged. "We went through a long planning session."

"Without me?"

"You were busy and it seemed the best not to get you upset right now. You are Death's daughter. Best not to upset his immortal highness now," Rory replied.

"Death's an idiot," I snapped.

"Having daddy issues?" Rory asked his eyes alight with mirth.

"Death said I had to 'close it from both sides', then doesn't tell me how. I don't know how to fix this and it's not being helpful," I replied.

"I'm sure it'll come to you when you least expect it," Rory replied.

I scoffed and then shook my head. "How? I have to close the portal if it opens from both sides. If I don't, it'll stay open and continue to rip until this world is engulfed by those parasites."

Rory shrugged. "I'm not that versed in magic to know what to tell you. I see you have the infamous Mistress Kable working with the witches."

"How do you know her?"

"She led a saucy life when she was younger, much more liberated than other witches. A refreshing mind," he replied.

"Tell me you didn't." I scrunched my nose up.

"Me? I don't know what you're talking about." His answering smirk made me shudder.

"Eww, that's like trying to imagine your parents doing it, yuck, yuckity yuck!" I rubbed at my eyes then shook my fingers in his face as if flicking water at him.

"Well, on that note, I think it's time Cole took you home. For all our sakes, stay there. We have enough to do right now and I can't pull any of my people off their duties to follow you and keep you safe." Rory's kingly control slipping back into place.

"Oh, I'm sorry, your Majesty, for the inconvenience. I don't need either of you to keep me safe." I stood.

"Just this once stop being so bloody stubborn and let us help you," Rory said.

I stood stock still, then slowly twisted to face him. "I know you're stressed. I can tell. But I am not your subject. I will take care of myself. I appreciate the effort you're putting in, but do not tell me what to do."

Rory ran his hand through his hair at his temple. "You are so bloody frustrating."

Cole growled in warning.

"I'm done." I moved past both men, took the stairs quickly and grabbed my jacket from the girl at the door. I threw it on as I stepped deeper into night and walked through the shadows to the tree in our garden. "Fuckers."

"You shouldn't swear like that," a voice said.

I jumped and spun around fists raised.

Mistress Kable was hanging a string of lights from a low-hanging branch further down.

"You scared the shit out of me." I put my hand on my heart. It was pounding like it was trying to do an alien escape and burst out through my sternum.

"Well, now I know where Jessie gets her walking ability from. I figured you'd slip up, eventually. I had you pegged as later though. That was sloppy of you." She hopped up to link a strand down the next branch.

"Sorry I disappointed you." My tone was neutral, but I was ready to deal with anything she threw at me. I'd fought stronger witches before.

"You have dark magic. You can shadow walk. Not much else for me to know is there?"

"Do you want to make something of this?" I shoved my hands back in my pockets.

"I don't have to. You're the reason that Josie is stronger than ever. Jessie, I guess died and somehow you brought her back. That's the only way a shifter could have the abilities she does. I've read about it from a long-forgotten book," she replied.

"Not forgotten enough if you've read it."

"I spend a lot of time in libraries. Books are more reliable than people," She stepped back from her work and then gave me a knowing smile. "Now you have to be powerful to bring a child back from the dead."

"Your point?" I flexed my fingers as much as I could in my pockets.

"There is no point. You don't use your magic often."

"No, I don't need to. I get along fine without it."

"But you have so much, you could do amazing things."

"My family thought so, right up until the point where they tried to kill me."

She tilted her head at me. "That might put a damper on it, for sure."

"Look, I'm sorry, but I'm exhausted. I'm going to bed." I pushed away from the tree.

"Of course, remember that even though you don't use it, you do need to practice."

"I'll keep it in mind."

I reached the back door to Coven House and bumped into Josie laden with more strings of fairy lights.

"Lucy, Cole called to find you." Josie juggled the strings.

"He can keep looking. If anyone wants me, I'm not home. I'm going to get sleep. Unless someone wants their nose rearranged, don't let anyone disturb me."

Josie let out a laugh. "Oh, feisty Lucy is fun. I can hex them. Come on, I've wanted to hex the vamp since we met him. I might hex Cole for fun, too. Whatever he's done he deserves it."

"Fine, hex away. Just remind them that I don't need them. I'm fine on my own."

12

— · —

The next morning, I took the dogs for a run and came home sweaty but happy. Dogs don't ask idiotic questions or try to control you. They wag their tails. If you want to shout at stupid things, they'll bark along with you in case there's a bird or cat somewhere they can't smell. If you stomp your feet at the shifter, you caught hiding in the bushes, keeping an eye on you, the dogs think you're getting ready to chase them. They accept me for me with all my faults, no questions asked.

I chewed over my conversation with Mistress Kable from the night before. I still couldn't figure her out. She was helping Jessie in a big way, but the statements she made about me left me feeling a little off kilter.

I had not seen hide nor hair of my grandmother anywhere in Wayland City, but I knew she was here somewhere, hiding, biding her time to attack.

"Package for you." Josie held a box in her arms as I entered the room.

"Did you check it?" I eyed the white cardboard box suspiciously.

"Of course, no hexes or curses or anything magical about it."

"Fine, I'll open it here. Be ready." I grabbed the scissors from the second drawer.

"This feels like one of those films where you've got seven seconds to defuse a bomb before it blows." Josie leaned against the bench to get a better look.

I sliced open the sides and lifted the lid. A bunch of yellow roses sat in the centre with a small note card.

"Read it, read it," Josie said.

I lifted the card. "I'm sorry. Cole."

"Ooh, maybe you're finally making some headway with that stubborn lump of man-flesh," she chirped.

I picked up the flowers. They were tea roses and their scent was divine. Underneath the roses, I spotted an old leather-bound book. I put the roses on the bench and lifted the book out. Turning it over in my hand, I flipped the pages open.

"He knows you well." Josie picked up the roses and placed them in a vase.

"Maybe," I replied. "It's an old history book. Why would he gift me this?"

"What's it on?"

"History of Encounters with Fae and the Faerie Realm, by Hubert somebody." I flipped the next page open.

"Well, it's pertinent, that's for sure. You going to read it here and now?" she asked.

"I may as well."

"Can you take a shower first? Not to be painful or anything, but you stink of wet dog and sweat." She sniffed the roses.

"Sure. You doing much today?"

"The girls and Mistress Kable are working, Jessie's coming over soon for her next lesson,and we're going bridal dress shopping for Sarah," she said.

"Good luck with that." I gave an exasperated grunt.

One thing I hated more than anything was shopping for clothes. Josie was my personal shopper, buying things for me she knew I'd wear and occasionally throwing in an outfit I wouldn't ever buy for myself, but she knew I'd look good in.

"Oh, didn't we tell you?" Josie said with a sing-song tone.

"What?"

"You are part of our Coven and you are part of the bridal party, so you have to come too," she said.

My stomach sank like the Titanic. "No, I didn't agree to that."

"No, take backs. Our Coven has to represent. You live here, you get to dress up like we have to." Her grin widened to Cheshire Cat level.

Whining didn't come natural to me, but I couldn't modulate my tone enough to hide my annoyance. "No, come on Josie, you know how bad I am at formal things. I hate shopping. I'll mess up the wedding. Just let me hide in the background."

"Oh Lucy." Sarah came into the kitchen. "Good. I heard Benji tried to take you on the dance floor."

"He lost, of course."

Josie raised a perfectly plucked eyebrow. "You don't dance."

"Oh yes, she does. She caused quite the scene at Benji's bucks' night last night," Sarah said with a giggle.

"He tried to do a head spin, TJ was vomiting after one beer and I wanted to put him in his place." I tried to put a bit of nonchalance that I didn't feel into my voice.

"Lucy, you dance? You've never danced with me." An accusatory frown deepened on Josie's forehead.

"I had a bad day and had a drink or two and well, he challenged me. I won though. Did he tell you that?"

"He told me that most of the guys in his gang nearly fainted and now they can't stop wondering why the hot crazy dog lady didn't ditch her day jobs and go stripping, she'd make megabucks with those moves," Sarah said.

"Stripper moves?" Josie's face blazed red.

"No, I mixed hip hop with belly dancing. It felt right."

Josie grabbed my hand. "You danced? I'm hurt. Why have we never gone out dancing?"

"Because when I dance that happens." I pointed at Sarah.

"What? I didn't say it was bad." Sarah feigned innocence.

"I lose myself and have to get into a few fights to get off the dancefloor. It gets ugly." I moved away from the two witches.

"Yeah, no wonder. I heard the vamp and shifter were ready to punch on over you. I want you to dance at my wedding," Sarah said.

"No, I can't."

"Lucy, we need someone to dance. It's Coven tradition, fertility festival. You wouldn't want me to end up infertile now, would you? Cursed at my wedding because you wouldn't dance for us?

Benji told me you're freakin' awesome at it. Come on, you owe me," she said.

"How do I owe you?" I flicked at some dirt under my nails as my stomach knotted.

"I bought you those joggers." She pointed at my shoes.

I stopped what I was doing and stared at her. "You can't blackmail me over a pair of shoes."

"People have gone to war over less." Sarah pulled one of my roses out of the vase and sniffing it. "This is divine. We need to incorporate yellow roses into the flower settings."

"Come on Sarah, you can't do this to me. I hate being in front of people."

"A true friend would do anything to help a girl on her wedding day," Sarah said.

I looked over my shoulder at Josie for help. She shrugged one her shoulders, then put her hands up in acknowledgement.

"You danced without me. That kind of betrayal ain't going to help you here," Josie replied.

"Fine."

Sarah's smile was back larger than ever. "You will?"

"Fine, I hate it when you gang up on me. It's not fair."

"I have to find you the perfect outfit. This is going to be so much fun," Sarah replied.

I glared at Josie who scrunched her nose at me. This was going to end badly. I knew it.

I stomped into my room with book in hand and managed not to slam the door. I didn't want Kable or anyone else coming up to interfere in my business. How do I get roped into things? Because I have a massive guilt complex and can't say no. I lay on my bed and hit myself on the forehead with the book. As I did so, a page tumbled loose.

"Oh." I levered myself up onto my elbows and reached for the page.

The page in question didn't look like it was a part of the book. Instead, it appeared older, the writing more jagged, almost script like. I sat up straight, put the book down and picked up the paper. The words Blood Wytche and Fae jumped out at me. I don't know if Cole knew this extra page was in the book or not, but my intrigue was well and truly roused.

The paper talked of the pact between the Blood Wytches and some Fae who would enhance the Wytches power for sacrifices. I'd heard a similar tale growing up. It was my grandmother's obsession, immortality with magic. I shuddered at the thought of her attaining the power. The chaos she would unleash to attain her goal was something I couldn't allow. I'd been born to stop her. My mother had given her life for me so I could do this. A dreadful longing swept through my chest. I'd grown up without parents. The only family I had was my grandmother who treated me like a tool to use, nothing more. She'd tried to kill me once already when I turned sixteen and 'came' into my magic. Unfortunately for her, I'd failed the test and blew up half the Blood Witch coven. They had thought me dead, or at least that's what I'd hoped they had. Now I knew better. I'd never been free of her. She had been biding her time until I gained enough power to be of use to her again.

The paper had similar markings to the carvings on the portal. It jogged my memory. If I was going to this ridiculous gala thing to make sure she didn't attack the event, I would need a dress. I put the paper and book down and shuffled over to my wardrobe. I could wear the dress I wore to the Shifter Ball, but it was colder now and I didn't think I could fight well in such a flowy skirt. I hadn't told Josie or the witches I was going to another gala. They'd descend on me and try to girlify me. I loved their attention, but I was more comfortable in pants. After searching for a few minutes, I gave up. Most of my clothes were jeans and t-shirts or active wear. A couple of nice jackets and a dress or two. Nothing which said 'gala' presentable.

"Damn it."

There was no use. I'd have to go shopping. I grabbed my phone and checked my bank balance. I had enough to get what I wanted, but I would need to sell a few bits of metal if to cover things. Which reminded me I hadn't been to Rory's shop in a few weeks. I grabbed my jacket and my deep winter boots which were lined with fleece. Even at this hour, I bet it would be open. Vampires kept weird hours and now that Sciorsaidh was gone I wondered who was manning the shop. I'd been meaning to check it out.

"Where are you going?" Josie asked as I pulled up the hood of my jacket.

"Teakettle Lane."

"You going to Rory's shop?" Her face brightened; a smile tugged on her lips.

"Yes, I need some more metal and there were a few things that might be acceptable as a wedding gift."

"Don't move. Josie's skirts flew behind her as she raced off to her room.

"I wasn't going to be long."

Sarah came back into the room from training. "What's going on?"

"I'm going out to find you an appropriate wedding gift."

She offered a grin. "Anything saucy?"

I arched an eyebrow. "Not really. I know a shop that might have some nice things for you and Benji and your new life together."

"Okay, I won't ask. Secrets are good. But don't tell Benji..." she said.

"Don't tell Benji what?" Benji said from the front room.

"Ah, you're late." Sarah passed by me to wrap her arms around his neck and pull him in for a kiss.

"Don't tell me what?" Benji asked.

"I'm going shopping. Apparently, you can't be trusted with secrets," I smiled with all my teeth.

He stepped protectively back from me. "Oh man, you're mad at me about the dancing?"

"Am I?" I folded my arms in front of me.

"Come on Lucy, you've got some crazy dance moves. I thought my boys were going to have heart attacks on the club floor. I know there were a few red-eyed vamps staring," he replied, with a shiver.

"That's the last time." I didn't finish my sentence. I'd promised to dance at their wedding. I needed to learn to say no without all the guilt.

"You still didn't beat me," Benji replied, his arm wrapped around Sarah's side.

"How many vamps did you turn on with your half-arsed head spin?"

"Hey, I was getting ready when you pulled out the siren moves."

Josie came stomping back down the stairs and greeted me with a huge smile. "I'm ready."

"You don't have to come with me. I can go to the shop without all the fuss," I replied.

"Who's going shopping?" Jessie ran up from downstairs.

"Aren't you supposed to be finishing your markings?" Sarah asked.

"Mistress Kable said I did, so now I'm finished for the day." Satisfaction radiated in Jessie's voice.

"Did she now?" Sarah detached herself from Benji.

"Yep, Dad's busy with pack business so I get to hang out with you guys for a while. Mum's out of town on family work," she said with a worried frown.

"Well, Josie and Lucy are going shopping for a wedding present for me," Sarah replied, her tone mild.

Jessie stared at me with her big brown expectant eyes.

I put my hands in my pockets and shrugged. "I was going to have a look. I wasn't sure I'd get anything. I have the gala thing tomorrow night."

"A gala?" Josie said with a frown.

"Vampires are showing off."

"You've got nothing to wear," Sarah and Josie both said.

"I know. I was going to get something while I was out."

Josie grabbed Jessies hand. "Girl's trip!"

Triumph was etched on Jessies cherubic face. She had won this one. "Excellent."

I threw my hands up with dramatic flair and spun slowly around scanning the room for an out. "Why do I do this to myself? I should have told you I was going out to get menstrual pads or something."

Sarah screwed up her nose. "We've got heaps of them in the storage cupboards. Your excuse wouldn't have worked. You should have tried to lead with you needed to go renew your driver's licence or something."

"I do have to do that soon. Thanks for the reminder," I replied. "Fine, but I'm not going all girly this time. I need to fight in my outfit."

"Why?" Jessie asked.

"Because the wicked witch might attack and I need to fight her." I realised the moment I said the words what I'd done.

Jessie frowned, her mind racing. "She's going to be there?"

"No, I hope not. You can't go." I waved my hands at her before she responded. "And if you shadow walk, I will tell my Dad and he'll stop your access to the shadow realm."

Shock flooded Jessie as she gave me an expression of betrayal.

"I mean it. I'm not letting you get hurt, ever."

"Hey, let's not think about that. We need to go get the car and head to the shops. Jessie, you get front seat. Lucy's nasty, so she gets to sit in the back." Josie grabbed the keys from the bowl on the kitchen bench.

Jessie rounded her shoulders and walked slowly after Josie towards the garage in silence.

"Don't mind her, she'll get over it in a minute," Sarah said.

"She's young. She'll do something stupid. I can't let her get hurt. I've lost too many that I love."

13

Our trip into the city was uneventful. Josie was telling Jessie all sorts of stories of growing up a witch and hexing the mean girls in her school. Jessie sat quietly, listening. Guilt reared its ugly head again in my stomach. I had to stay strong. Jessie was too precious to go up against a Blood Witch. I didn't know the full extent of her magic yet, but my grandmother would rip it out of her and leave a smoking husk in a blink of an eye with no remorse.

"We're here." Josie turned her car off.

The shop was deep in Teakettle Lane, an older part of the city that held many used books stores. Rory had set up the shop as a front for all sorts of business opportunities he could transact in daylight. His club was his night time office. I doubted he would be awake right then, but you never knew.

We pushed open the door and the tinkle of the bell should have alerted someone to the fact that there were customers. I'd seen no one else in the shop except the creature who had been held captive there for years. The tang of aged shelving hit me. Usually the shop was spotless, except for the areas around silver artefacts. No one had dusted in a few weeks. Small piles of dust were left scattered around.

"Oh, what is this place?" Jessie crinkled her nose.

"This is a curiosity shop," Josie said. "I found a Dragon Riders set in mint condition never out of the box for twenty dollars."

"Really?" Jessies face picked up. "Can I look around?"

"Yep, go for it, but if you feel something's off, don't touch it," I said. "Some things can leave a nasty zap."

Jessie ignored me and flounced off down the shelves, picking up everything that caught her eye and giving them a sniff before moving to the next thing.

"She'll come around," Josie whispered.

I shrugged. "Better angry and safe, then the other."

I walked down one aisle. There were many little nick knacks which appeared to be about over a hundred years old, they were still made of beaten metal, no circuits or plastic involved. I knelt down and found a little jewellery box which had a lid enamelled in ebony. When I opened it up, it played a melody while a little ballerina spun on the spot. Jessie would like this. I grabbed it and then headed further into the shop. There were several sets of silver knives set at the back of the shelving which I grabbed and then I found a beautiful little tea set with tiny red roses around the rim. I flicked my nail against the cup and it tinged. A sign that it was fine china and not some imitation. It was perfect for what I wanted to get Sarah and Benji. Well, Sarah really. Benji wouldn't care if he drank from an old mug. I took my gifts up to the counter and placed them ready to pay.

Jessie yelped from two aisles away. I spun and ran towards her. Ready to fight whoever had tried to harm her. Josie beat me to her by a fraction of a second.

"Are you alright?" Josie asked.

"She didn't realise I was here." Raoul's thick accent was even more prominent for Jessie's sake.

"You don't sneak up on people," Jessie snapped.

"I usually can't sneak up on a shifter. Something must have caught your eye and you took your guard down," Raoul replied.

Jessie growled low, her hand clutched around a bangle. "Try me vamp."

"Hey, that's enough. Raoul, apologise for scaring Jessie. Jessie don't fight the vampire, I don't have time to explain to your dad why you're starting an interspecies war right now." I folded my arms across my chest.

"Sorry Jessie. I should have announced my presence." Raoul bowed with a flourish.

Jessie stared at him for a moment as if weighing up if she should fight the suave vampire. "I'm sorry."

I nodded at both of them. "Jessie, what did you find?"

"A bangle, it's gold with green stones in it. Mum would love it." Her eyes were alight looking at the bangle.

"Emeralds?" I asked.

"Jade." Jessie held it out to me with an iron grip as if we would have to pry it from her dead hands if we wanted it ourselves.

"You're right. That is lovely jade. How much does the docket say it is?"

"Too much." She looked up at Raoul, her brown eyes widening almost teary.

"Would you like it?" Raoul asked.

Jessie stared at him as if he had said the stupidest thing she'd ever heard, then nodded her head. "Yes, but I have no money."

"Well, seeing as though you promised not to kill me with your extraordinary shifter powers you can have it as a blood price for my life." Raoul leaned down and patted her on the wrist.

"I can't. Dad said I'm not allowed to talk to vampires." Her voice trailed off.

"You didn't kill me when you had the chance. That means I owe you a debt. This bangle repays the debt in full, would you deny me the honour of paying a debt?"

She shook her head, her blonde pigtails flaring out as she did so. "No."

"Then it's yours, but best not tell your father where it came from. I don't think I could take him on, especially if his daughter is so fierce," he replied.

"You sure?" Jessie clutched the bangle.

"It is a debt paid," Raoul stood and brushed the dust off his knee.

I swept my gaze around the store. "You need someone in here to clean this up."

"We do," he replied. "But we're short staffed at the moment."

"I'll talk to Benji. He has friends that need a job."

"The gangsters? Letting them in here, with all this?" Raoul gave me a shocked expression.

"Yes, believe it or not, they do have morals. They won't rip you off too much," I said. "Besides Mr Chop Shop, you've dealt with them before."

"That's why I'm hesitant to let them in here." A shiver rolled through him.

Josie stood staring at the two of us and then honed her gaze in on Raoul. "You're the bartender."

"Yes," he replied.

"It's daytime." She pointed at the window where sunlight was dappling through onto the benchtop.

He nodded.

"You're a vampire and it's day time." Curiosity rolled through her voice.

"Yes, sometimes we can rise and tend the shop if it's necessary."

"Okay." Her frown showed she didn't believe him, but she was too polite to pursue the matter.

"Do you need anything Lucy?" Raoul asked.

"I have some things on the counter I want. I'll transfer money into your account once you tell me the price." I then as Jessie shuffled closer to Josie.

"Of course." He moved swiftly around me with liquid vampire grace.

"I have a few things." Josie grabbed Jessies free hand and pulled her towards the counter.

She had found a set of amethyst earrings and a matching necklace set in a white velvet cushioned case. Jessie's eyes widened as she let out a sigh.

"You like jewellery?" Josie asked.

Jessie nodded. "The departed showed me so many pretty necklaces and things."

Raoul's eyes shot up, but he said nothing. He scribbled a number on a piece of paper and handed it to me. I took it from him and sent him a small smile in return.

I glanced at Raoul. "Have they found out who burnt the Shack?"

"Not yet, there was a body found. They think it was the arsonist, but it was too badly burned," he replied.

"The Sugar Shack was burned?" Josie asked.

"I forgot to tell you."

"My dad is looking into it, with that funny police woman." Jessie's face took on a crestfallen appearance. "No more doughnuts."

"Detective Pearce isn't that funny," I mumbled.

"She looks at the world cross eyed," Jessie said.

"She's not cross-eyed," Raoul and I both said.

"No, she sees things, but she refuses to see them. She's gotten better, but her old partner, the one with the moustache not to hunter, used to yell at her a lot. She couldn't hear him, but he yelled all the same. He was cranky. I'm glad he's gone," she replied.

"Don't." I held my hand up to Raoul who took the information with a straight face.

"I have no idea what you mean," Raoul replied.

"We all have secrets," I reminded him.

"Indeed, we do. It seems there are more and more around you," he replied. "Always a pleasure."

With that, Raoul faded into the back of the shop.

Josie stared at the spot he'd stood in. I twisted my shoulders to study her and then directed my gaze at where she was staring. The shop window had let in direct sunlight, right where Raoul had stood. He should have gone up in flames, but he'd stood there without care. Josie me offered me a look of horror and then understanding.

"Did you do that?" she asked in a voice barely a whisper.

I clutched my purchases to me. "It's a long story."

"Always is." She gathered her things as she mumbled to herself under her breath.

The idea of vampires being able to walk in daylight was an abomination in the thoughts of the other supernaturals. Similar to witches that could harness dark magic and shifters that could shadow walk. I had accidentally changed so many things in the past year and I didn't know what would happen if the wrong people found out. A distant shiver rolled down my spine, leaving tiny spider webs of worry clinging to my soul.

"Can I see your bracelet?" I asked Jessie as we walked back to the car.

She hesitantly handed it over. It was nine carat gold with jade embedded at intervals, little wolf carvings had been laid between the stones. Jessie was right, it was a perfect gift for a shifter.

"I got you something." I handed her back the bracelet, which she snatched quickly and shoved in her pocket.

"What?"

"I had one like this when I was a girl. I'd keep all my important things in." I held out the jewellery box to her.

Her eyes lit up. "It's pretty."

"Open it."

She did so and the ballerina spun to the music. "That's the song the maiden sings."

"Which maiden?" Josie asked, unlocking the car.

"She died. She was pushed off a cliff by a man. She's gone too," Jessie said.

"We'll get them back."

"Or we'll get revenge," Jessie whispered.

I hugged her. "I will kill her. She's my kill. But I will need your help."

Jessie nodded and then settled into the car seat still holding the box.

"Well, on that note. Where are we going to get you an outfit?" Josie asked, trying to improve the mood.

"I want an overcoat which can be used as a dress and pants," I replied.

"But it's a gala." Josie tried hard to control the whine in her voice.

"Then let's make it a fancy coat." I stuck my tongue out at her through the rear vision mirror.

"Fine, I know someone who does those." The car purred to life.

I peered out the window towards the street and noted two shifters fading into the background. Lucy duty got a bit more complicated with the alpha's daughter and the coven head being in the same car as me. I wondered what they'd tell their boss when they checked in. Who was I kidding? Brad and Cole probably knew everything we'd spoken about. I was getting sick of being the centre of so many people's attention. I understood why they thought they had to, but in fairness I was the one who had killed the Blood Witch and the Witch Hunter. I could handle my grandmother.

As soon as the thought popped into my head, I knew I was fooling myself. I'd always be the little kid standing before her waiting for the punishment that she would mete out because I wasn't perfect at a spell or hex. My heart pounded thinking about it.

"You okay Lucy?" Jessie asked from the front seat.

"Huh? Yeah, I hate shopping." I pushed aside the anxiety doing flips in my stomach. I did hate shopping, I hated the way it made me feel less than adequate. I hated the way the assistants stared down their nose at me when I didn't know what the latest fabric or trend was. I hated the uselessness of owning a piece of clothing that would be outdated within a few months. Most of all I hated the superficialness. Life was worth more than a few sequins. I'd told Josie this repeatedly and she still insisted that I shop with her.

"She does. You should see what she used to wear before she moved in with us," Josie said.

"Really?"

"It was awful. Tragic, even. She had two pairs of jeans, one was so thin in the butt that I thought every time she sat down it would rip," Josie replied.

"Yeah, yeah. Some people aren't fashionistas." I waved my hand.

Jessie guffawed. "But you're a witch. Witches love clothes."

"Not this one. This one would rather be out fighting bad guys than standing in a cubicle while some nasty women stare down their noses at you, telling you that you're not pretty enough or not thin enough to pull off a look."

"They don't do that to me," Josie said.

"No, because they recognise you have money."

"You've got money?" Jessie asked me.

"Not really, I could, but it's not important."

"I have some money if you need it," she replied.

I reached over and patted her on the shoulder. "It's okay. Let me show you what I can do."

I took the silverware from the bag beside me and held them in my left hand. I then pulled the metalsmithing magic from inside me and melded it to the silver. The metal flowed in and out of my fingers as if it was a snake coiling about. I then pictured the sword I wanted to make and pushed the image to the metal. It flowed into the shape with relative ease.

"That's amazing." Jessie let out an excited squeak.

"It's something I was born with. No one knows really, so this can be our secret?"

"Yes. Can you show me how to do it?" she asked.

"I don't know. I don't know if it's something that can be taught."

"But if you could you would?" she asked.

"You bet I would."

"Can you turn metals into gold?" she asked with a sparkle in her eye.

"Yes, but I try not to."

"Why?"

"Because if I made everything gold, then gold would lose its value. It wouldn't be worth the same because I'd made too much. It's expensive because it's rare."

"So, jewels are the same?" she asked.

"Yep. The less likely you are to find it the more expensive it is."

"Sort of like friendships, huh?" she asked.

"Yes, like friendships," Josie said. "Some people don't realise how rare it is that they have people willing to help."

"Point taken," I muttered.

"We're here, let's go find this woman something that won't embarrass us in public." Josie shot a wink at Jessie.

"Will these things be safe in the car?" Jessie asked, putting her jewellery box and bangle on the console.

"This is a witch's car," Josie replied. "I've warded it and placed hexes all over it. If someone tries to touch it, they'll come out with boils on their bum."

"Can I learn that?" Jessie asked excitedly.

"Mistress Kable taught me everything I know," Josie replied as we locked the car.

"Mistress Kable is going to kill you." I nudged Josie as we walked into the high-priced store.

Josie gave me a small push me back with her shoulder. "She'll love it. She loves students who are curious,and boil hexes are her specialty."

"Remind me not to get on her bad side."

Josie laughed and followed me in. We'd been here before to get my other gowns. I remembered the snooty service officers, but their faces changed the minute they saw Josie, going from disinterested to fawning in a heartbeat. I sighed. It was going to be a long day.

"Alan, Maeve, we need a new look," Josie said. "One that says bad arsed bitch who won't take shit from no one."

The two tittered at Josie's use of language and then set off into the stacks of high-priced clothes with glee. I sat on the soft couch and waited for the parade to begin. Jessie whispered something to Josie and she nodded. Jessie ambled over to several dresses, running their fabric through her fingers with a soft smile settling on her. Josie called her to another stack of dresses and the two of them started talking about flow and cut. I zoned out. If I was a princess, this is where I'd shop. But I'm not, I'm a security guard who is more tomboy than princess.

The first round of dresses was too fluffy, too restricting, or wrong colouration. Josie rejected everything. Jessie had a strange glint to her eyes and wandered off. I tried to keep a magic eye on her progress in case she shadow-walked, but she stayed in the store rummaging through dress racks. The next round of dresses was entirely too revealing.

"I can't wear this. Half my boobs are showing and one arse cheek. It's a gala event Josie." I was not willing to walk out of the change room to show the dress off.

"Fine, we'll keep going." Josie smile lit up at my frown.

"Just something which lets me run and fight in, but keeps me warm, that's all I want." I threw my own clothes back on.

"Is it an outdoors event?" Josie asked.

"Yes, kind of. It'll be indoors and outdoors, but I'm not hanging out inside."

"I wonder why I haven't received an invitation." Josie's casual tone let me know that it bothered her. Josie was passionate about everything. If she was yelling or swearing, she was fine, the minute she slipped into a calm and collected demeanour you were in trouble.

"It is a last-minute thing that the vampires are putting together," I replied. "I have to go because of things, but you wouldn't want to hang out."

"I wouldn't." She picked at the hem of a feathered dress to the side of her seat.

I stared at her artfully trying to avoid begging me to intervene, and then sighed. "I'll tell him to invite you."

"Yes, you will. If I'm postponing a wedding, he'll have to give me an invitation."

"Okay, I'll text him." I pulled out my phone.

"Look at you being all caught up with technology," Josie said.

"Don't mock me. This is hard enough as it is."

"Josie, come here," Jessie said from three racks away.

"Coming." Josie bolted out of her chair and disappeared behind more dresses.

I sat back down on the couch and concluded my text to Rory, putting three exclamation marks on it in case he didn't think I was serious. I need the witches willing to work with the vampires and shifters and the last thing I needed was Josie with her nose out of joint about a party. I shoved the phone back in my pocket and waited.

"Close your eyes Lucy." Jessie waved her two hands at me, her eyes bright.

"Okay, why?"

"Just, it's you. You'll love this one," she replied.

I had my eyes firmly shut when the assistants whispered together with Josie. I heard the fitting room curtain open and a hanger placed on the hook.

"You can look now." Jessie also had broad grin staring up at me.

"You want me to go try it on?"

"You will wear it like a warrior." Jessie pointed her finger at the dressing room.

"Yes ma'am." I gave her a mock salute.

"It's Circassian, I forgot we had it in," Maeve the assistant said.

I stepped into the fitting room. There were no mirrors inside. They were out in the rest of the room. I stood before a military looking long emerald green velvet coat with silver embroidery down the sides and latches across the chest. The high collar opened at the neck and the coat was latched shut above the breast. The dress coat opened to show a set of silver pants with pockets that you wear underneath. The embroidery on the arm depicted oak leaves and the wide silver belt which went with the coat had a tree design built in. I put the pants on, then the coat, which was long enough and flowy enough to be a dress. The buttons were a bit of a pain to do up, but the outfit worked. There was a loop in the belt that seemed to allow me to attach a sword to it.

"Come on, Lucy, show us." Josie;s voice was close to the curtain.

"Step back, this is going to be interesting." I pulled back the curtain to the change room.

"Holy mackerel." Jessie had her two hands in front of her mouth holding in a giggle.

"Do you like?" I stepped out of the tiny change booth and twirled in place for her.

The coat's skirt was done in panels which floated freely from each other, each panel lined in embroidery on the sides. It was warm, but not overly so and had a bit of give in the shoulders and chest which I would need if I fought anyone. I deliberately hadn't seen the price tag yet. I would do what I needed to do so I could buy it.

"You look like a kick arse warrior woman from days gone by," Josie said.

The assistants nodded along with her, though I don't know if they were convinced that this was appropriate for a gala.

"I'll take it."

"She said you would," Jessie murmured.

"Who said?"

"The little old lady that was over there." Jessie pointed towards the back of the room.

I scanned the room. There were other shoppers, but no one matching Jessie's description. "Who? Can you show me where?"

"Come on." Jessie dragged me with her to a rack at the far end of the room.

I stood still when we got there. My grandmother had been here and I hadn't sensed her. Panic rose in my chest, my heart squeezed tightly and I couldn't breathe.

"Lucy? Lucy are you okay?"

I stood staring at the spot Jessie had pointed to. Grandmother had left me a present. A diamond pendant which had belonged to the Dorchasas line for generations. I'd seen her wear it to formal occasions many times. Now it stared at me like a loadstone.

14

I bent down and grabbed Jessie by the shoulders. "Jessie, when I tell you, I want you to grab Josie and run the shadows back to the house. Can you do that?"

Jessie frowned. "You told me I'm not allowed to."

"Jessie, that was the wicked witch you talked to."

"But she was kind," Jessies face dropped. "She didn't smell like a witch."

"No, she can hide her smell. You need to take Josie now. Walk her out of here. I need to count on you to do this. I am going to find the witch," I said. "Go now."

Jessie nodded, her eyes flaring amber like her alpha father and then sprinted back to Josie. She grabbed her arm and pulled her away into the shadows behind the fitting room as if Josie weighed nothing at all. I sensed her slide into the netherworld and breathed a sigh of relief. The two assistants stood staring at me dumbfounded.

"I need to see your footage of this area, it's important." I picked up the brooch.

"You need to pay for the dress." Maeve pointed at the till. The smell of her cloying perfume was laced with sweat as if she knew suddenly that her shop was in trouble and she was trying to make the best of it while she could.

"Here's my card, ring it up, while you." I pointed at the man. "Take me to see your footage. There was a lady trying to kidnap the girl here. I think there might be a sex trafficking ring trying to target your customers."

They both stopped open-mouthed and stared at me.

"Please, I need to see it so I can take it to the police."

"Shouldn't we get them now?" Maeve asked, ringing up my dress.

"I work with Detective Pearce who's in charge of this operation. We had a hunch something might happen. That's why we're here. I need to see the footage."

They nodded and then Maeve handed me back my card.

"Do you want to change back into your clothes so I can wrap them up while you look?" she asked in a timid voice.

"What? Oh, yes. Sorry, I'll do that, won't be a second."

It took me far longer than I wanted to take the coat off, but I handed it back to Maeve while I followed Alan to the security office. It was a fruitless search. I could see Jessie from the angle of the camera, but my grandmother had hidden herself well, so we couldn't get an adequate view of her. I thanked him, picked up my outfit and withdrew to the car. I didn't need Josie's keys to start it, being a metalsmith had its advantages. I worried what I would tell Brad about Jessie almost being taken by a Blood Witch while

I was with her. I searched around for the shifters who should have been watching and protecting us. There was no sign. That was not good. I grabbed my phone and dialled Coles number. There was no answer. I texted both him and Brad to find out where their people were. I had a bad feeling about what they would say.

My phone rang and I picked it up without thinking.

"What the bloody hell are you doing?" Josie screeched at me.

"I'm driving one handed while I talk to you," I replied. "Any minute now Pearce is going to show up and drop a big fine on me for breaking the law."

"That was horrendous, never let Jessie do that to me again," Josie said.

"Shadow walk? It's not bad."

"It was awful. Why did you get her to do that?"

"My grandmother was there. She approached Jessie and suggested the dress. She was right there and I didn't feel a thing. She could have got Jessie." My heart was still racing.

"Damn."

"We need to redo the wards, again."

"I'll get the girls onto it."

My phone trembled in my hand. "I've tried contacting Cole and Brad and they're not answering. I think the shifters that were tailing us are dead."

"She got through them. Jessie says she didn't feel like a witch. How is it possible?" Josie asked.

"Blood Witches drain the power from others, so they can shape change and it makes them not feel like a witch for a while. It reasserts itself the longer they are in form."

"She could be anyone and we wouldn't know until she attacks." Despair crept into Josie's tone.

"I'm going to fix that."

"Why didn't she attack us?" Josie asked.

"Hang on, I'm getting another call. I'll be there in a minute." I hung up.

"Cole," a male voice came over the phone.

"It's me."

"Everything okay?"

"Do you know where the tails you had on me are?"

"They were still with you half an hour ago when they clocked in with us," Cole replied.

"Do you have trackers or something on them that you can find them?"

"Sort of, why?"

"My grandmother came near, she spoke with Jessie." I winced at the silence which greeted my words.

It took Cole around four seconds before he cleared his throat. "Is she okay?"

"She shadow-walked back to Coven House. Grandmother can't get her there, she's safe."

Cole spoke after a moment's pause. "Brad is on his way to get her,"

"I'm sorry. I was supposed to keep an eye on her. It's my fault she came near Jessie."

"The shifters are behind some store. They're not answering," Cole said.

"Send someone to retrieve their bodies. I'm sorry I couldn't keep them safe."

"I'll be at the house as soon as I can." Cole hung up.

I dropped the phone onto the seat beside me as I stopped at traffic lights. The door burst open and Pearce landed in the seat beside me. Screaming and patting her arms.

"Drive, fuck you," she screeched at me.

"Holy shit Pearce, what are you doing here?" I pushed my foot onto the accelerator and took off faster than I'd ever had.

"Get me out of the damn light you moron, how can I protect you if I'm on fucking fire, Driver?"

Pearce was wearing a long, black coat and hood which covered most of her body. She had thick black gloves on and was huddling out of the light from the window.

"Faster." She gritted teeth, her fangs extended, giving her a sibilant hiss to her words.

"I am going faster. If I go faster still, we'll crash," I yelled back at her. "You sat on my phone."

"It'll live. Just get me indoors quickly." She had a hint of pain in her tone.

"We're coming up to the garage now, hold on." I jumped the curb and slid the car down the driveway to the open garage door. "I thought you could handle some sun."

Pearce panted in her seat when the garage door slid shut behind us. "Fuck this for a bad joke. I need some of your blood."

"What?"

"I need to day walk properly, you're it. I need you to do to me whatever you did to Raoul. How can I protect you if I can't walk in the sunlight? This is a shit job I tell you." Her fangs still extended, Pearce's face went through several micro-emotions before settling on worried.

"I'm not giving you my blood." I hopped out of the car keeping it between me and the detective.

"It works doesn't it? I need to work in the daylight. Those fucking shifters couldn't do the job, so it's up to me." She got out of the car and stomped towards me.

"It could kill you," I replied. "I was desperate with Raoul. It nearly killed him."

"I'm tougher than that pretty boy. Just give me your arm and we'll get this over with." Pearce's tone was police procedural grey, as if this was another crappy part of her job.

"No."

"Lucy." Pearce's eyes glowed red.

"Don't even think about it, creature of the darkness!" Mistress Kable shouted at the door her arms extended, green magic rolling off them in waves.

"What the fuck? Driver, who's the psychotic librarian?" Pearce shook her head and advanced towards me.

"Kable, I've got this. Pearce is a friend." I held on to the box with my gala outfit while trying to wave the witch off.

"No chance, she's gone red eyed. She'll leap on you before you can blink," the witch replied.

"Mistress Kable, it's okay, that's Detective Pearce, she's helping us." Josie emerged behind the witch in the doorway.

"I need to do this. You don't understand. Driver is in danger, you know that, so give me blood and I can help fix it." Pearce took another step toward me.

"You creature of deceit, step away from the girl before I put you down for good." Kable's magic caused her hair to flow out like brown and purple dandelion fluff in a windstorm. Crazy maths teacher cosplay was working for her.

"I don't have time for this Driver. Put away your witch, let's get this done." Pearce put her hands on her hips.

"Mistress Kable, it's okay. This is Detective Pearce, she will not pounce on me, she will stop the red eye thingy that's happening right now and we'll go have a cup of tea in the kitchen to sort this mess out." I moved towards Pearce to show my faith in her not ripping my throat out.

"This is a witch's domain." Kable pulled back some of her magic.

"Yep and Pearce has saved our lives before. We owe her."

Josie whispered something in her teacher's ear and the witch shut her magic down. She sighed heavily, her hand on her heart and moved towards the kitchen. I nodded thanks to Josie and shoved my dress box into Pearce's hands.

"Don't damage it." I walked past her.

Pearce rolled her eyes a little. "I'm not your freakin' slave."

"Nope, but you want something from me and so you'll carry that for me."

Josie had Jessie helping her in the kitchen, setting out little cakes and biscuits onto plates while the kettle boiled ready for tea. Jessie stopped and stared at me, then used her shifter speed to run and hug me around the waist, burying her head in my stomach.

"It's okay." I hugged her back.

"I should have torn her throat out." Jessie's words came out with a half sob. "I'm sorry."

"No, remember, she's my kill. You don't move in on someone else's kill, do you?" I let her go and knelt to face her.

She wiped her eyes. "No."

"I called it a long time ago."

"She was right there, though. She was a little old lady," Jessie said.

"I know. She's a master at disguises, uses stealth to pick her prey and then waits to attack."

Jessie mulled over my words. "We're better hunters than she is."

"Yes, we are." My knees creaked as I stood.

"Need some oil for those old knees Driver?" Pearce dropped the dress box on the table.

"Jessie, could you put that box on my bed?" I gave Pearce a shitty look.

"Yes." With the swiftness of a shifter, she flew out of the room.

"So, are we going to at least talk about this?" Pearce slid a chair out from the table and sitting down with fluid grace.

I blinked at her, trying to tilt my head towards the witch still itching to wipe the vampire off the face of the earth.

"Mistress Kable, is it?" Pearce asked.

Kable stood up to her full five-foot two height and placed both hands on her hips. "I am."

"You know anything about the disturbance at the academy three weeks ago?" Pearce voice held a light and breezy tone.

Oh no, I knew that tone. She had something on Kable and was leading her into a trap. I wanted to warn the witch, but I was of two minds about whose side I was on.

"You mean the one where a student tried to blow up the faculty coffee machine so I hexed her powers, as this was the fourth attempt she had at destruction? Objectionable Defiance Disorder my butt, she didn't have any of the symptoms, she decided she wanted to get her own way." Kable stared Pearce down.

"Do you know who she is related to?" Pearce asked. Her voice still calm.

"Yes, she had told me several times that she was the niece of our current state representative. I told her she could be the Queen of Sheba for all I care. She will not use poor circle form in my classroom," Kable replied.

"Ah, youth," Pearce said.

"Indeed, too much pride and not enough humility," Kable replied.

"I know how that is. You work hard, you put in extra hours and then they try to take it from you." Pearce scratched the back of her neck.

"Youth is wasted on the young." Kable slid a chair out opposite Pearce and sat down.

Josie picked that moment to bring the tea and biscuits. She offered me a quizzical look and I signalled with my fingers slightly not to interfere.

"You see Mistress Kable, Lucy here has an ability which I need to take advantage of. I'm head of the police division and we've been tasked with getting rid of a Blood Witch threat." Pearce picked up a macaroon and placing it on a plate in front of her.

"Blood Witches are nasty, takes a lot to stop them," Kable replied.

"I know. That's why I'm willing to face death if I need to in order to stop this woman before she hurts our city," Pearce said.

"Oh, for goodness' sake, she's going the martyr route," I muttered under my breath.

Pearce's squint quelled my retort. Kable tut-tutted at me for poor manners. I grabbed three biscuits and shoved them in my mouth before I could say something nasty.

"As you were saying," Kable said.

"I have worked as a police detective for years. I've only been turned. Is that what we call it?" Pearce asked no one in particular.

"Yes, turned I believe." Kable took a dainty bite of a cake.

"I was turned after I tried to save Lucy and Jessie from a Witch Hunter," Pearce said.

Kable grabbed her chest. "NO."

"Yep, turns out my partner on the force was an undercover Witch Hunter and he tried to kill Jessie and Lucy here," Pearce replied. "I died stopping him, so the Vampire King turned me after I died."

"Oh, dear," Kable replied.

"But I can't work during the day. The old ultraviolet radiation burns vampires through clothes. Can you believe it?"

Kable nodded her head.

"Now, it's believed that Lucy, with her magic can help me overcome my UV sensitivity, but she doesn't want to help me, even though I died for her." Pearce picked at the biscuit in her hand, a note of longing in her eyes as she did so.

"Well, it's her duty. You've sacrificed for her," Kable replied.

"See that's what I think. You work hard, you do everything you can to help others and then when you need help." Pearce spread her arms wide.

Mistress Kable appeared to ponder her words cautiously, then turned her attention to me. "Would what she's asking work?"

I pursed my lips. "It has a high rate of failure. She's likely to die for real this time."

"But there's a chance you could help her?" Kable asked.

"A small chance." I sighed and grabbed another cake to shove in my mouth.

"Then why won't you? She did sacrifice for you," Kable replied.

I pushed back in my chair. "She would be a day walker."

Kable nodded, waiting for me to continue as if I was answering a maths question.

"A day walker, a vampire that could walk the streets during the day." I put both hands behind my head.

"Lucy, I thought better of you. I didn't realise you had these prejudices." Mistress Kable used her disappointed teacher's tone, the one that would usually have you cringing in your seat in front of your classmates.

Luckily for me, Josie was sitting, studying her biscuit and not sniggering behind her hand at me, squirming in my seat.

"Yes, but a day walker. If word got out, then our city would be flooded with hungry vamps trying to either get the cure themselves or kill me before I could turn anyone else."

Kable looked over her shoulder at Pearce. "Who would you tell?"

"No one, she's already done it once. I know it works. I need to work both day and night to protect her and everyone here," Pearce said.

Kable nodded and then she glanced over Pearce's shoulder. I craned my neck to see what had her attention.

Jessie was walking over, holding the page from my book tenderly in her hands. Wonder filled her expression.

"Jessie, what do you have?" Mistress Kable asked. Her curiosity spiking.

"It's about the shadow lands," Jessie said.

I tilted my head, from what I'd read the shadow lands weren't even mentioned. "No, it's about Blood Witches."

Jessie held the page out to me. "If you turn it sideways and look through the shadows at it, there's an answer there. Look at it through both sides."

"Ahh, right."

"May I see that?" Kable asked, holding her hand out to Jessie.

Jessie placed the paper into the teachers' hand and stepped back.

"It's old, pre-witch war old," Kable muttered. "She's right. There're two sets of writing on this. You can't see it unless you tip it, but I can't read it. It's not in a language I understand."

Jessie patted her teacher on the arm. "It's okay, it's in Drevnian. The language has been dead for thousands of years. They used to worship Death and Life, but had weird things through their noses."

"How do you know this?" I slowly rose from my chair to take the paper from the teachers' hands.

"Death told me," she said.

15

—·—

I swallowed and tried to remain calm. "I thought you were trying on my shoes or playing with the swords I have in there."

"Nah, they're nice and all, but this is more important. You need both sides Lucy, that's what I needed to say to you." Jessie yeawned.

My phone rang in my pocket. It was a text from Cole. They were at the doorway but couldn't enter because the wards had been changed.

"I'll go let them in." Jessie raced off to the front door.

"Shit," I stared at the two witches and the vamp. This was another complication I didn't need right then.

Jessie could talk to my parent without me there and could read ancient languages. I had changed her more than I realised. I had brought her back from death and I knew that every soul that comes back goes through changes. I had no idea my magic would affect her this much. I shivered at what her parents, especially Lauren her mother would say when they found out her latest abilities.

The shifters had serious faces as they entered the kitchen behind Jessie. I frowned and tried to signal Cole, but he was focused on Pearce.

"The shifters were killed," Cole said to her.

Pearce nodded. "Thought so. They'd never leave their post."

"I'm sorry about letting Jessie near the witch," I said to Brad.

"If she can fool Jessie, then she could fool all of us. Jessie has the best nose out of all the pack." Brad wrapped his arm around his daughter.

"I was busy looking for Lucy's dress, so I wasn't being careful." Jessie eyes were downcast, her shoulders slumped as if ashamed.

"It's okay. She got past me as well," Josie replied. "And I'm Coven Leader. I feel bad, but I'm going to learn from my mistake."

Jessie nodded.

"We'll do detecting spells in the morning, Jessie," Mistress Kable said.

Determination ebbed from Jessie, but she pressed her lips tight, as if trying not to give away a secret. I wondered how much I had changed her and if she would thank me as she grew older for all the trials she'd go through now she had magic as well as shifter abilities.

"Jessie, you said Death told you how to read this writing. Do you mean your powers?" Kable asked quietly as she studied the lines one more time.

"No, Death. It tried to use a wolf's form but the hind legs were too weird looking, so we talked in cloud mode," Jessie replied.

I nodded. I preferred that mode as well. Death tried to accommodate my feelings and appeared as an older human, then an elf and finally a cloud. Cloud mode let me remember who and what Death was. Entropy was another inevitable force in the universe, like gravity.

"Ah, well that explains it." The witch gave her a look which showed Jessies answer was as clear as mud.

"The shifters might help me." Pearce turned to face them.

Brad's eyes darkened, but Cole remained neutral. When he got like this, I couldn't tell if he was readying for a fight or trying to calculate how many socks his washing machine had eaten on the last cycle. I made myself a promise that I would never play strip poker with him unless I wanted to lose. The thought of playing strip poker with a hunky lumberjack sent my body responding. I cursed my brain for those stray thoughts and hoped to high hell that Cole couldn't tell what was going on in my nether regions. He kept his cool demeanour focused on Pearce.

"As you have said the witch got to your men. I have asked Lucy to help me protect her," Pearce said.

Coles eyes flashed bright blue then settled back to his normal colour. "Go on."

"If Lucy gifts me a few drops of blood I will overcome the UV skin issue I have and can follow her without burning. You can pull your other operatives off her and focus on keeping your pack safe. I know that run on your compound last night taxed you," Pearce said.

"What run?" I stared holes into Cole and Brad.

"The witch tried our defences at the pack house," Brad said.

"Why didn't you let me know?"

"You were busy," Brad replied. His tone shut down any reply I could have given.

"So, you see Lucy, they have children to protect. I only have to protect you. You're the one this witch wants. Rory and his crew can't come out in daylight, but I could, if you help me." Her voice was neutral, something I'm sure she learned in the police academy. When speaking to others, remain calm and you'll win any argument.

"You don't understand Detective. This could kill you, permanently. Or it could do some real damage. I don't know the ins and outs. I only know that I was desperate with Raoul." I scratched the top of my scalp. A hot flush poured through my face and neck. I hated that I had kept my magic under wraps for so long to keep safe that I didn't know what I could actually do. And I hated the fact that if I did use it, the magic would warp those I used it on and change them beyond normal.

"Lucy." Cole moved closer to me, worry creased the wrinkles in the sides of his eyes.

"It's okay." I paced away from the table. "If I did this and you were changed, say, if, because it could do some bad things. What happens then? You become a day walker. You will have a target on your back not only from the human world, but from the supernatural as well. Especially the vampires. The others who are hounding Rory will come after you with brutal force."

Pearce shrugged. "I've spent my life facing down many people who had the power and authority to do vast damage to those I loved. I didn't shy away. I didn't choose this life, but it's what I've got. If there's a way I can do my job better than I'm going to do it. Not because I want power, but because it's right. Someone has to step up and do the right thing and it sure as hell won't be those narcissistic jerks who've sat on their arses for centuries lining their pockets."

"Pearce is right," Kable said. "As much as the thought of a day walker sends shivers through me, someone has to step up. The witch covens have been fighting for decades and evil keeps spreading. The other supernatural communities are the same. They're only thinking of themselves instead of the greater good. Pearce is willing to lay down her life to protect others. I vote yes."

"It's not a vote. It's condemning her to being different, to having to hide herself and her abilities for centuries. It's not being able to be true to yourself because doing so could get everyone you care about killed." I walked slowly around the bench so it stood between me and the rest of the people.

"It's okay to be scared." Jessie's big eyes bored through me with sympathy. "I'm scared all the time, but Mum said that if something scares me, I have to scare it back. That way, at least I'm not alone in my fear."

I bit my lip and put both hands on the bench. The cold marble soaked through my body as I tried to calm my racing heart.

"Thank you, Jessie you're right," Kable said. "If this goes wrong Detective are you willing to take the consequences?"

"Of course. I've faced men holding guns to my head and not backed down. I've given my life once before to save others," Pearce replied. "I know the stakes. But if this witch does what she intends, then nothing I do will compare if I can't stop her."

"It's not you who has to stop her."

"No, it's you. But if something happens to you before you can then I can't live with that," Pearce replied. "There have been seven attempts on your life recently."

"Seven? I thought only two." I tried to do the mental math.

"Seven. Your shifters here caught three, the other four were mine. Rory tried to hustle in on one, but he got distracted by someone dancing on the club floor and missed the knife headed your way. Stupid fool," Pearce said.

"Who's sending them?" I leant my elbows on the bench and bent my head down to touch the marble.

"First couple were witch hunters," Cole replied.

"The rest we think are your witch testing your powers," Pearce replied. "So far you're doing a lousy job at keeping yourself safe."

"I know." I was not willing to lift my head off the cool marble. If I could drop into the depths of the rock, I could hide and no one would find me. It wasn't possible, but if there was somewhere I could go where I could not have all of this hassle and gloom I'd jump at the chance. I glanced up at the expectant faces.

"So, man up, give me the blood and I can keep you safe until you have to slit this bitch's throat," Pearce said.

"Detective," Kable said. "Children present."

"It's okay, I've heard Dad say worse when his football team is losing," Jessie said.

"And they lose all the time," Cole said under his breath.

Brad's pain leaked through, apparently it was too soon to talk about his team. Cole shrugged.

"Fine." I pushed myself off the bench and slapped my hands together. "But if this goes wrong, you won't be coming out of it. I'll walk you through the mist myself and make sure my parent keeps you in there. No coming back."

Kable's eyebrows arched and she appeared to be about to ask a question but thought the better.

"I can accept that." Pearce's facial features were still neutral. I'd give her one thing. She could go up against Cole in a poker match and probably win, although she'd have to stretch up a bit to reach eyeball level with him. For a police officer, I often forgot how small she was. She had a way of projecting herself, which made a person feel small.

"We'll do it in the training room. The wards there will stop any prying eyes," Kable said.

I nodded and followed the rest of them down the stairs.

"Does anyone have a knife?"

"I could bite your wrist," Pearce offered.

"No, you'd take too much and I don't know what that would do." My heart raced at the thought of a vampire latching on to me. It was the stuff of my childhood nightmares. I shivered and pulled my sleeve up.

Cole reached out and transformed his index finger on his left hand into a wolf's claw. I frowned.

"That's a cool trick," Kable said beside me.

I jumped at her closeness. I didn't realise when she'd come up behind me.

"Pearce you need to lie down." I let out a long breath.

Josie stood on the outside of the circle we were standing in, Jessie was on the stairs beside the door. I think she might have thought she was guarding the door, but I'm sure Brad put her there in case she needed to flee. Kable stepped back onto the other side of the circle and lifted her hands at the same time Josie did. A thin green shield emerged between the two. They'd trapped us in a temporary ward. No sound or magic would escape the boundary unless they shattered.

I shook my arm and knelt beside Pearce. Her blonde hair had come out of her usual slicked back bun. I hoped I wasn't about to kill her, but my mouth had dried up so I couldn't say a word.

Cole reached out and pricked my wrist to the side of a major vein. Blood swelled out of the opening and I tipped my wrist over Pearce's open mouth far enough away that she couldn't grab it if she convulsed. Brad was kneeling at her hips ready to stop her moving while Cole would take her head and neck. Both shifters had glowing eyes. Brads a golden amber, Coles an electric blue. Their alpha and sigma powers were fully on display. As an honorary part of their pack, I sensed the pull of those but ignored them and let the blood fall.

Pearce swallowed and then gawped at me with blood-soaked eyes, her fangs fully extended. I pressed my other hand to my wrist to stop any more blood from flowing and stood up. Pearce lay there, licking her lips.

"It's sweeter than I've usually had, nothing too fancy to write home about." Pearce tried to sit up.

"Stay down," Cole growled, his eyes ablaze with shifter magic.

"No, honestly, I don't know what they were...argh." Pearce tipped her head back and screamed. Her body seized up and then shook terribly.

Jessie let out a little yelp and grabbed the door handle ready to run.

"It'll be okay." I watched as Brad and Cole held the vampire's flopping body down as much as they could. "This is normal."

"She's strong," Brad murmured, sweat rising on his forehead. His large arms strained to hold her down.

"It'll take a couple of seconds." I could not control the worry in my voice.

Cole kept his gaze firmly on Pearce who was attempting to shake her brains out of her skull. He clamped his hands tighter on her head and pushed down.

"Don't crush her skull," I whispered.

"She's stronger than I thought." He gave a grunt, the muscles in his forearm popped as if with great strain.

"Yeah, it's the small ones you need to look out for," Kable said from across the circle.

She should talk. Odd witch.

Pearce's seizures subsided and then her limbs went limp. I stood back and indicated to the men to let her be. Josie and Kable kept the ward in place in case things went wrong. I closed my eyes, hoping that she wasn't dead dead. I didn't think I would survive being interrogated by the police captain about this situation.

Pearce took a long breath in. My body sagged with relief. I hadn't truly killed her. I nodded to the witches to lower the ward and we moved back to give the vampire some space.

"Fuck that for a bad joke. Never do that to me again." Pearce wiped her face with her sweaty hands. "That was like the worst trip I've ever taken."

"You did drugs?" I was not able to stop the shock from registering on my face.

"Got duped into it by a high school boyfriend, he's the reason I became a cop. Thanks Josh, what a dickhead." Pearce stood on shaky legs.

"How do you feel?"

"Fine. Bit tired, but nothing different." She rolled her shoulders and kicking out her legs like she was warming down from a heavy weights' session.

"Well, do you want to go test it out?"

Fear flew across her features, then she shut down and changed into cop mode. With a sigh, she tried to take a step and almost fell over. Cole grabbed her arm and steadied her.

"Lucy, whatever you've got packed in those veins I want no more of it. This is harsh." Pearce pushed herself away from Cole with shooing motions. For an independent woman, I think having to rely on a man caused her more pain than the seizures.

"I warned you." I led the way out of the room, and stopped when we got to the back door. We chose the back yard in case things went wrong. We didn't want any neighbours or others to see. "Are you sure you want to try this?"

"Just have fluff ball there throw me back into the room if I catch fire." Pearce pointed at Cole.

"Did you call him fluff ball?" I shook my head.

"I've seen him following you around in his wolf form. He's a fucking fluff ball. Pity he's not that cute in human form or I could be attracted to him," she replied.

A stirring of jealousy rose from my midsection.

"Ha, see your face," Pearce pointed at me with a giggle. "Shit, am I drunk?"

Pearce pirouetted and then let out a full-blown laugh. "Didn't think I'd feel this ever again. On second thought Lucy, bottle it and we'll make millions from the supe side of life."

"Go into the sunlight you idiot." I pushed her down the back steps with both hands.

The full afternoon sun was blazing down in a last reprieve before twilight hit. Pearce stumbled down the stairs and landed flat-footed on the ground.

"Who gets off pushing a poor vamp into the sunlight? I should arrest you for endangerment of a hot cop." Pearce fixed her collar and gazed around the yard. "Nice azaleas, you need to get some fertiliser on them though, they're waning."

"You know about flowers?"

"Dad loved them, grew them to place in shows and that sort of shit. He was a good man," she slurred, putting her hand up to shade her eyes. "Fucking sun's hot though."

Cole whipped down the stairs past me with vampire like speed and threw her back up into the shade before I could blink.

"Fuck off fluff ball, I was saying it was hot, look no fire," Pearce said from the patio floor with another giggle. "I'm so fucking funny I amuse myself."

"I think I might want to record this and show it back to you whenever you put on your 'I'm too cool for school cop face' you do."

"Nah, can't do that. I'd have to tell everyone you coughed and farted at the same time when you got scared the other night," she retorted.

Cole trudged back up the stairs to stand beside me. "Drunk Pearce is interesting."

"Yeah, but I think the hangover is going to be nasty."

"I heard that, don't get hangovers stay drunk, come here Loosey Lucy, come here and let me drink your blooooood." Pearce sent herself into fits of giggles.

Mistress Kable walked up beside her, knelt, her knees cracked as she did so and punched Pearce in between the eyebrows with a magic filled punch.

16

— • —

I gasped as Brad and Josie jumped in to pull her away from the vamp.

Pearce was out like a light. Kable stood up and pushed away from her captors. Wiping her hands of her magic.

"She asked me to," Kable replied. "She said if she started acting like a fool, I had every right to punch her in the face."

"I don't think she'll ever live this down." Josie spoke under her breath.

"I'm going to hold it against her for the rest of her undead life."

"Let's get her inside," Brad grumbled.

"Well, she didn't burn up," Jessie said beside her father. "So, it worked?"

I stared at Pearce's limp body cradled in Brad's arms. "Maybe? Hope so, otherwise she got drunk for no reason."

"Well ladies, this has been educational," Mistress Kable said as Brad dropped Pearce onto the couch. "I will see you tomorrow. Jessie, we'll practice detecting magic."

Jessie grabbed her hand and walked her to the front door while I stood staring at the unconscious detective.

"Hope she's okay."

"She seems to not burn." Cole wrapped his arm around my waist.

I leaned back against him. "Could you imagine having to explain to the police Captain that I let his best cop fry herself to a crisp?"

"French fried cop wouldn't go down well."

My stomach rumbled at his words. "I guess we've done all we can. Hopefully, it worked. If not, we're back to square one?"

"We'll figure it out. We always do," Cole replied.

I sighed and turned away from the vamp. "You hungry?"

"I'd like to stay, but I have to go help Brad." Cole's face spoke of more than hunger.

"Well, I'm hungry. Damn."

"What?"

"Sugar shack is down. Don't know what I'm going to do."

"You've got a fridge and a frypan," he replied, raising a dark eyebrow.

"There's a reason I don't cook."

"Did you ask Lucy to cook?" Josie asked, walking past us.

"Shut up witch." I shook my finger at her.

"He asked you to cook, he's in for a treat." Josie scampered back from me.

"I can do chocolate eclairs well, even you agree." I placed both hands on my hips.

"Yep, that's true. That's it, your one and only talent in the kitchen," she replied.

"I think she might be more talented in the kitchen than you think," Cole said beside me.

"Eww, nope, nope, nope. Not going there." Josie laughed and waved her hands over her face as if to scrub the thought out.

I couldn't help the blush that flamed through me at his words. We had done little in the kitchen yet. Every time we tried someone would interrupt us with life-or-death situations. Just my luck. I had the hottest guy interested in me, but I was getting no action because the universe was conspiring against me.

Cole leaned down, placed a kiss on my forehead and left.

I stood there watching him walk away and sighed.

"Get in the kitchen woman. Sarah ordered the entrees. They're in the fridge. We're going to sample them," Josie said.

"Aren't we supposed to wait for the rest of the girls to get back from their trip out?" I pulled up a seat at the bench.

"Nope, they're on their girl's night, we won't see them for ages." Josie took out a tray loaded with different edible delights.

"Did we not get invited?"

"Your dancing did you in. They were afraid you'd take all the limelight from the bride and well I'm their mother, so no one wants to hang out with me while they're getting frisky," Josie said.

"We're hardly old."

"Young people these days." She took a caviar topped fritter.

"They don't know how to live on the wild side." I picked up one of the cheese creations, inspected it carefully before popping it in my mouth.

"Not like Pearce," Josie said with a guffaw.

"I should have recorded that."

"She would rip your arms off and shove them down your throat if you did," Josie replied.

I shrugged. "Welp, at least she didn't die."

"Again."

I toasted Josie with a little prune wrapped in bacon. "Again."

"You talking about me?" Pearce said at my elbow.

"Hell!" I fell off my seat and managed to grab the benchtop on my way down so I didn't hit the floor.

Pearce glared down at me with a fang filled grin. "Now who's on the ground?"

I snarled at her and drew my magic to myself.

"Settle down Driver, if I wanted more of your blood I'd already be at your throat. I've had enough to last me a few lifetimes. That shit hits hard." Pearce grabbed a little tomato creation and popped it in her mouth.

I shot up from the floor. "Don't."

She bit into the food and chewed slowly, her face taking on a sublime joy. "This is good."

Fear stilled Josie. She glanced quickly from me to Pearce and back. I widened my eyes at her. I didn't know what the hell was going on either.

"I'm going to feel this in the morning, but this is good." Pearce's belch would have been welcome in a beer sculling competition.

"You still drunk?"

"Nope, that's out of my system, but I have a ringing headache," she replied.

"That's from Mistress Kable." Josie's face still filled with worry.

"She can throw a hefty punch. I'll have to ask her to spar with me. Never underestimate short people." Pearce popped another hors doeuvre into her mouth. "Bloody fangs."

"You sure you should eat?" I grabbed another treat for myself.

"Nope, but it's been a while. Liquid diets suck," she licked her lips. "Actually, now that I think about it, I don't feel hungry anymore."

"You might want to talk to Raoul. He can't drink human blood anymore."

"Yeah, when I interrogated him for Rory. He spilled his guts."

"You interrogated Raoul?"

"I had to make sure he wasn't a liability to the vampire king." She waved a caviar laden cracker around.

"But he's been with Rory for centuries."

"Vamps!" Pearce's disgust was palpable.

"So, you feel different?" Josie asked.

Pearce shrugged. "No, maybe tired, which I haven't felt for a while."

"Does this mean you've pulled day time Lucy duty?"

"You can't get rid of me, I'll be on you like a shark to blood." She gave me a fang filled grin.

"Yay me." I waved a biscuit around limply.

"Could be worse," Pearce said.

"How could this get worse?"

"You could still have Tucker on your tail," Pearce chewed again trying to work around her fangs that kept extending and retracting as she bit down on the cracker.

I shivered. "He's such a creep."

"Yeah, I've caught him stalking you a few times. He runs crying to his daddy," she said.

"What does he want?"

"You embarrassed him. For a narcissist, that makes you enemy number one. He'd sell his soul to the Blood Witches to get back at you," she replied.

"We need to deal with him," Josie said with a snarl.

"He'll get what's coming to him." Pearce wiped her fingers on the napkin Josie had placed in front of her.

"I was going to go by the Sugar Shack and see if I can get some clues why they were targeted."

Pearce shook her head. "That's a police investigation. Can't do it during daylight hours. Have to wait until tonight."

Pearce picked up the paper Kable had left on the table. "This yours?"

I nodded. I'd forgotten the cryptic note in all the goings on.

"Feels weird."

"How so?" I watched as she turned it over in her hands.

"Like it's trying to hide from me. You know that feeling you get when you think you can feel someone looking at you, but when you turn, there's no one there?" she asked.

I let out a snort. "Every moment of my life."

"Well, it feels like it's hiding something. Who's is it anyway?" Pearce handed it to me.

"Mine." Anxiety grew within me. "It was hidden in a book Cole had given me. I forgot to ask him about it."

"Well. Nice seeing you and not dying." Pearce stood. "I have to report in."

"Cops or vamps?" I turned the paper over in my hand.

"Both," she said with a sigh. "Idiots the lot of them. Don't know how they ever survived this long."

"They're shady bastards who throw their weight around to get their own way?" Josie took the tray away from me and placed it back in the fridge.

"That's about right." Pearce zoomed out the door.

Josie shook her head. "She's going to be trouble."

"Do you think I did the right thing?"

Josie stopped and bit her lip. "You did the only thing you could? If that helps any?"

"I don't know. I wonder if I gave her more trouble than she can handle."

"Well, she's got the balls to take care of it," Josie replied.

"Why do we say that? 'She's got balls' when a woman is competent?"

"Don't know. Maybe we should say her uterus is tough?"

"Can you imagine. Jeez, you've got a uterus the size of a grapefruit!"

"So, what do you do with that?" Josie pointed at the piece of paper.

"Jessie said Death spoke to her about the paper. I might have to have a chat tomorrow to get the full story. It's got more than one side."

"Tomorrow night we're going to the gala," Josie said.

"You going to wear anything outstanding?"

"Well, I do have some new things in my cupboard," Josie touched her hair.

"I guess that's what we're doing tonight."

"Yep, or we could sneak out and go clubbing, get drunk and pick up awful men to use and abuse," she replied.

"I'm too tired for that."

Josie grabbed my wrist. "Come on, let's go choose a dress for me to stun the crowd."

Later, after several trips to the kitchen for more ice cream and snacks, we'd picked out the dress she would wear to stun the crowd senseless. I put my boots back on and grabbed my jacket.

"You going to check out the Sugar Shack?" Josie rubbed her eyes, it was late and she'd been up for a very long time.

"Yeah, I'm sure Pearce or another vamp will be somewhere nearby. You should go to sleep."

"I was going to stay up to make sure the girls got home, but I think I'm done in for the day," Josie replied.

I nodded and pulled the hood over my head. It was the middle of winter and I needed all the protection I could get. Wayland City didn't get snow or anything to make it a magical winter wonderland, instead we got sleet and slush that made the city a drab hellscape to walk through.

"You want to take my car?" Josie asked.

"I think I will walk there."

She offered a quizzical look. It was a long way on foot to the Shack. I could tell how tired she was by the time it took for her to understand what type of walking I was going to be doing.

"Isn't that dangerous? Couldn't you get trapped in there?" Her voice low with worry.

"Death's daughter, remember?" I pulled my gloves on, stomped my feet and headed out the back door.

Dropping into the shadow realm wasn't that hard, but it did leave me exhausted. I knew that with time, if I kept doing it, I would get better at it, but I'd had little time to practice. Witch law had stated it was banned, that those who walked shadows should be eliminated. Magic had rules, I wasn't following them. The laws said a lot of things about people who didn't fit into their normal witch world. I knew now that was a way to contain the people. If they could walk the realms, then new ideas might come into things and the leaders would lose their power. In the end, everything came down to power struggles. Those who had power and those who were subjected to the will of the powerful.

I pushed my way through the mist to the back of the Shack. The building used to sit on a big lot near the bay. I timed it so that I would appear from behind the dumpster. On my appearance, I heard a screech.

I turned and found Sergeant Offord standing in front of me with her gun drawn.

"On the ground now," she yelled her gun held firmly in her hand.

"It's me, it's me." I knelt.

"I don't know who me is," she replied.

"Lucy Driver, it's me Lucy." I extended my hands up into the air. The ground was cold and slushy and the slush was soaking through my jeans.

"What the absolute hell are you doing here? Where did you come from? I checked behind that bin." Offord had her gun still pointed directly at me.

"I was there. You looked past me." It was the best lie I could come up with.

"Are you telling me I'm losing my mind? There is no way in hell you were there." She shook her head.

"Please don't shoot me," I replied. "My knees hurt and now I need to pee."

"Get the hell up," Offord said and then with another deep look at me she put her gun back in its holster. "Don't ever sneak up on a police officer like that. You'll get yourself shot."

"I thought you'd seen me." I kept the lie simple and it would pass.

"What are you doing here? It's late, the place is shut." She pointed to the burned-out husk of the Shack.

The smell of ash and accelerant was overpowering. Even though the fire crew had ensured, it was completely out I expected to see tiny embers blazing away. The devastation of the building hurt me on a deep level. This was a part of my sanctuary. They fed me, listened to my woes and had welcomed me to Wayland City when I was all alone. Emerald and Marty deserved better. My social justice warrior raised her metaphorical fist, enraged. They would not get away with this.

"I wanted to see it. I'm mad someone did this." I shoved my hands into my jacket worried that Offord would know how close I was to vow revenge and becoming a vigilante in that moment.

"You and me both. The forensics have been here. We'll find out things in a few days," she said.

"Why are you here?"

Offord stared at me. "I'm on patrol."

"Really?"

"No, but if you tell Pearce or anyone else, I'll shoot you," she said.

"I won't."

"It doesn't sit right. The Shack has been here for decades. Marty does the best burgers."

I nodded. It was the truth.

"Then some fool comes along and blows it and himself up for no reason? What's the motivation? He didn't get enough fries with his Deluxe? Something's not adding up."

"That's how I felt. Where did they find the body?"

Sergeant Offord strode ahead in her police officer in a hurry stride. I struggled to keep up with her. My thighs were burning like I was in mile three of a run.

"By the burners in the kitchen," she turned her flashlight over to where the greatest damage could be seen.

"Can we go in there?"

"Why?"

"Maybe we'll find something they didn't?"

"You think you know more than forensics? Go right ahead, this I've got to see," Offord said.

I didn't reply as I picked my way through the rubble, trying not to disturb anything. The stench of ash and burnt plastic still hung in the air. Sergeant Offord walked behind me, following my lead. I knelt down when I got to the crispy bit of the kitchen.

"If this is where the fire started, why doesn't it smell of accelerant?"

"See, that's what makes little sense. Why would this guy drop here and not throw the bomb or whatever and leg it? The doorway is three steps away?"

Offord scratched the back of her neck.

I stared at her in the dim light of her flashlight and then sighed. "I'm going to use some magic in a minute. Please don't shoot me and don't tell anyone I did this."

"I thought so," she replied.

"What?"

"You're a witch in hiding, aren't you?" Offord replied.

"Sort of. How did you know?"

"My grandmother was a witch, but it didn't pass down to us. We get feelings about people," Offord said.

I nodded. "Yep, I am, but I don't use it often and I'd rather no one know."

"You'd better hurry then, because the patrol will be here soon. I have to get this done before they get back," Offord said.

Crouching low to the ground, I steadied myself and sent a tendril of my magic into the dust, stirring up the ashes as I did so. Slowly a scene formed in front of our faces.

"Turn the light off."

The Sergeant flicked it off and the ashes rose to show the face of a male with a look of horror on his face. He appeared familiar, but I couldn't place him.

"I've seen him before," Offord said.

"Do you know who he is?" I had the same feeling. I'd met this guy somewhere, but had no direct link to him.

"Can I take a picture?"

"I don't think it works that way. You can try."

She pulled her phone out and snapped. "Shit, nothing."

"Do you think you could get someone to draw him? He's obviously the arsonist, but the look on his face doesn't look right." I stood up and turned around. I wondered what I would see if I pushed my magic behind me where he was looking.

Lights blinded me for a moment as the patrol car pulled into the parking lot. The crunch of the wheels evaporated the ghostly remnants of the magic.

"Shit, move," Offord sprinted to the bins.

"Hold my hand." I reached out to her.

"What?" Sergeant Offord placed her back to the bins in the darkest spot, her chest heaving.

"Trust me." I grabbed her hand.

17

I pulled her with me through the shadows to the spot outside Rory's nightclub where I'd emerged before.

"What the absolute hell was that?" Sergeant Offord pulled her wrist away from me with force. "What did you do? There was darkness, like the type I had in my nightmares and then we're here?"

"Don't tell anyone, please." I stepped back from her and collapsed on the ground. I'd walked too much in the shadow realm and the energy it took was taking its toll. I lay back my chest heaving trying to catch my breath.

"Who's going to believe me?" Looking down at me, worry etched in the sergeant's brows.

I rolled over onto my knees and made my way up to stand beside her, wiping my hands on the back of my pants. "What would have happened if they found you there?"

"I'd have to explain to the Captain and he's already in the worst mood ever. He'd demote me to desk duty," She searched the street around us. "Now tell me how you did that."

"It's something I can do. It takes a lot of energy and right now I need sugar."

"Only the vamp club here. You want to go in?"

"Are you on duty?"

Offord shook her head. "No dummy, that's why I was hiding from the patrol."

"Okay, no need to get snappy. Fine, come with me. The least I can do is get you a free drink," I replied.

"That I can get involved with." She followed me to the front entrance.

It was a slow night. The usual line up to get in had waned. Tiny was sitting as he ever did on a small stool by the entrance. His smile lit up as we walked towards him.

"You out again tonight Lucy?" Tiny the bouncer stared over my shoulder at the Sergeant.

"This is Hazel, she's with me." I gave him a squinted gaze.

"I know Hazel," Tiny said and then smiled at her, "are you in trouble hanging out with this hell cat?"

"No, but she offered a free drink so I'm here," she replied, leaning in and giving Tiny a hug.

"I should have known you'd know the bouncers."

"More than that," Tiny said. "She saved me from some foreign buggers a few years ago. I owe her."

"Well, that's good you can pay for her drinks then." I patted him on the shoulder as I walked past.

"You get your drinks free," Tiny said with a puzzled look.

"My humour is wasted," I muttered and pushed the door open.

The club was pumping out lots of music that I'd never heard before. I took three steps into the bar when Joseph grabbed me and whipped me up to Rory's office, another vampire grabbed Sergeant Offord before she could draw her pistol and she landed beside me on the couch with a pissed off Vampire King pacing back and forth in front of us. The men shut the door as they backed out quickly.

"What the actual?" Offord attempted to pull out her gun.

"Don't. It's okay." I put my hand over hers before she could do something idiotic.

"It's not okay. Since when do the vamps treat guests like this?" Offord asked.

Rory stopped his pacing and stared directly at us. He was seething. His fangs had extended longer than I'd ever seen and his fist were bunched by his side.

"I pissed him off, obviously," I whispered to her out of the corner of my mouth.

"I was coming for a drink, not to have to fight the vampires," she replied, not taking her eyes off the vamp or her hand off the gun.

"Does she need to be here?" I asked Rory.

He stared at me, too livid to speak.

"It's me you're angry with, so how about you let her go before you say something stupid? She needs a drink."

"I just, I just," Rory stammered. "You…"

The far door of the room slammed open, rattling the shelves on the wall it hit as Detective Pearce stalked in gun drawn eyes blazing. "Step away from them before I blow your head off."

"You see..." Rory yelled at me. He was almost frothing at the mouth stabbing his finger towards Pearce, his knuckles white with rage. "You see."

"Offord, you good?" Pearce asked.

"Yeah, typical Thursday night, what about you?" she replied, still holding on to her gun in its holster.

"Ancient male, taking things the wrong way, now having a tantrum because he didn't get his own way," Pearce replied, her gun still directly aimed between Rory's eyes.

"So usual Thursday night," Offord replied.

"Okay everyone, we're going to put the guns down, we're going to retract our fangs and Sergeant Offord is going to go down and have a drink with Tiny before you yell your heads off at each other. Do we understand?" I used my best pre-school teacher voice in the hopes someone would listen.

Rory stared at me, then shook his head. At his signal, Joseph came back into the room and offered his hand to help the Sergeant out of the room.

"You sure you're okay?" Offord asked before she took a step.

"Yep, he's having a crisis at the moment, when he puts on his big boy panties we'll chat about how rude it is to snatch women out of the bar in front of his patrons and try to scare them."

Offord stared at Rory. His fangs had retracted back into his mouth.

"Maybe some men need to learn a bit of manners in the future," Offord said.

I nodded. Pearce kept the gun tightly trained on him.

"Good to see you Pearce," Offord said.

"You two," Pearce replied.

Once the sergeant had left the room, I glanced over to Pearce. "Put it away."

"He started it," she replied.

"And you both know that I could finish it before you could even move a muscle." I kept my voice low and calm.

"Try me," Rory said.

"Now, now, your high and mightiness, stop the tantrum."

"You!" He stabbed his finger at me in the air. "You made that!"

"No, you did remember? I told you not to and you did. So, her being a bloody pain in the arse has nothing to do with me, I warned you." I stretched my arms out over the back of the couch as if I had no cares in the world. It was a nice leather couch, soft and well maintained. I eased further back. "Nice couch, how much was it?"

"I'm right here Driver." Pearce ignored my question as she put her gun back in her holster.

"I know."

Rory put both hands in his hair as if he was attempting to pull each follicle out by its roots. "I can't deal with this."

"What?" I didn't throw him my innocent look because we both knew I was beyond that.

"I told you not to do anything that would raise suspicion and you've gone and turned her." He put his hands out beside him as if he was trying to part the Nile.

"She asked," I replied. "Nicely for once."

"Are you both idiots? You must be to do this," he said.

"I'm getting the gun out," Pearce replied.

"No, let him rant, he has every right to." I waved her hand away from her holster.

"Don't patronise me. I'm the King," he said.

"So, act like one," Pearce murmured.

He spun to face her. "You are my subject. You will obey me."

"I'm not. As we both know, you used Lucy's power there to help you turn me, so if anyone's in charge, it's her. As much as that pisses me off to say it. It's true," she replied.

"Shit." He turned to the small bar against his wall, drew out a bottle and took a giant swig directly from the neck.

"That bad, huh?" I asked.

"Do you even know what you've done?" He took a long swig of his drink almost draining it in one go.

"I helped a girl out. She can now walk in the daytime without burning to a crispy fried chicken."

"You made two. One would have been a fluke, but two? No, two is evidence that it works. If this gets out, we're all doomed," he said. "I can fight one or two, but the Council?"

"There's a vampire Council, of course, there're witches and shifters, so of course the vamps would have one." I leaned further into the leather. "So, you want me to take care of them?"

Rory and Pearce both stared at me dumbfounded.

"You think I can't?"

"You stupid little girl. I have spent weeks trying to protect you from them. Weeks going back and forth, trying to ensure that no one knows about you. To keep your secrets safe. And you blow that up in my face." He slid to the floor. "Do you not care about your own safety? Why do I even bother?"

"It needed to be done." I gazed over at Pearce, but she stood still and kept her gaze directly on him.

"They will take everything," Rory said.

I walked over to him and knelt beside him, taking his hand in mine. "I won't let them."

Rory let out a humourless laugh, more of a cough than a laugh and then stared directly at me. His eyes were dark and sunken as if he hadn't slept in weeks. I hadn't noticed when I first came in due to the rant he was throwing, but now I stared at him I could see he was under a great deal of strain.

"Do you want me to help you?" I asked.

Rory shook his head. "And do what?"

"I can help you know."

"I am the Vampire King of Wayland City. What could a no-name security guard offer me that I would ever think of accepting," Rory struggled to his feet pushing me away.

"Rest."

He blinked and then shook his head again. "I give up. I've tried to keep you safe, but you run head first into danger."

"That's why I had to do it," Pearce said.

"You didn't, you wanted to. You'll be hunted and dissected and I won't be able to do a damn thing." He pivotied his attention to her.

Pearce shrugged. "I'll make it work."

"Fuck my life," he said.

"Unlife?" I offered.

"What?" He frowned as he focused back on me.

"Unlife, or undeath, whatever it is." I waved my hand dismissively.

"It's not a time for jokes. They'll come here to Wayland. They'll rip this place to shreds trying to find you. Raoul I could hide, but this." He pointed at Pearce, "and you?"

"We'll deal with it when we have to. Right now, we need to stop my grandmother from tearing open the fabric of reality and inviting truly scary creatures into our world."

"There's no winning with you is there?" he asked.

"Just give in to the flow, Rory."

"I hate it when you call me that," he mumbled, taking another swig.

I walked over to him and crouched onto the couch next to the thousand-year-old vampire. "This stroppy look is not good on you. I'm sorry I make you mad. I didn't want any of this. I have to work with what I have."

He peered at me, his green eyes softening. "They will take you and I will be powerless to stop them. I have fought them before and been banished here."

"I won't let them touch anyone." I put my arm around his shoulders and gave him a hug.

Rory always smelled like cinnamon and apple pie. Tonight though, he smelled of pain, a tangy blood rich aroma. I grabbed the bottle he was drinking from and sniffed it.

"Give that back," he said.

"What are you drinking? I thought it was bourbon, but it's synthetic blood." I passed the bottle back to him. "What have you done?"

"You gifted me one drop. I took more from Raoul, but it doesn't work," he said with a discontented smile. "It doesn't work."

"Do you want me to help you?"

"No. I am fine the way I am." He patted me on the knee.

"You still mad with me?"

"I believe I need to lie down for a while. I'm not as young as I look," he replied.

"Well, that's good," I said. "Because you look like crap. Stop drinking this garbage, it's not doing you any good."

He laughed, a slow chuckle that built into genuine laughter. I could imagine him as a human, with his young family enjoying life. The joy that he'd had taken from him by the Fae. The thought brought me back to my senses.

"I will stop her, you know."

"I hope for all our sakes you do. It took everything I had and then some to contain one Fae. I could not stop a horde." He stood fluidly and reached down to help me up.

My body ached and I was glad he used his strength to get me onto my feet. Shadow walking took the energy right from my body. I didn't want to admit that I wasn't at my best after doing it. I dusted my pants off and then glanced over at Pearce.

"Well, shall we?" I asked.

"I'm standing here, minding my own business." Pearce leaned against Rory's desk. "Are you done with his majesty?"

"I guess so." I tilted my head to look at Rory studying the bottle of synth blood in his hands. "You good?"

"I will be." He didn't meet my gaze.

"Okay, then yes, time to go."

"Nichole," Rory whispered.

I stopped in my tracks. I'd never heard him use her real name before.

"Yes?" Pearce replied.

"Watch for signs. Alert me if there are any," he replied and disappeared into the darkness of the far hallway.

She stood there for a moment and then turned back to me with an exasperated look.

"What's that about?" I asked.

"The Vampire Council might show up any day. He wants to be ready. He's been working day and night, cooking up a plan to defeat them."

"Do you believe it will work?"

Pearce scratched at her chin. "Maybe, but we've got a Blood Witch to kill first."

"We do indeed."

18

Friday was busy. I didn't have a security shift until the weekend and running the dogs was a quick sprint. I was done before I knew it and had the day to figure out what I was going to do if my grandmother attacked at the gala.

"What if we set up wards around the perimeter and then have a series of secondary and third wards inside? So, they close up on her and only open one at a time?" I sat upside down on the couch.

Josie was lying on the rug by the fire, testing her magic. "What Jedi style?"

"Sort of. It could work."

"She's more powerful than that, you could have one hundred wards, one on top of the other and it would only drain a bit of her power to break them." Josie sent a spark of purple power out from her finger tips towards the flames.

"Too much concentration, let it flow through you." I waved my finger upside down at her.

"Thanks genius, this might be easy for you, but it feels so wrong," she replied, sparking out more purple tendrils that fizzled when they reached the fire. "Ick."

"You're a white witch trying to use dark powers. Of course, it'll feel yucky. Get rid of your morality, your preconceived ideas of what's right and wrong and realise it is only power. How you wield it decides whether it is good or bad, not the actual energy itself. AC, DC, same electricity, goes a different way is all," I flipped my body over to crouch on the end of the rug. Blood rushed out of my head and I had to steady myself while the wooziness left me.

"I still feel wrong," she replied.

My phone pinged as I stood.

"Who's texting now?" Josie turned off her magic and sat up.

"Sergeant Offord."

"What has she found out?"

"She could get the drawing guy at the precinct..."

"The drawing guy? You mean the sketch artist?" Josie said.

I waved her to shush. "Yes, them. She got a picture done. Do you remember this guy?"

I held my phone up to show her the picture. Josie leaned in and squinted, then leaned out and scrunched her nose.

"He looks like a douche," she replied.

"Yeah, but I've seen him before." I looked back at it. I texted back that I couldn't remember his name but I'd definitely met him before.

Offord told me she'd discretely ask around and see if anyone knows him. There had been no missing persons reports filled in on anyone matching his description, so she'd keep checking.

Sarah and the rest of the witches emerged from their rooms in the early afternoon. Sarah straggled her way to the medicinal cupboard to brew up a large batch of hangover cure. It was in the green jar, two tablespoons in a pot and boil that stuff. It smelt like the devil, but it fixed the problem.

I gave her a salute as she downed the cup in one go. "Bad night?"

Sarah belched unladylike and then nodded. "Too good. We tried to get into a drinking contest with some shifters at the bar over on Macey Lane."

"Rookie error," Josie replied.

"Know that now." She poured herself another cup.

"Careful, you could push yourself so far past sober you'll go to blurt," I warned.

"My head is blurt already. No more shots, ever," Sarah groaned.

I put my phone on the bench and grabbed a drink from the fridge.

"Who's this?" Sarah asked as she stared at my phone.

"That's the guy who died burning down the Sugar Shack."

"What a jerk," she said. "Emma, come look at this."

Emma was one of the younger witches who didn't say boo around the house, especially when I was around. I hadn't seen her for a few days, but she was always there, doing her lessons.

Emma peered at the photo and alarm registered on her face.

"You know that guy?" I used my quiet voice, trying not to scare her more than I did already.

"That's Chad, he's one of those money guys," Emma said.

"Chad?" Josie asked, walking into the kitchen.

"Yes, you remember, the bossy jerk who tried to mansplain how to make a coffee a few weeks ago, Sarah," Emma replied.

"We've had more than a few of them lately." Sarah rubbed at her temple.

"Yeah, he was with a couple of other douchebags." Emma pushed the phone back to me.

"Well, we have a name, sort of. Do you know anything more about them?"

She shook her head. "Only that he had 'almond milk latte with a double shot of expresso, hold the milk'."

The way she intoned her voice might have been a perfect copy of Chad's. It certainly gave creep vibes. I texted the Sergeant with the name and hoped that would narrow it down.

"Well, that's one less coming in harassing the girls," Sarah said.

"Who's harassing the girls?" Benji asked, coming into the kitchen. He brought a bunch of mint and sage with him.

"The douche-nozzles with the fancy coffee." Emma took the greenery off him.

"Oh, those schmucks. 'Don't you know how my father is?' Yeah, we get them some times." Benji rubbed Sarah on the lower back. "You okay, baby?"

"She's hungover," Josie said.

There was no sympathy in her voice. I thought maybe she was a little sore from not being invited out to a good time, but I couldn't be sure.

"That's not like you, you usually can drink the gang under the table." Benji hugged her and kissed the top of her head.

"She tried to go head-to-head with the shifters." Emma let out a snigger.

"It was a matter of honour," Sarah replied in a small voice. "They tried to call us wimps."

"Well, they were cheating," Benji said. "Those bastards have a fast metabolism and can out-drink everyone, except the vamps."

"I know that now," Sarah replied with a wan smile.

"Hey Benji," I said.

"Yep Driver," he replied.

"Back to the shmuck who wanted to know if you knew his father. Do you remember if he told you who he was?"

"Nah, I was getting ready to get the knuckle dusters out and have a bit of a biff. TJ was there to back us up in the kitchen if I needed him," Benji said.

"Damn, I know the words, I've seen the face before." I scratched at my ear.

"It'll come to you when you are busy with something else. Always does for me," he said. "Hey aren't you two going to that schmancy gala thing tonight?"

"Yep, we are. Probably should get ready."

"I'm on patrol tonight, so don't make a mess. I'd hate to come save your arse again," he replied.

"Keep dreaming Credz." I flipped him the bird.

"Oh, she acts all tough now." He gave a little hoot at my hand signal and then turned back to his fiancé wrapping her in his arms.

"I think I'm going to be sick with all that kissy crap," I yelled out.

"You're jealous," he said.

He was partly right. I was jealous when others were so open with their affection for one another. I had tried to be more open with

Cole, but I clammed up when anyone else was around us. Not that I didn't like him or have feelings for him, it was I hated when others tried to nose into my love life. My affection was not to be advertised across a billboard. It was to be treasured. A long shiver rolled down my body to my toes. Who was I kidding? Right now I was so happy to get any human touch I'd even given Rory a hug.

I had a quick shower and then pulled my hair up into an easy up-style, pinned it in place and did my makeup. Josie had bought me some magnetic lashes that would mean I didn't have to go too heavy on the mascara. It took several tries and a social media video tutorial to get them to sit straight. I was learning new skills every day. I took the silverware I'd collected out of the bottom drawer of my dresser and liquified the metal and placing it on my stomach and back like a thin chain mail corset. Then I put on the pants and overcoat dress. No one would know I had the metal under my clothes unless they held my waist. It pinched a little, but nothing I couldn't handle. It was better to have it for safety than go in with no weapons at all. As Cole was the only one I was going to let near me all night, I wouldn't worry about anyone discovering it before I needed to use it. I would definitely need it before the night was out.

I walked out to the kitchen to find the coven having a game of Dragon Riders. There were teaspoons and snail forks being wielded as weapons against the advancing army of the dead. Benji had invited a few of his old friends over. It was amazing how fast his friends said yes to hanging out with such eligible witches, when they would run away from me if I approached them. Ah, to be young and insane again.

"Hey, hot stuff Lucy," Benji stabbed at a potato that had been designated a zombie in the game.

"Thank you." I gave the outfit a twirl and then curtsied at them.

"It looks dangerous, yet alluring," Emma said from the end of the table.

I pointed at her with a grin. "That is exactly what I was going for."

"Well, you hit the nail on the head," Sarah replied. "Are you going to wait for Josie?"

"Yep, she'll be awhile won't she?" I let out another sigh.

"Who'll be awhile?" Josie walked up behind me.

I turned and saw the strapless midnight blue ball gown with beaded pearls at the bodice flowing down into almost feathers at the hem. It was perfect against her alabaster skin and flaming hair. She'd done a treatment and her hair was almost the colour of deep fire. She offset her outfit with pearl drop earrings and a pearl clutch.

I stared at Josie. "Don't you look amazing?"

The Coven all stood and bowed to her.

"See they think so too."

TJ was stunned and stood mouth agape not knowing where to look. The dress certainly emphasised her breasts and small waist. Benji nudged him and he blushed furiously.

"Thank you everyone. A girl tries her best," Josie replied.

"We taking your car?"

"Yes, it's the best way to escape early if we need to." She threw the keys to me.

"You trust me to drive?"

"I am not going to get this dress damaged, besides you have pants on under there," she said.

I shrugged and strode to the garage.

"Don't get into trouble," Benji yelled as we left.

"I'll wait until your shift starts, you know that," I yelled back.

The gala was being held at the museum, so it was a fairly short drive, however, parking the car was a bit of a nightmare. Cars were backed up around the corner.

"I'll drop you off and go find a park," I said.

Josie offered a disparaging look. "You will not. I'm on Lucy duty until we get into the museum. Do not make me look incompetent in front of Pearce."

"This should be fun." I turned down the small alley that I'd once been accosted in by Harrold the hobo. Thinking of him brought a wave of sorrow. I hadn't been able to save him from the Witch Hunter.

"How did you know this street existed?" Josie whistled at the narrowness of the parking space I'd found.

"Long story," I replied. "Do you want to place a few extra hexes on the car, though? In case, you know?"

She nodded and took out a little bag from inside her pearl clutch. "I came prepared."

It took her around two and a half minutes to finish her spell-work. When she was done, the car was hard to see, so anyone who was trying to steal cars would be discouraged from seeing it and then if they tried to break in, they would get sick fast. Some hexes were worth the effort.

"Shall we?" She held out her arm to me.

I linked mine with hers and shot her a smile. "Yes indeed. It should be a marvellous evening."

"I hope to make a statement. The cities best and fairest will know they've been outclassed by the witches again."

"Always."

The entrance to the museum bustled with major business owners and their partners all trying to be noticed by the local media pack. Cameras flashed as different small screen stars sashayed down the purple carpet posing at several points so they could get maximum exposure. Trust Rory to bring out the big guns when he wanted his event noticed. I drew my magic around Josie and I, the last thing I needed was photographs of myself or her entering the building.

Right outside the entrance was a beautiful sculpture of pure silver that danced in the wind. When I'd first come to Wayland City, I was amazed it was still intact. Normally any precious metal in a town like this would have been fair game. Josie had let me know that the sculpture was heavily warded and the supernaturals avoided it anyway, no one wanted to touch pure silver.

"That tickles," Josie whispered as we strode down the carpet towards the red rope signifying the entry point.

Tiny was on bouncer duty for the function. He greeted me with a low bow and a whistle for Josie.

"I've never seen two more beautiful women in my life," he said. "You two are stunning."

I reached up, pulled him down to my level and gave him a kiss on the cheek. "You make a girl feel special. This is Josie, the Coven Leader. Josie this is Tiny, not his real name of course."

"Tiny or Tony?" Josie asked, batting her perfect eyelashes at him.

"For you, witch queen, I could be anything," he replied, in the suavest tone I'd ever heard him use.

"Careful Josie, he steals hearts and then leaves you in the cold." I waggled a finger at him.

"I think that adds to his charm," she replied.

Flirtation was second nature to Josie, but the look she sent him was more than her casual best. For a moment I felt like a third wheel.

"Shall we?" I took her wrist and pulled her towards the entrance, breaking the spell of allure between the two.

She gave me a little sigh and walked away from the smitten vampire.

"You are going to break every man's heart here tonight."

Josie gave me a direct look. "That is the plan. Conquer."

"Okay, you conquer. I'll keep a lookout for wicked witches."

She gave a low cackle. "Don't you remember? We are the wicked witches."

19

— • —

We stepped into the main gallery.

"Holy shit," I muttered, staring up into the vaulted ceiling sparkling with a myriad of twinkling lights. Rory had pulled out all stops, chandeliers lined the ceiling and chamber music from a four-person string ensemble came rolling towards us as we walked further in.

"Classy," Josie mumbled, looking around with a mysterious smile plastered on her face.

"Maybe I need something to eat though, or I'm going to get cranky soon."

"Is that the time?" she said.

"Huh?"

Josie pointed at my stomach. "It's got to be eight thirty. Your stomach normally throws a tantrum about that time."

I shrugged. It was true. Annoying to be so easily read, but my stomach did keep its own clock and heaven help me if I didn't abide by its terms and conditions.

We made our way over to the buffet table and Josie was soon surrounded by men wanting to compliment her on her gown. She sent me a small wave and swanned away with a smile still firmly attached. I bit into my pastry. The filling was apple and raspberry, not too hot that it would burn my tongue and tart enough to have my tastebuds tingling. It was good. I took another bite. I'd have to find out where Rory got the catering from, they might become my new best friends if this is how the food was going to go for the evening.

"You do look elegant." Rory sidled up from behind a curtain.

I swallowed the last of the pastry and hungrily searched for more. "Are you playing mysterious man tonight, Rory?"

"No, I'm avoiding the curator. She's not delighted that I brought so many delicate artefacts into view tonight." He kept his head low.

"You look handsome as ever," I said. "You still mad?"

"No. Just worried."

"Do you think she'll turn up tonight?"

"Let's hope she does. We have a few traps ready to spring on her if she's here." He faded back into the shadows.

"Fine then." I snatched another pastry as I stepped away from the table.

I'd be back I promised my stomach as I made my way around the room looking at all the display cabinets. There were some beautiful pieces of pottery that I was drawn too, but nothing screamed magic to me. The down lighting highlighted so many tiny nuances that I half wished we could stop the gala so I could read all the notes the potters had inscribed in the clay. I nodded to a few women and men that met my gaze, trying to work out who I was. But I made sure I kept my haughty and aloof facial expression, trying to discourage the crowd from actually talking to me. I heard Josie's tinkling laughter in the next room; she was a hit, men surrounded her while women openly gossiped about her look. At least one of us was having a good time.

My nerves were ready to explode at any minute. The worst feeling was knowing that somewhere out there my grandmother was watching me, judging me and getting ready to attack me. I'd survived many of her scathing judgements before, but this time I was an adult and could fight back. I shivered at the thought of letting go of my magic to stop her. She'd grown more powerful than before and I didn't know if I could counter all her spell-work fast enough to defeat her.

While chewing over this thought, I sensed a familiar warmth coming towards me and craned my neck to see Cole striding past several groups, his eyes firmly locked on mine. He was wearing a black tuxedo with green cufflinks. He'd shaved and appeared to belong on a magazine cover. My heart skipped a beat or two at the heat his gaze triggered in my body. I kept my aloof look but inside my body wanted to react completely differently to his presence. He smelled of chocolate and decadence. I licked my lips and he shot me the edge of a knowing smile. Damn it, I couldn't hide my emotions from the man. I preferred him in wolf form when he was like this.

He took my hand and kissed it. "You look amazing."

"I know right, look it has pockets." I did a half twirl with one hand in my pocket extending the overcoat to flare out.

"It does," Cole replied, keeping my hand in his.

"You matched my dress." I pointed at his cufflinks.

"Of course."

"Where's Brad?"

"They're here, spanning out, keeping an eye on things." Cole walked us into the next room. "Josie's enjoying herself."

"She's an extrovert. She lives for these things."

He bent to whisper in my ear, "I can't stand them."

"Me too. I'd prefer to be outdoors running or hiking or something."

We came around a cabinet of curiosities and ran into the police Captain and Detective Pearce speaking in hushed voices. Pearce had her professional face on. She was in a purple ball gown that covered her shoulders and had beading going across the bodice.

"Captain, Detective Pearce, are we interrupting?" Cole asked, coming to a standstill beside the two.

"Ah, Mr Elliott, Miss Driver, it's nice to see you at a formal occasion. I thought you didn't enjoy socialising much Elliott," the Captain replied.

"It's for a good cause," Cole said. "My company always strives to be charitable."

"It is indeed, ah I see the mayor over there, you will excuse me I do have some business to tend to," he said, making short work of high tailing it away from Cole.

"What did you do to him?" Pearce asked, clinking the side of her glass with her finger.

"He tried to muscle in on pack business. We sorted it out. He's been very accommodating ever since," Cole said.

"I would have liked to have seen that, such a pompous arse." Pearce stared over at the Captain's back.

I tilted my head, the movement got her attention back to us. "Now, now, he's not your target tonight."

"Have you had a walk around the exhibit?" Pearce asked.

"I've only got here. I was going to go through to the next room where the portal is."

"Very interesting pieces in there. Some might be a bit too risque for you Driver." She gave with a hearty chortle and walked off.

"She's hard to gauge," Cole said when Pearce had disappeared into the crowd.

"I think she works hard at that," I replied. "What are you smiling about?"

"She won't take crap from the vamp." Cole's tone full of mirth.

"She makes his life a living hell." I tried not to smirk at the thought. I liked Rory. Despite everything, he tried to do the right thing. But I was glad someone else was a pain in his neck more than I.

"Good." Cole moved with me to the next part of the exhibit. The warmth from his body was nice, I leaned in to his shoulder as we walked along.

Brad appeared across the room and made a small hand signal, Cole sighed and they leaned down to whisper in my ear. "I'll be back."

I squeezed his hand and kept inspecting the crystal necklace in the display while he went and sorted out whatever was going on.

"You are mesmerised by the actual pieces and not the glamour of the patrons," a deep male voice said beside me.

I tilted my head to answer and my hackles immediately raised. The mayor was standing beside me. His pasty face and bulging eyes were testament to a life not well lived.

I smiled politely. "My friends enjoy the social side of things. These types of things are not my first choice for entertainment."

"Sometimes we have to appear to let people know we exist," he replied.

"I'm sure there are far more entertaining people around who need the spotlight more."

His countenance was that of annoyed, as if I had bugged him a million times asking are we there yet and he was at the end of his tether. Perhaps his small talk wasn't going the way he'd planned. "I know little about you Miss Driver. The captain told me he cleared you of any wrong doing."

"I was at the wrong place at the wrong time and witnessed some terrible things. Luckily our brave police officers could save the day. Their budget might need a top up soon. They seem to be going above and beyond the call of duty." I nodded towards Detective Pearce. I wondered if she was tuned in to my conversation. She was close enough for her vampire hearing to pick up, but she might have been busy focused elsewhere.

"Indeed. You are at the wrong place and wrong time a lot. In fact, it's almost as if disaster follows you around." He wiped the side of his mouth with a handkerchief as if talking to me left a distaste on his tongue.

"I don't know why, I report to the police anything I see, like a good citizen." I picked at a phantom piece of lint off my sleeve.

The mayor was about to throw another jibe at me when his son, Tucker sauntered up to us, half-drunk already.

"Well, well, what have we here?" Tucker slurred.

The look of contempt his father shot him was palpable, but Tucker ignored it and glared at me. He took no effort to hide the furiousness bubbling to the surface. He seethed at the constraints his father had shackled him with and by the looks of him if his father wasn't there, he'd unleash his emotions on me in a violent storm. Pity, I could punch him in the face, but I had to remain calm.

"This has been an interesting conversation, Mr. Mayor, but I'm sure you have better things to do." I gave him a nod.

"You have no idea what's coming for you and all the abominations." Tucker's tone turned harsh as he glared.

"That's enough," the mayor hissed. "Get a hold of yourself."

Tucker glared at him and then left without another glance.

"I apologise for my son," the mayor said.

"Families can be complicated."

He nodded and then walked away, fisting his hands as he did so. Tucker was in trouble. I peered over at Pearce who sent me a slight questioning tilt of her chin but I shook my head and traversed the room, staring at the museum pieces. Many hadn't been displayed for years apparently, so I was excited to get a free viewing. I kept my magic carefully in place. I couldn't sense any other witches nearby.

If my grandmother was here, she was keeping an incredibly low profile.

I walked around a display of silver gauntlets I thought might have belonged to Rory himself from years gone by and saw him standing stoically beside the main attraction for the evening. The silver portal stone was displayed in the middle of the main room. I'd done a loop of the wing and ended back where I started. Rory was making small talk with some patrons, their greying hair and outfits had me thinking they were old style money, not too gaudy but enough to show they were wealthy. I moved to the side of the room and grabbed a glass of water from the staff. Josie's laugh rang out from the other side of the room, but I didn't go to her. She could hold her own with these people. Cole and the other shifters were absent, a small gnawing sense of dread chewed at my spine.

Someone grabbed my arm and pulled me into a small alcove so fast I didn't have time to yelp or get my magic ready. My glass spilt onto the floor, but I managed not to drop it. The stink of old alcohol and sweat hit me.

"What the hell are you doing?" I pushed Tucker away from me with enough force that he hit the wall behind him.

"I know what you are," Tucker spat at me. "I'm going to make sure that you and all your abominations are wiped out."

"Piss off Tucker."

"You are going to get what's coming to you and I'm going to be there to see it," he snarled again his hand balling into a fist, his face so close I could see the glue on his veneers.

"Is your daddy going to let you out to play?" I sneered at the patheticness of this drunken fool.

He raised his fist. "My father has nothing to do with this, but I'm going to enjoy you being flayed alive."

"Why? Because you're too much of a pussy to do your own dirty work? What's wrong Tucker? Not enough balls to do it yourself?" I stepped closer to him.

Our noses almost touching. Magic hummed under my skin. As a human, he couldn't see it, but witches would sense the power resonating through me and run. Unfortunately, no one was running yet. Maybe this was what my grandmother had set up. Force me to expose my magic to the public and then swoop in to attack while I was trying to hold them off.

Tucker threw his fist towards me with a grunt. I ducked under his weak attempt and punched up into his solar plexus, deflating his lungs. Tucker curled up on himself with a groan, but then recovered faster than I'd hoped and straightened up. His mouth had flecks of foam forming at the sides, throwing out another punch, which I stepped back from.

"You fucking dog lover, I'm going to fucking kill you," Tucker said as he tried to land more punches.

I snapped my body out of the way of his fist and his punch blazed past me. I questioned if I should teach him a lesson, but before I could kick him in the back of the head both Rory and the mayor were in the small room with me as Tucker fell onto his knees. I assumed Rory had taken him down, but he'd used vampire speed, so I couldn't be sure.

"Get a hold of yourself," the mayor hissed. At first, I didn't know if he was addressing Tucker or myself. His face livid. Tucker had embarrassed him while he was trying to drum up support for his next electoral campaign. I wondered how long he'd tolerate his sons presence if it meant losing money.

"I think he might need to go home. I'm sure Miss Driver won't press charges for his attempt to attack her, if you get him away now." Rory's urbane tone had a razor edge to it.

The mayor stared at Rory for a moment and loathing spread across his face as he bent down and pulled his son onto his feet. "This never happened."

"Mr mayor, I've heard stories of your sons many indiscretions that you have covered up before," I said. "Take this as a warning. Another attack on me, or anyone I hold dear will be met with the law."

The mayor gritted his teeth and appeared as if he would explode.

"There is an election coming up, do nothing stupid that might cost you the vote." Rory stepped between us.

"I'll fucking kill you." Tucker pointed at me.

"Take your son home and teach him some manners," Rory said.

The mayor struggled to hold Tucker's arm as he dragged him away.

"I did have it under control." I wiped my sleeve.

"That's what I was afraid of. I get a feeling Tucker has more to do with this situation than I assumed. If I let you deal with him now, we might miss our link," he replied.

A small group of onlookers had kept a safe distance from the alcove now chittered about the audacity of the mayor's son to embarrass him at this event. Rory's vampires moved in and started changing the subject with glowing eyes, the conversations faded as the mesmerisation took hold.

"Nifty trick." I flicked my fingers at the vamps moving the patrons away.

"It takes a bit of energy out of us. Can't do it for long. Those will need a top up soon or they won't be able to fight when we need them," he replied.

"Good to know."

"What was that snail doing?" Rory asked, fixing his collar.

I put my glass down on a side table and it was immediately scooped up by staff. "He hates me and was trying to swing his dick in my face."

Rory's eyes shot up.

"Not really. He has an issue with me. I think he's projecting his insecurities with his father really."

Cole came striding into the room.

"Ah, here's your knight in shining armour now. Bit late really." Rory nodded his head to another patron who passed by.

Coles eyes blazed then settled as he got closer. He'd heard the remark. That was the problem with supernatural's. They could hear your whispers across a room, there were no secrets around them. Cole's gaze travelled slowly up and down my torso, his eyes lingering on my waist, he frowned, noting my sleeve.

I shot him a smile as he stopped beside me.

"You missed the fun," Rory said. "Excuse me, I need to go speak with some people."

Cole held my hand and walked towards the entrance with me. "Are you okay?"

"Just a stupid misogynist trying to lord it over little old me."

"He'll be taken care of," he replied, his jaw clenching.

"Leave him, he's involved in all this somehow and I want to find out all the details."

"I know ways to get the information out of him," Cole replied, mildly.

"No, let him drop himself into the mire. If he has anything to do with my grandmother, she'll eat him up before we can even get near," I said. "She doesn't tolerate imbeciles."

Cole winced as if a dentist had drilled too far into a tooth and hit a nerve and then spun facing the darkened alcove, his eyes ablaze with righteous fury. Before I had time to react, Jessie ran from the darkness. Her pyjamas were torn, blood dripping from long slashes down her arms and legs.

"They've killed my Mum!" she wailed as she collapsed in Cole's arms.

20

Fury raged within me. My grandmother had attacked the Alpha's house while we were distracted here waiting for her to arrive.

Shit

I'd underestimated her.

Shit.

Brad and the other shifters ran to us, as Cole cradled Jessie in his arms. His body was still, almost vampire like. The patrons in the room took one look at his face and fled.

"What happened?" Rory asked from beside me.

"My grandmother." My hands blazed with uncontrolled magic as I fought to keep my anger under check.

Brad took Jessie, his face not registering any emotion except confusion.

"The house." Cole's voice was barely a whisper as the shifters set themselves to fight.

"I can get you there faster." I grabbed his hand.

"What about the rest?" he asked.

"I don't have that much power, I can walk with one." My voice was loud over the extreme quiet of the supernaturals surrounding me.

Cole nodded, then tilted his head up to speak with Brad who loomed beside him. "Get there as fast as you can, I will try to do what I can."

"We will come too," Rory said.

Cole nodded once as he dragged me to the alcove, into the shadows, as if he could warp space. I steadied myself and stepped into them, my mind a jumble of emotions and thoughts. We stepped out into the garden behind Brad's house, where Jessies treehouse stood.

Cole dropped my arm and ran towards the house.

"Cole, no," I yelled, following him.

My grandmother had wreaked havoc. The house was ablaze and several bodies of shifters were lying where they had tried to defend themselves. My heart sunk as I let my magic loose. It was too late to hide it. Grandmother was here, she was waiting for me. She'd chosen to attack those who she decided couldn't harm her instead of confronting me head on. Bitch.

Cole let out a rage filled cry of despair as he made it into the main room. Jessie's mother was still clinging on to life but the other pack members had fallensurrounding her. Their limbs torn from their bodies with an accuracy that was completely in line with Grandmother's handiwork. She had had over a century to perfect her technique.

I flooded the room with magic, trying to discern if any of the shifters lived as Cole gently knelt beside Brad's wife, lifting her head into his arms whispering words of comfort as his eyes blazed artic blue.

There were no other survivors. I counted at least eleven shifters' dead on the property. Several humans who I'd guessed had joined my grandmother to firebomb the place. My grandmother had attacked and fled, or probably had never been here. She was not one to get her hands dirty if the occasion didn't absolutely need it. How she got people to do her bidding still worried me. She was not one for a soft word and the motivation to attack a shifter compound would have had to have been massive for any of the attackers to risk it. The woman needed to be stopped.

I turned my head as I heard a gurgling cough. Lauren, Jessies' mum, clung to life, barely, as Cole whispered to her to hang on. I strode to them and knelt beside her. My resolve hardening. I was sick and tired of the way my grandmother assumed that the world was hers. That others didn't matter in her grand schemes. I didn't matter. As long as she got the power she was after, she would condemn the world to hell. Fire raged at the back of the house and a similar fire rose my spine. She would not win.

"I've got this."

"No," Lauren croaked, her eyes on Cole. Her body was desperately trying to repair itself, however her life energy was draining faster than it could renew.

"You have little time."

A tear rolled out of her eye as she tried to shake her head. "No."

"What about Jessie? She needs you and Brad." I kept my magic tightly wrapped around me like the smoke clinging to the house. I needed to do this. To set this right. Sometimes in your life when you know the course of action you have to take. Even if it goes against all sanity. This was like that moment.

"No." Coughs wracked her chest as more blood seeped out of the wounds to her arms and torso.

"Cole, hold her."

He kept his eyes on Lauren, as if silently communicating with her. Then spoke. "Brad will be here soon, he's coming, hold on."

"Cole, she's not going to last. Let me help." I didn't touch either of them in case I triggered metamorphosis which would end Lauren's life faster than it was already.

"She said no," Cole replied. His voice was dry, almost as if he was reading the words.

Lauren managed a one-sided smile. The other side of her face, which was turned away from me was swollen with bruises. She closed her eyes with a nod.

I stood up, unable to process how to react. I could help stem the bleeding, which might give her time to heal herself, at least allow her to stay with us long enough for Brad to say goodbye. Cole ignored me and held on to Lauren, cradling her like a newborn.

I turned from them, frustration, anger, guilt flooding through me with equal ferocity. The wards on the house had been obliterated. It would have cost my grandmother a lot of energy to do so. Why attack here? I was at the gala. She wanted me more than anything.

Jessie. She wanted Jessie.

I turned back to Cole and Lauren. "She wants Jessie."

Cole glanced up, Laurens eyes blazed gold.

"She's going after the pack. They have Jessie. Let me heal you. That bitch is going to get your girl and you are lying here choosing to die instead of protecting her. Some mother you are," I said. "If you won't save her, I will."

My words hit home with both of them and if they could they would have torn my throat out in an instant. The anger in Cole's eyes was hurtful, but I could live with that. Jessie was in danger.

"Do it," Lauren snarled through her misshapen jaw. Her body was trying to shift to attack me.

Cole held her still as I dug into the shadow realm to pull as much energy as I could. Magic flooded over Lauren.

"Step away Cole." I gritted my teeth at the pain I sensed upon touching her. It was amazing that she had lasted this long, nearly all of her internal organs had been pulverised. I could flood her with the energy her body needed to heal itself, but I was no surgeon. "Use the energy, heal."

She let out a mighty howl, full of pain and rage. Her body thrashed on the floor. Claws extended from her fingertips. I pushed more energy in, not thinking about the consequences of lending her my magic. We would deal with that when the time came.

"Lucy," Cole growled from the other side of Lauren.

"She has to do this herself. I'm giving her the energy she needs. She has to transform." I watched as Lauren's body flipped off the ground and exploded into a massive black wolf that stood head height with me.

"Fuck," Cole said.

I was about to agree with him, but Lauren bared her incredibly long, furious teeth at me. My words must have hit a nerve.

"Jessie." I let out a gulp. "She's after your daughter."

Lauren took a step towards me. She stood eye to eye with me, the most massive wolf I'd ever encountered. I thought Cole was huge, but Lauren made him look like a puppy.

"Lauren." Cole's eyes blazed with his power. "We have to get to Jessie."

Lauren snapped her teeth back at him. I pulled my magic back to me and turned my back on her, running towards the front door.

"Fine, I'll save her," I said over my shoulder and ran at my top speed.

I could only run for a short time, but I'd hoped that I could distract Lauren long enough to stop any challenge she was about to throw down at Cole's feet. My plan sort of worked. Lauren was bounding after me, silent and deadly. Cole had taken a moment to change into his shifter form, his body dwarfed by Laurens. They would catch me soon. I'd spent way too much energy to maintain the speed I had. I slowed down, my chest heaving, trying to suck in as much air as I could. Lauren bounded past me with a snarl towards the pack.

I waved Cole on as he slowed down to check on me. "Go. Protect her."

He bounded off after the massive wolf, guided by some instinct shifters have. I stopped and leaned against the fence surrounding the local football fields. Running in a gala dress wasn't easy, especially with the metal underneath my clothes.

Fire engine sirens blared in the distance, responding to the fire at the house I supposed. Police sirens came from a different direction. The shit storm was about to hit. Humans had attacked the pack. Regardless of who they were affiliated with the pack could not, would not, let this stand.

I rested my forehead on the cold metal pole. My life had become so crazy I missed the simpler times of going to work, keeping my head down so no one would bother me. My phone buzzed in my pocket.

"What now?"

"She got the portal," Pearce said. The bitterness in her voice was palpable.

I switched the phone off and grabbed the metal railing. The dim street lights flared outward as I tried to control the absolute rage and fear coursing through me. She'd attacked the pack to distract me, so she could steal the portal right from under my nose.

I should have known.

I should have known this would happen.

This was how she operated. She divided and conquered. She had followed Sun Tzu's strategy. Turn your enemy on itself. I was no match for this woman. She'd had decades to perfect her plan. I was floundering around putting out fires left and right. She was running rings around me. How was I supposed to fix this? I pushed back from the fence and stalked down the road. I could shadow walk back, but if I turned up raging with magic, I'd expose myself to the entire city and then the Vampire Council would be onto me in a heartbeat. I was damned if I did and damned if I didn't.

I'd underestimated my grandmother. She was four steps ahead of me at every turn. Bitch.

She'd taken out so many shifters and the humans who had helped her would be linked somehow. I needed to focus on that. She was getting help from humans and it had to be someone high up. None of the attackers had any trace of magic, so that ruled out the witch hunters. From Rory's report, the group in this part of the state was wiped out already.

I'd been running on adrenalin for so long that I'd forgotten how damn cold it actually was. My teeth chattered the longer I walked. I hugged myself to preserve some of my body heat, but it was futile. Wayland City winters were brutal. The dress was wonderful, but not cut out for the outdoors. I was about to call Josie to come get me when a familiar car drove towards me from the industrial section. It slowed down beside me.

"Benji, give me a lift." My teeth were clacking as I pulled the passenger side door open.

"Shit woman, weren't you supposed to be at the gala thing? How come you're all the way out here? You get kidnapped again?" Benji asked, giving me the once over to check for damage.

"Long story, things turned to garbage. I need to get back to the gala." I cranked the heating to full as I shifted the central air vents to focus on thawing me out.

"Righto, I've got an extra jacket in the back if you want it," he said.

"You know the thing I like about you Benj?"

"My amazing masculinity?" he suggested.

"Nope, I tell you my night's gone to shit and you accept me at my word."

"Lucy, I've seen your crazy nights and some not so, nothing phases me anymore."

We drove back to the museum in silence, which is exactly what I needed. Soon enough, I'd be in the thick of trying to figure out how to deal with all the mess my grandmother had made. For now, I needed to not ponder on things. The heater was making big strides in warming my hands, but I still had a hard time getting my body to stop shivering.

"You're in shock," Benji said, placing a hand over mine as I shivered again.

"What?"

"Whatever you've done, your body is reacting to it by going into shock. We have to get you some medical care or it could be bad." His brows were etched with worry as he slowed down for an intersection change.

"I'll be okay, I've overdone it." I wrapped my arms around my chest.

"I'm taking you home. The rest can deal with all that shit. If you go out, there you're going to get hurt," he replied.

"But."

"No buts," he replied.

"You like big butts."

"I cannot lie," he returned with a grin.

"Fine, take me home. They'll make me take some crappy drinks that'll taste like garbage."

"They're not so bad, try some cocktails TJ's come up with, they make the worst of the girls drinks taste like a chocolate thick shake in comparison," he replied.

"I'll keep that in mind," I said. "You're not having him in charge of drinks at the wedding?"

"Nope, he's best man. I'm worried about the speech, but it could be worse." Benji pulled into Coven House's driveway.

"Tell Sarah I'll be back in an hour," he said as I stumbled out of the car, trying to find my footing before he took off.

Most of the witches had gone to bed, so I opened the fridge door as quietly as I could. Hunger gnawed at me as I dragged a block of cheese out and hacked a chunk. It wasn't the sugary delight I needed, but it would sate my stomach for a little while. I wanted to curl up and sleep. I'd spent so many years suppressing my magic and now that I was using it all the time my body wasn't content. I was magically unfit.

I dragged my sorry body to bed, chewing on the cheese. Benji was right, other people could deal with the fall out for a while, I needed sleep. The mess would still be there in the morning. With that thought in mind I undid my dress and slung it over the chair in the room's corner. If I had more energy, I'd rinse the sleeve out so it didn't stain, I'd have to beg one of the white witches to help restore it. I threw on a pair of shorts and singlet and crawled under my blankets. They weren't as soft and snuggly as Coles, but they would have to do.

21

I awoke to snoring in my ear. The light from the morning broke
through the cracks in the plantation shutters on my window.
My legs were pinned to the bed. Cole. He'd snuck into my room,
which should be impossible as I warded it. Or had I? I'd had
nightmares. Too much cheese will do that to a girl. I reached out
to push Cole over slightly so I could get more comfortable and
encountered fur. Cole was still in wolf form. He must have been
exhausted from last night. I tried not to wake him as I slipped out
of bed. My knees cracked as I stood and then my spine let out a
series of crackles like bubble wrap bursting in sequence as I twisted
to check I'd not woken him. I was sure he'd wake, but he kept
snoring. He must have been exhausted.

Josie was clattering around in the kitchen when I made it out
of my bedroom, the aroma of spicy bacon rising from the pan she
tended. My stomach gurgled its approval.

"You okay?" she asked, noting my dishevelled appearance.

"Bad night."

"I gathered that, hence the oversized fluff ball on your bed," she
said her voice low.

"How'd Cole get in?" I scratched at my exposed stomach.

"He came back as I was getting in, said nothing, pushed past me and flopped on your bed. You were so gone you didn't even budge." Josie handed me a plate.

"I overextended myself," I murmured.

"Benji said you were done. He was worried and had Sarah and Mistress Kable checking on you every hour until we got home."

"Benji worries too much." I bit into the bacon as I hopped up on the stool opposite her.

"Someone has to." She was about to say more when her eyes flared and she looked away quickly her face blushing red.

Cole sauntered up to the bench. He'd commandeered a pair of my grey track pants. They were snug and left nothing to the imagination. He'd forgone the shirt. None of my t-shirts would have fit that chest.

"Are you okay?" His voice was husky from lack of sleep.

"You can go back to sleep. I'm okay, but you look haggard." I tried desperately not to lose eye contact.

"Bacon!" Sarah shouted as she hurried into the room with some of the other girls. She stopped and let out a breath. "Woah."

"There's enough for everyone," Josie said, in a matter-of-fact tone. She, too, was trying not to eyeball Cole and his semi-naked-ness.

Cole accepted the plate she offered him without a word.

"Lauren okay?" I asked.

He winced at my question.

"She's mad with me, isn't she?" I dropped the bacon I was about to bite into.

He put one hand on my lower back and leaned close to me. The heat of his breath on my neck sent shivers rolling down my body as my brain tried to compute whether they should be full of fear or longing, or a bit of both.

"She will be fine. You saved her. She is not satisfied with your words, but you were right." Cole leaned back and ate more of his breakfast.

I nodded. I'd changed her. I didn't know what those changes would do, but she was alive because I leant her energy to heal. I'd taken the energy from the shadow realm and things like that always had a way of backfiring on me.

Josie sat on the other side of me. "Your grandmother is good at strategy."

My stomach dropped and I pushed my plate back. "I feel like she's so many steps ahead of me that I'll never defeat her."

"I like your streaks Lucy, very chic," Sarah said, grabbing more bacon.

"What?" I stared uncomprehendingly at her.

She waved her hand around her own head and nodded at me. "The white streaks, I think they might be the new trend we've been trying to start. Looks very glam."

I spun to face Josie and Cole who were staring at me. "I've gone grey?"

Josie nodded. Her body stiff and formal, as if we were standing in front of a school principal about to get in trouble. "Seems like you have."

"Shit." I munched down on more food. "I overdid it. Lucky my fingers didn't rot off."

"How bad did you have to overdo it to turn your hair grey, Lucy?" Josie asked with a warning tinge to her tone.

"I may have nearly passed out and ended up chatting with my dad."

"It's okay Lucy, it's a trend," Sarah said. "Within a couple of days, only the elite will have this hairstyle. You watch."

I turned and stared at her. Sarah always searched for the positive. I swear we could be neck deep in mud and she would devise a way to make it appear like a spa day.

"Thanks," I said without cheer.

"Gotta go." Sarah put her dishes in the washer before she left.

I focused back on Josie. Cole was busy devouring the rest of the breakfast without sound.

"My grandmother has the portal, but can't open it. Rory is trying to hold off the European vampires from invading. I need to work out how to stop both." I pushed the last morsel of bacon around my plate with a fork.

"Rory can work on the vamps. We have to figure out what your grandmother's next move is going to be." Cole's rumbly tone brought shivers down my lower spine.

"She's always two steps ahead of me." I tried to reduce the whine in my voice.

"If you were her, what would you do?" Josie asked.

"I'd eliminate anyone who might stuff up my big moment." I'd spent years under my grandmother's tutelage and so the tone I used was close to her own.

"So, who's been helping her?" Cole took my plate from me.

"They're as good as dead," I said flatly. "She leaves nothing behind that could compromise her power."

"We wait for someone to die?" Josie asked.

"Never trust a Blood Witch," Cole said under his breath.

"It's true." I pressed my lips together. After taking a long breath, I shook the tension out of my neck. "She will make sure nothing gets back to her. So those involved will suffer mysterious deaths rather quickly now she's got the portal."

"How do you make deaths mysterious?" Josie asked half-jokingly.

"They die of natural causes en masse."

"This should be interesting," Cole said as he busily stacked the dishwasher in a more logical manner than the witches had.

"But shouldn't we stop her?" Josie asked.

"These are the people who've been trying to eliminate Lucy. Who burned down the Sugar Shack and other businesses? Perhaps we should let nature take its course?"

"Nature?" Mistress Kable asked as she barrelled through the front door. "I swear it gets harder to get through that door. Is someone messing with the wards?"

I rubbed the outside of my arms, for some reason I was cold, as if someone had just walked over my future grave.

"Well, I don't know about you, but I'm tired of mucking about," Kable said.

"If you have a plan for stopping the most powerful Blood Witch in history, please let me know," I snapped.

"Ah, you need sleep," Kable said, tut-tutting as she poured herself tea. "But as they say, no rest for the wicked. Your problem is the portal. She has it. You don't know how she's going to open it and if she does, the world is in for a terrible time."

"Thank you Captain Obvious," I said as Cole touched my knee with his.

"Hold the sarcasm, young lady. I'm getting to it," she replied.

"Please, continue."

"The vampires ran a gamble and lost. We can't find her. I've tried scrying and get nothing. She certainly knows how to hide in plain sight," Kable replied.

"We know." Josie wiped down the bench.

"So, we need to create a distraction, one that your grandmother can't help but get involved in," Kable replied.

"How?"

"We need to sacrifice you," Kable replied.

"What?"

Cole had gone still, a predator about to pounce.

Kable raised her arms and used her hands in a flapping downward motion to stop the yelling that had started at her suggestion. "Hold on. We obviously don't sacrifice you, but if your grandmother thinks we've abandoned you, then she'll come for you.

Right now, she hasn't attacked you personally because you're too strong in this house with all these powers here. But on your own..."

"She's got a point. You said she needs you to open the portal," Josie said.

"I think so. I'm the only one that's been able to do anything like it so far."

"She can't do anything even though she has the portal, because you're the key?" Mistress Kable asked.

I nodded.

"Well then, it's simple. You need to be isolated and she'll come at you, then we grab her from there," Kable replied with a grin.

"Simple." I pushed away from the bench.

"It's all we've got so far," Mistress Kable replied, clicking her purple nails on the tabletop.

"I'll think about it." I stood and strolled back to my bedroom, Cole following silently. He closed the door behind us and then wrapped his arms around me.

"Why me?"

"Why not?" he replied.

"There's other people out there that could handle all this much better than I could. I'm sure of it," I rested my forehead on his shoulder.

"Probably, but you've got the job for now," Cole replied.

"Yeah and I'll stuff it up like I always do."

"Pity parties aren't your style," he replied.

"No, I usually run straight at the problem and whack it until it goes away."

"I will bring the popcorn." He kissed the top of my head.

I wanted to snuggle closer into his arms, the heat of his body warming mine to end up being dangerous for both of us. My body responded enthusiastically to those thoughts. Why couldn't I hide from all this in his arms? He smelled divine and the caress of his hands grounded me in a sense of safety I'd never felt before in my life. I'd always been hypervigilant since childhood. Any moment could be one of pain, yet here, with Cole, it was right. But we wouldn't be safe until she was gone from my life.

I pushed slightly back and stared up at him. "She's going to kill everyone. I don't know how to stop it."

"She will try, but she's on her own. You've got us," Cole said.

I squeezed him and then stepped away. The strange note was still sitting on my night stand. I had tried little to decipher what it meant. Cole sat on the end of my bed as I grabbed it.

"This supposedly has the answers, but it reads like gibberish to me." I held the paper up to him.

"Didn't Jessie say you have to be in both worlds to see it?"

"I forgot," I replied.

"You've had a lot on your mind."

I turned the page over. I could sense, rather than see that there was more to the paper than it appeared, but the answers I was seeking were illusive. I let out a sigh.

"Didn't Jessie say you had to look at it from both sides?" Cole's voice was low and calm, as if he was treading lightly across an unstable bridge.

"Yep, here goes nothing." I closed my eyes.

Dropping into the nether realm was not something I would ever get used to. I gripped the page in my hand. Its weight was even heavier in this realm than my own. I opened my eyes and glanced around. The same grey cloudy void stretched out before me.

"Right, well," I said to myself and brought the page up so I could view it. I let out a quick squeak as the thing in my hand undulated. It wasn't so much a page as a group of living words circling themselves in silvery snake-like motions. "That's new."

The words slid back around on themselves. They mentioned the Fae and the dangers. Right, that stuff I already knew. "Tell me what I need to know."

The words kept repeating themselves and sliding into a sort of animated Mobius strip. Fae, danger, Fae, danger. I wanted to throw the words to the metaphorical ground around me. Both sides. I needed to look at it from both sides. I turned my hand around with the words still circling themselves.

"Clever girl," Death said from the void beside me. "I knew you could do it."

"No help from you," I grunted.

The words were changing slowly. The frustration built within my gut. I needed to know how to stop this now.

"I've helped more than you know," Death replied, materialising.

"Then tell me how to stop the portal or at least shut it down if she opens it. I have to protect this existence." I gazed at the words as they formed what could be gibberish or goblin speak or even Elven runes for all I knew.

"It takes time. I'm not allowed to step in," Death said.

"Who doesn't allow you? You're Death, entropy, you should have no one bossing you around."

Death grunted as if I'd hit upon a detail too complex to contemplate. "There are more things in this existence than you know, Horatio."

"Spare me the bad theatre. I've mucked everything up and now I have to make it right."

"Yes, you barge in and shoot without thinking lately," Death replied.

"What was I supposed to do, let Lauren die?"

Death stared at me, its face placid, unphased by my outburst.

"I couldn't. Her daughter needed her. She'll have to live with the changes."

The words circling my hand were now turning a slight green tinge. I bit my lower lip, trying not to bump or disrupt the process.

"You took energy from this realm and infused a shifter with it. Change is inevitable. But your willingness to change fate is worrying," Death replied.

"I didn't change fate. She wasn't dead. I gave her energy to live. I didn't know it would do that to her."

"Perhaps you should learn what it can do before you wield the power."

I twisted my body to face my parent and tilted my head, cautious not to jostle the words still streaming over my skin. "You going to teach me?"

Death showed me a tight-lipped smile on its generic face. "If it was allowed, but no. Figure these things out."

"Well then, I'll keep making mistakes like this," I replied.

"At the expense of your own life?"

"If need be."

"Perhaps caution should be your new mantra. Don't bring someone back. Don't stop someone going. Don't change the laws of the universe. It's their time. Let them come to me."

"I'll keep that in mind next time," I snapped.

"There it is, you're ready now." Death dismissed my frustration like a butterfly flittering away from an unproductive flower.

The words were fully green now. I stared at them. I knew what I needed to do.

"It's the only way." Death patted me on my shoulder.

"Shit."

"Indeed," it said. "But if you do want to save this realm and others from those parasites, then it has to be this way."

"Fine." The nether realm disappeared as I came back to the normal world and found Cole staring intently into my face, as if ready to shake me back to reality if needed. "Hello."

"Are you okay?" Cole asked as his eyes lit with shifter glow.

"Yep, my Dad's a dick, but that's the way of the world, isn't it?"

"Did you find what you needed?" He still had his hands on my shoulders as if he was arguing internally whether to push me away or pull me in to his embrace.

"Unfortunately, yes." I pulled him into me. Burying my face into his neck. He wrapped his arms around me gently, as if he was afraid to hurt me.

"What can I do?" He whispered.

"Just hold me," I mumbled back.

"I can do..."

My door burst open, Josie's bangles clattered as she lifted her arms. "Lucy, sorry, um, we need you. There's a situation."

"There's always a situation." I stepped back from Coles' embrace. I shot him a small smile and spun to find the whole witch coven crowding my doorway. "What is it this time?"

Josie pointed her hand out of my room. I rolled my eyes and plodded out to the main room with a huff as the girls shuffled out of my way.

The police captain was looming in the front entrance of the house. He had splashes of blood and gore still clinging to his jacket and his eyes were wide in shock.

"What's going on?" I asked.

"Miss Driver?" he sputtered. "There's been an incident."

"Who?"

"Someone bombed downtown, several businesses went up in flames, unfortunately Mr O'Braihan's business was one of them. He's missing, presumed deceased."

22

—·—

Dread clung to my stomach, dragging it down towards my feet. This couldn't be happening. I'd just talked to Rory, he was helping me. I steeled myself, not willing to believe a word the captain said.

"Do you know who did it?" Denial was the first stage of grief. Deny the truth and it's not true. I could handle that. Deny, deny, deny.

"It looks to be the same method as those who targeted the Sugar Shack. The fire chief will let me know." The captain ran his hand over the edge of his cap.

"Why are you telling me?"

"Mr O'Braihan had stated in communications with me that you were his next of kin, should anything happen to him," he replied. His eyes were glazing over.

"Thank you. I'm sorry you had to tell me. Is there anything I can get for you?"

He shook his head. "There are several other families I have to speak to this morning."

Josie came up to him and offered him a mug. "Drink this. It will help."

"I can't," he replied.

"Drink, or I will inform the mayor that you have concussion and need to be in hospital," Josie replied.

The captain stared at her, his eyes trying to focus his normally steely will onto her. After a few heart beats, he gave up and drank the concoction. He winced as it barrelled down his throat. "What the hell was that?"

"Headache cure, also you'll have a bit more energy for a while, but you do need to see someone for your concussion. That bruise on the side of your head is looking nasty," she replied.

"I've had worse." He put his hat back on and adjusted it, wincing as it touched the bruise.

"Do we have any clue who's doing these bombings?"

He winced, then shook his head. "When I do catch them, they will rue the day."

I watched as he strode from the room.

"Why would Rory appoint me his next of kin?" I asked no one in particular.

"Do you think he's dead?" Josie asked.

My knees ached, I stretched them while holding on to the countertop, the pain didn't dull. "Rory wouldn't be taken out by a simple fire-bomber. I don't know where he is, but I'm pretty certain he's still around."

"Glad you're so sure," Josie replied, a shiver running down her body. "I'd hate to be the one who set fire to his club, though. He's got a reputation for a good reason."

"I should go out into the middle of city square and call her out. Have an old-fashioned showdown." I grabbed a grape from the fruit bowl on the counter.

"Blood Witches at high noon?" Josie asked.

"It might work." I shoved another grape into my mouth.

"We are not ready," Cole grumbled next to me.

I leaned into him and rested my head on his shoulder. "I don't think we'll ever be ready."

"I wish all this would stop. Sarah and Benji's wedding's coming up and I want it to be perfect for them," Josie grabbed a grape from the bowl and bit down hard, juice shot from her lips. She ignored it and grabbed another.

"I know. I want to find my grandmother and stop her. If we stop her, we stop the rest of the bullshit."

"So, what are we going to do about it? Do you want to go downtown?" Josie asked, her voice hitching on the last word.

"I have a few things I have to get before I can do that. In the meantime, I need you to redo our wards again. Someone has been testing them. I can taste the tainted magic from here."

"I don't know what else to do to stop this bitch from getting in here," Josie said.

"That's why I have to draw her out."

Cole's phone rang and he stepped away from me to answer it. I motioned to Josie to move to the practice room. She followed without a word.

"You're going to tell me some terrible news, aren't you?" Josie said as we warded ourselves into the circle.

"I spoke to my parent, it's not going to be pretty. My grandmother has spent a lifetime building up to opening this portal. She won't achieve immortality as she thinks. The Fae will syphon her magic from her and leave her husk where she stood. They don't have powers, they take others magic and use it for themselves like parasites. I was hoping to tell her this, to get her to stop, but she won't."

"What will you do?"

I wrapped my arms around my chest. "I have to kill her before she opens the portal, but it could open the portal. It's a no-win situation."

"How do you kill a Blood Witch?"

I swallowed my fear. "Messily. It's going to get very, very messy."

"What do you need us to do?" Josie's eyes were alight with concern.

"In the end, no one else matters. It has to be her and I in the fight. If anyone tries to come in with magic, she'll siphon them dry. I need everyone to stay out of the fight."

Josie shook her head. "No, you said before that you aren't strong enough to stop her. We are going to help you."

"I've changed my mind." I kept my voice to barely a whisper. I wish I could tell them exactly what I was planning, but knowing

Josie she'd try to stop me and if she told Cole he'd overpower me so I couldn't go through.

"No, not buying it," Josie said.

"It will work out. I have to figure out how to get my grandmother out into public view. Then when she goes to cast the power into the portal, I am going to stop her."

"Yes, genius, that's the plan you've been talking about, but you haven't mentioned how you'll stop her," she said.

"Death told me how to do it, so I'll trust they know what they're doing."

"Death can go suck it, for all I care. They have been little help at all," Josie said with a huff.

"On that, we can agree." I turned to watch Cole descend the stairs.

"Brad called. I have to go meet pack," Cole said.

"Keep them safe."

He nodded and moved with shifter speed back up the stairway. I missed running with him in his wolf form.

"Well, now we can get working on how to rip this bitch's head off." Josie wrung her hands behind her back as she paced back and forth beside me.

"Leave the violence to me," I half-whispered.

"She deserves what's coming to her," Josie bit back.

I nodded. "Yep, but it has to be me that does the nasty stuff."

"I can do nasty." Josie's nose turned up in defiance.

I reached over and patted her on the shoulder. "Yes, you can. But I have first dibs."

"I suppose you do."

"I'm going to go see what's left of the club, perhaps someone will give me a clue where Rory is."

"Do you think he's dead? I mean, dead-dead?" Josie scratched at the back of her neck, a sure sign she was tired and irritated.

"No. Rory wouldn't get taken out like that. I won't be long." I drew on the surrounding darkness.

"Wait." Josie reached for me, concern knitted her brows into a sharp v.

It was too late I'd stepped into shadow before she could touch me and slipped through the darkness to the netherworld. It was calming but discomforting in the void. You could literally walk for miles but get nowhere. I concentrated on my destination and stepped through into the alley behind the club. The usual stink of gutters overflowing and diesel fumes from vehicles was overpowered by the stench of burned wood and metal. The arsonist had done a good job, both the upper level and the ground floor were a husk. A tiny stab of anger pierced my belly. Rory had worked hard to keep his establishment going all these years. His collection of magical books and suchlike must have gone up in the fire. I hadn't even got to go through all of them. I gritted my teeth and leaned out to touch the remnants of the wall.

"Oi, Miss, step away from there, it's bound to collapse soon," a male voice yelled from behind me.

A firefighter was sifting through rubble further up. I held up my hands.

"Sorry." I shuffled back from the burnt bricks.

"It's not secured yet. We'll know more in a few days," he replied. The firefighter was around forty and appeared as if he'd had enough of the world's bullshit for one night.

"Okay. I had friends who worked here. I haven't heard from them." I made my voice trail off at the end of my sentence.

He nodded. "I'm sorry, we are still trying to piece together what happened."

I sighed and then let out a sniffle. "Is this the same as the Sugar Shack?"

The firefighter frowned and then scanned the surrounding area, his jaw tightened. "Don't know yet."

I thanked him and walked towards the main street where the entrance had been. Across the street, I saw a familiar lecherous face. Tucker, standing with a group of concerned citizens in a cordoned off area. A bolt of recognition hit me. The ghost I'd seen at the Sugar Shack, that was Tuckers friend, what was his name? Blaine? Chad? Something like that. That douchebag was in this up to his eyeballs. That meant if he was his father was too. I stopped the surge of rage swirling within me and tiptoed up to him.

"Tucker, come to see your handy work?" I asked.

He spun with a face full of fear and spite. "What did you say?"

I kept a distance between us, but I had my magic ready if he tried anything. He wouldn't get a second chance at attacking me again.

"I asked if you enjoyed your handy work." I pointed at the remnants of the building.

"If you don't get out of here," he said.

"You'll what? Call Daddy?"

He took a step towards me. "I should have ended you a long time ago."

I let out a chuckle. "Do me a favour, when you see Mistress Darklight again, remind her how incompetent you are."

At the mention of my grandmother's name, Tuckers face turned ashen.

"I don't know what you're talking about," he stuttered.

"She killed your friend, Chad, she hates incompetence. And now you've stuffed this up royally. The vamps were not to be touched, especially when the Europeans have their eye on this joint. Remind her of that, that you brought the European Vampire King's gaze upon her little escapades. She'll love that. If you're lucky, she'll kill you quickly, but I doubt it. She'll want to ensure you learn your lesson and good lessons take time. Hope it was worth it." I gave him a little wave of my fingers before I walked away.

I left him sputtering in fear, none of the other people had taken any notice of our conversation, or if they did, they were so far gone in their own fears that they didn't stop me walking away. I rounded the corner and let out a sigh of relief. I had fully intended to fry Tucker to a crisp if he had tried anything physical. Well not fry, exactly, more like make every nerve in his body feel like it was on fire before his brain shut in shock. I didn't use my magic to hurt, ever, but if Tucker was in this as deep as I thought he was, he would deserve the pain.

I had walked about two blocks when I noted the sensation of someone watching me coming from a grate in the pavement. I approached with nonchalance and bent down as if to tie a shoelace before I spoke.

"Hey Tiny, you shouldn't be hanging out in the gutters like this," I whispered.

"We're all right down here, need to talk though," he said.

"Where do you want me to meet?"

"Old river tunnel by the bay, give us five minutes?" Tiny's voice travelled from the grate with a lilt.

"Will do. Is he okay?" I couldn't hide the concern in my tone.

Tiny gave an exasperated sigh, before answering. "He's angry right now."

"Everyone else get out?"

"Yep, but Slayer and Raoul are hunting," Tiny said.

"Okay, see you in five." I strolled on.

The river tunnel was a failed project from last century and had been boarded up for decades, but enterprising teens and others had found ways into the system to have fun. I kept with the major tunnel, if I blundered around in one of the off-shoots I might encounter a vamp that didn't know who I was and that might end in disaster for it. I would rather keep the hurting to a minimum, save strength for the real fighting. By the time I'd got there, it'd taken me around ten minutes, more than I thought because I'd had to avoid the Pack patrols. I didn't want Cole to know I wasn't tucked up in Coven House. He'd worry and then he'd come and try to help. He was good at helping, but I wanted to deal with this on my own.

"Well, hello there." I wandered up to the tunnel's opening like a lone gunfighter in a western.

"Thank you for coming," Tiny said from inside the tunnel.

"Take me to him, he's going to be madder once I chat with him."

"Madder? Is that a word?" Tiny asked.

I gave him a well-deserved hug. "In my scrabble games it is, especially if it's on a triple word score."

"Do you mind if I carry you? It'll be faster," he asked.

"How fast do we need to go?" I shot him a grin.

"Fast," he replied.

"Lead the way, I'll follow."

Tiny shot me a worried glance. "No, we have to go vamp fast."

My grin grew. "I'm faster than that."

Tiny shook his head. "Lucy."

Before he could complete his thought, I shot forward into the darkness at vamp speed. I didn't go far as it was completely dark and I didn't have a light to guide me. My ego was writing cheques my body couldn't cash. I stopped and waited for him to catch up.

"But." he came to a halt beside me.

I held my arms out to him. "It's okay. I'm tired, you can carry me, this once. But if you want a race one day, I'll give you one."

The befuddled expression on this giant of a man was worth the entrance fee. I was tired and I had to admit I couldn't see in the dark, so I'd probably end up tripping on some old wiring and garrotting myself in the depths of the tunnels.

"Okay." He picked me up in a cradle carry position before speeding off.

I let out a laugh as we shot down many tunnels before we came to a halt at a junction.

"We have to climb here." Tiny placed me back on my own feet.

"No worries." I stared up at the solid metal ladder.

"I'll go first," he said.

"Lead the way." I swept my arm towards the ladder and stepped back.

It was a short climb. My arms didn't think it was that short and my muscles ached by the time I got to the top. I did need to go to a gym, my upper body strength was crap.

The ladder had led to a small hatch which opened into a well-lit garage. I dusted myself off after Tiny helped me out of the hole and then glanced around at the room.

"Fancy cars." I noted several old classics shining away to my right.

"His Majesty likes things that work well," Tiny replied.

"Take me to him, let's see what fun we can have." I strode towards the doorway.

Tiny opened the door for me, a worried frown niggling at the edge of his brows. "Go easy on him, he lost a lot of precious things in that fire."

I shot him a smile, and put both hands behind my back. "I'll be on my best behaviour."

Tiny let out a sigh that seemed preposterously small from his large frame. "We are in trouble now."

23

"So, the rumours of your demise are false?" I asked as I strolled into the room that Rory had designated his new office.

Block out curtains kept the sunlight at bay, a little lamp blazed away, giving minimal light to the luxurious room.

"They always say such nice things about me." Rory's voice came out in a tired drawl. His Irish accent was thick and there was a darkness under his eyes that betrayed the weariness we all felt.

"I found out who's behind the fires." I flopped myself into the small leather couch off to the side of the desk.

"A friend of yours?" Rory leaned back in his chair.

"Better."

"Go on then."

"Tucker, the mayor's son."

Rory shook his head. "That idiot couldn't light his own arse on fire even if you gave him a blowtorch."

I waved my hand. "I know, it surprised me, but he's part of it."

"How do you know this?"

"He flinched."

Rory shot me a quizzical stare as he poured himself a shot of some mysterious liquid from a decanter to his right. "Flinched?"

"I mentioned how disappointed the Witch Queen will be with him. Knowing he had not completed his job correctly and he flinched."

Rory got up and offered me his glass. I scrunched my nose up; it was too early for hard liquor and the tang coming from the glass was very hard liquor. Rory shrugged and downed the rejected liquid in one gulp.

"You okay?" I watched as he leaned back against the desk.

"Busy. Tired. Need to throttle people." He deliberately avoided my gaze by refilling his glass.

"Well, Grandmother will take care of Tucker, what are you going to do with his father?"

"That little prick has been a thorn in my side for years. Perhaps it's time to deal with him," he said.

"I think you need to sit back and watch his world crash around him. Blood Witches like to leave a clean slate once they're done."

Rory shook his head. "Can't let a Blood Witch live."

"Ah, that old parrot."

"In circumstances such as this I think you can indulge me in this one," Rory took another drink.

"That's my job."

"We have bigger fish to fry," Rory said.

"The Europeans?"

I hoped that he would deny the thought and I could go back to concentrating on grandma's evil world domination plot instead.

"I told you to stop, but when have you ever listened to me?" Rory asked.

"I have listened to you once or twice. Are they near?"

Rory shook his head. "I've been summoned."

I flinched. "Can you stall?"

"Nope, if I do then I'm defying the Vampire Council's will and me and all that is mine will be forfeit." He downed another gulp of his drink and then stared at me through bloodshot eyes.

"Do you want me to change you?" I squinted at the thought.

A brief, hopeful look passed, but he shook his head. "I must be as I am. They will test me and mine. If I am changed, then it gives strength to the rumours."

"Okay, but what about Raoul and Pearce?"

"Raoul, technically is not mine. He's Josephs. And Pearce." He gave a derisive snort. "Pearce is her own man, woman, vampire, whatever."

"She's gotten under your skin."

"I regret the turn." His voice was small and with no power to his words.

"Where is she?"

Rory waved his arm about. "Somewhere fucking things up for humans and vampires. She's a one-man agent of chaos."

"She is efficient at what she does." I waved the fingers of my hand and bit at my bottom lip. Looking over at him I noted the reddish stubble on his jaw. He needed sleep. "So, you survived another attempt on your life and livelihood, what next?"

Rory shook his head. "Don't skirt this argument. The change in Pearce is obvious, she's got a tan for God's sake."

"There are lots of fake tan products on the market that are superb right now."

"We can sense fake tan a mile away, usually an easy meal walking. No, she has been out in the sun, standing in the sun. I'm glad that most of my people are asleep by the time she's parading herself around the place," Rory replied.

I set my jaw. "I can ask her to keep her suntanning to a minimum? What if she wears tanning lotion, that way she'll smell like it."

"I wish I'd never met you," Rory said.

"Well, when we can't change the past, we adjust to the future." I used the quote Josie had had sitting above the café bar.

Rory shot me a look so loaded with sarcasm I wondered how it had travelled across the small space between us. "You keep changing things. It has to stop."

I held my hands up to him. "How about I stop once I've gotten rid of my grandmother and her attempt at ripping the fabric of reality apart?"

"What are we going to do to stop her? She's got her claws into everything in this city. My people are living in fear," he replied.

"I plan to track her down, call her out in a western type shoot out away from large crowds, break the portal so it can never be used again and kill her. Don't know exactly how I'm going to achieve this, but it's a work in progress." I shifted in my seat. Listing out what I had to do was easy, actually achieving it would be hard.

"So easy." Rory's dull tone betrayed a pinch of fear.

"I came to see if you were alright. Thanks for naming me your heir, but I don't think I need all your money."

Rory frowned. "What do you mean?"

"The Captain came and told me that you'd named me next of kin, that's when he informed me you were dead." A frown threatened to break out in my face in response to Rory's frown deepening.

"Lucy, I never named you next of kin. No one knows our connection." His body was rigid, as if he was contemplating a fight-or-flight scenario.

"I'm so stupid." I flexed my hands.

Drawing my magic to me used to hurt, but now it was like the painful buzz a joke zapper button gave you.

Rory had his phone out. "We're compromised."

I bit my bottom lip again. "Fuck."

He then pocketed his phone and stepped towards me. "Never a dull moment with you around, Driver."

I shrugged my shoulders and gave him a weak smile. "I try to serve?"

"I had centuries of dullness. It was peaceful. Nice even." He buttoned up his suit.

"Yes, but you enjoy chaos. It's when you shine." I offered him a hopeful expression that fizzled within seconds.

Rory's expression was not hopeful. He lowered his fangs and prepared to fight whatever was coming our way.

There were shouts down the corridor as the sound of fighting drew near.

"Can you get your men to retreat? I think I can get us out of here without all the mess."

The muscles in Rory's face barely moved, but I could tell he was livid at my words. Rory was once a king in his homeland centuries ago. He'd probably been in more battles than I could list. Retreat most definitely was not one of his favourite words. So, I put my hand in his and drew the darkness to us.

"Get them to retreat, we're going to take a walk."

He stared down at me and then pulled his phone out again. "Retreat. Yes. I'm fine. No. Go."

He let out a long hiss as he put his phone back in his pants pocket. "Let's do this."

I shot him a maniacal grin and pulled him into the shadows with me as the door to our room burst open and Wraiths poured in ready for the kill. Pity I had little metal on me, a slaughter of Wraiths would have worked out the kinks in my neck. I smiled at the thought of the fun I could have had. With a shake of my head, I held Rory's hand in mine as we walked through the shadows.

Rory dragged behind me as I hurried us down the long nothingness. His footsteps grew slower and slower until I turned and faced him.

"Are you okay?" My words were barely heard in the soup that surrounded us.

"This is it?" His voice was tiny and frightened.

"No, this is shadows, different thing. This isn't your afterlife silly, come on." I tugged at his hand.

Rory snapped out of his stupor and followed me once again. It took a few seconds longer than I wanted and again I heard a susurration from far off calling me. I ignored it and kept striding towards my entrance back into the world of the living. I'd chosen the basement where I'd left from. Rory would be safe in a witch's den more so than in the myriad of safe houses he had around the city.

"Who was calling you?" Rory's whisper was loud in my ear.

"Ignore it, I do." I deposited him back into the reality of our world.

Rory shook himself off as if brushing snow off a jacket in winter. "That was awful, please don't do that to me again."

"It's not the afterlife, it's shadows. Faster to get around." I slapped myself on the forehead.

"What?" Rory glowered, his fists tightening, ready to fight.

"I'm so stupid some days."

The sound of Josie coming down the stairs jolted me back from my thoughts.

"Why are you stupid?" Josie and Rory both asked at the same time.

The puzzlement on Rory's face appeared as if he was slightly constipated, on Josie's it held a touch of fear.

"I've been shadow walking, there are others who can do it, I think my grandmother can. She'd know when I walked. We have to tell Jessie not to walk until I've dealt with the bitch." I strode past the two of them.

I was hungry, infuriated with myself and fed up with all the rubbish we were having to deal with. If only I had a sweet grandmother who was content with knitting and baking. That would have been good. Instead, I ended up getting a grandmother who was hell bent on world domination and immortality.

"I think I'd rather face the Wraiths, walking in the shadows leaves a feeling of ick all over me." A shiver rolled through Josie as she recalled her experience.

I turned and smiled at her. "You hate cleaning up Wraith entrails worse."

She grinned back. "You need to be less messy and I wouldn't have to."

"No chance." I took the stairs two at a time.

It was daylight, Rory stayed in the basement. Josie followed me and headed straight for the coffee pot to drown her ick away.

I called Cole. He would let Jessie know to not shadow walk. It was a quick call. I had the feeling he was dealing with things I shouldn't get involved in. Cole didn't enjoy talking on the phone. Scratch that, Cole didn't enjoy talking a lot. He was the polar opposite of Rory, who could talk the ear off a corn stalk at fifty paces. Rory did love the sound of his own voice. I let Cole know that the police Captain was compromised as well. I would have to tell Pearce. I would have to tell her. Rory would insist on it. Sometimes I wonder if I shouldn't have run away before all this began and start over without all the mess.

"So, what now?" Josie opened the fridge.

I plunked myself down at the counter and rubbed the back of my neck. "Now I'm going out and confronting her."

"So, no big plans, then?" She pulled out a container of cheese and meat and antipasto before setting it on the bench in front of me.

I grabbed a slice of cheese and salami. "Nope, you?"

"I thought I'd go watch my friend annihilate the Blood Witch Queen, come home, host a wedding and then collapse into bed with a nice slice of cake." Josie shoved food into her mouth.

"Sounds' like a plan. What type of cake?"

"Double mud." She put another piece of cheese onto her plate.

I was about to reply when Detective Pearce stormed into the kitchen, her face glowering.

"Someone's not having a good day," Josie said under her breath.

I put my hand under my nose. "What is that stench?"

Detective Pearce held up her arm and turned around. "Oh, this? This stench? The one that reeks of a mix of tanning oil and an off avocado?"

I scrunched my nose. "Not so much avocado, what have you done?"

"Your mate has decided that if I'm walking around in the sun, then I have to have an excuse why I'm not burned to a crisp. He came up with the solution." She shoved her arm towards us. The stench shot forward like a sickly miasma.

"Rory?"

"Who else?" Pearce pulled up a stool and started in on the antipasto and cheese.

"I don't understand," Josie scrunched her nose and leaned away from the vampire detective.

"Rory's grand plan is the witches have come up with a UV protection for vamps, however it smells this bad and no vamp in his right mind will want to wear it. Thus, I will be the only vamp walking in daylight." Pearce winced as her fangs descended at the same time she tried to bite down on a stuffed olive.

"Oh, that's the best he could come up with?"

"It was that or I would have to disappear until the vamps stop sniffing around," Pearce replied.

"It does have an odour." I waved my hand in front of me.

Pearce shot me a gaze that could strip four layers of paint off an old railing in seconds. "You think?"

"There's no way you can sneak up on anyone now." Josie grabbed a couple of glasses and pulled out some wine from the fridge.

"I told the vamps this was a stupid idea, I hate my life some days." She accepted a glass as Josie poured for her. "Keep going."

"Well, Lucy here is going to go out in broad daylight and confront her evil grandmother and repair the tear in the fabric of reality, so you got here in time, smell and all." Josie gave a sardonic smile.

"Thought she'd do that." Pearce drained her glass then holding it out to Josie to refill.

"It's the only way to keep everyone safe," I muttered munching on another olive.

"Neither here nor there, you are the type to martyr yourself no matter what," Pearce replied.

I clenched my jaw at her words. They were true, to a point, but I didn't enjoy hearing it, anyway. "The captain is compromised."

"Tell me something I didn't know." She swirled her wine around in the glass before downing it in a single gulp.

"You want the bottle?" Josies eyebrows arched in worry.

"Fuck it, yes." Pearce swiped the bottle out of Josie's hand with vampire speed and sat.

I thought about having a stiff word with Rory about his schemes, but the reek of Pearce had me pushing away from my seat.

"The captain's been getting kick-backs for a while now. I've had a few friends trying to figure out where it's coming from, but it makes sense now. The mayor, the Captain. This bitch has her fingers in all the major players in this town," Pearce said.

"Not the supes," Josie said.

I put my hands behind my neck, linking them together and leant forward. "If she could, she would."

"So, you're going to go out, fight to the death and then what?" Pearce let out a soft burp that smelled worse than the fake sunscreen solution.

"Yes, do you have a better plan?"

Pearce scrunched her eyelids as if contemplating the problem and then shook her head before taking a final swig of the wine bottle. "Nope. Let's go do this then."

I let out a soft cough and looked up. "What?"

"Now, let's go now. Get this over and done with. We have a wedding to prepare for and the daylights waning. You don't want to fight in the dark, that'd be stupid," she replied.

"Okay then." I sent a half shrug towards Josie.

Josie shook her head as if to go along with whatever hair-brained scheme Pearce was up to.

"You got any better plans?" Pearce asked, looking between both Josie and I.

"Nope."

"Good, let's go." Pearce put the empty bottle onto the countertop.

I followed her out the front door to where a bunch of people I was vaguely familiar with were milling about. Some had placards and appeared to be ready to picket, what cause they were picketing for I didn't know, but they were ready. I stopped on the front steps. Emerald and Marty were among the crowd, I could also see Mistress Kable and a few women I recognised as older witches hanging about.

"Um, Pearce."

"Yeah, yeah, I've brought a few helpers along." Pearce waved her hand nonchalantly. "Ignore them, they're going to take care of the dickheads who try to interfere."

"Like?"

"Corrupt police, politicians, politicians' sons... you know the drill." She strode past the group.

"We're going to the city square?"

"It's high noon Driver, where else would we fight the Blood Witch Queen?" Pearce stared at me as if I was delusional to think anything else.

"Fine. Go then." I pointed for her to lead the way.

"Bossy," Pearce shot back.

"I'm going to die in a few minutes, I can be bossy if I want to."

"Oh yeah, do you need any weapons or things like that?" Pearce put her hand on her service weapon.

"No, it won't help."

"Ah well then, let's go stomp some blood witch arse."

The crowd followed us to the bus stop, where two buses were waiting. I focused my gaze at Pearce who shrugged as if she hadn't orchestrated all of this. I blew out a worried breath and stepped onto the bus. The crowd piled on, several older members tried to tap their bus passes but they were assured by the drivers that they didn't need to, the ride was free.

"Nothing's ever free from Wayland Council," an older lady replied.

Pearce stood up from her seat. "The supernatural council have provided the busses, you're welcome, if you have any shopping you need to do after we are done, please do so, the busses will run all day for your convenience."

This announcement brought cheers from a few and frowns from some of the older types. They were right to be wary of police detectives shouting free bus rides. There was always a catch. The bus ride included a few songs to cheer everyone up. A couple of older men waved their placards at the surrounding streets but stopped when Pearce sent the look of death at them.

"I feel like I'm on an excursion for school," I whispered.

Pearce's face curdled into a full-blown grimace. "No, we're on the bus ride to hell, it's a one-way ticket."

The bus pulled in beside the museum. It was town central. The sculpture was turning in the breeze, sending little rainbows of colour around the courtyard.

The doors to the bus opened as the bus driver yelled for all those passengers departing to use both the front and back exits. This received a riot of cheeky calls about back exits. No matter how old people were there were still naughty little kids among them.

I stepped out of the bus and made a direct path towards the sculpture away from the crowd. Pearce tackled me as a bullet shot past and lodged into the base of the sculpture.

24

—·—

"**A**re you hit?" Pearce asked with one hand covering her head, the other reaching for her weapon at her hip.

I glanced up at her, lying prone across my body, protecting it with hers as the elderly placard waving crowd surged forward, yelling obscenities in the shooter's direction.

"No. You're pretty damn heavy, can you stop squashing me?" I struggled to breathe.

"Nope, someone tried to shoot you." Pearce had her weapon out, aiming it up towards where she thought the gunman might be.

"Don't shoot anyone, we can't be sure who's doing the shooting."

"Someone isn't going to be alive for much longer," Pearce muttered under her breath.

"Pearce, you good?" A woman's voice yelled from the other side of the sculpture.

"Could be better if some random wasn't trying to shoot the place up, Offord," Pearce replied.

"Typical Wayland City," Sergeant Offord replied with a hitch in her voice.

"You good Offord?" Pearce adjusting herself off me to peer around the legs of the sculpture.

"Never been better." Her words came out with another hitch, as if she was fighting for breath. "Might need to lie down for a bit more though, some buggers' gone a shot me in the leg."

"Fuck." Pearce peered at me. "Wait here, don't fuckin' move."

I grimaced as she scooted sideways around the base of the sculpture with her revolver drawn still aimed towards the area the shots came from. I took a deep breath in and lifted my head up. The building the shots came from was further down the square, one window on the second floor was slightly ajar. I guessed that's where the shooter was. We were effectively pinned down until someone took the shooter out.

"Hazel, you had to get shot, didn't you?" Pearce asked loudly from the other side of the sculpture.

"Just doing my patrol, if I'd known there'd be an active shooter, I'd have called in sick today," Offord replied, with a heavy dose of sarcasm.

"I told you not to come out today," Pearce muttered.

"Yeah well, my luck I get shot and bleed out before the hot paramedics turn up." Offord coughed again and ended with a grunt of pain.

"I can fix this," Pearce replied.

Offord hissed at whatever Pearce was doing to her. "Don't make me into one of those, you know how much of a bitch I'd be if I was immortal with all those powers, best to keep me here."

"Fuck," Pearce yelled.

The rest of the placard waving crowd were still on the ground waiting for help. I didn't think anyone would get here in time to save the sergeant. With a quick breath, I drew the shadows to myself and slid inside. I didn't care whoever saw, I had to do something. I stood up and strode forward through the small shadows that were thrown by the trees and the sides of buildings. Once inside the targeted building, I raced through towards the room; the shot had come from. The door was locked, but the shadows under the door were long. Enough for me to shift through. It hurt and my head was throbbing. I would pay for this, but it needed to be done.

I stepped out in the closet beside the bed and grabbed the metal rod and hangers, trying desperately not to jostle them and make any noise. The metal flowed around my hand as I shaped it into a short blade. I drew it across the back of my hand to coat it with my blood to seal the edge. Rage boiled over, temporarily blotting out my headache. I could hear movement in the room, the shooter was still here. With singlemindedness I didn't normally show, I pushed the closet door open slightly. The man was still crouched at the window, weapon still in hand.

I searched for anyone else who might have accompanied him, there was no one. I took a step towards him. This man was dead and he didn't even know it. No one attacks my friends without consequences.

The door exploded inward as police rushed into the room. I stepped back into the closet, my heart racing.

"Hands up, get your hands up now." Voices shouted towards the shooter. "Turn around, get on the floor."

I could still kill this guy. I could send a small piece of metal directly into his skull and they wouldn't be able to stop me. I could drain him of all his energy before they could draw another breath.

The man turned around, dropping his weapon before kneeling on the ground. It was Tucker, the mayor's son.

"You can't touch me," he hissed. "I'll be out before sundown."

The sneer he shot the police had me ripping off the tip of my blade, forming a small ball between my fingers. If I was going to kill him, I'd have to do it now.

"I wouldn't be so sure about that," one officer said. "You shot a police officer."

"Doesn't matter, never does," Tucker replied.

"Someone read him his rights, bag the weapon," another voice said.

I dropped the little metallic ball onto the floor and slipped back through the shadows towards Pearce and Offord.

"Where the actual fuck did you go?" Pearce snarled as I emerged beside Sergeant Offord.

"It was Tucker."

"What?"

"The shooter, Tucker is the shooter." I stared aghast at the amount of blood that had seeped out of the police sergeant's leg.

"Help me, paramedics will be here in a minute, but I can't stop the bleeding," Pearce said.

Hazel Offord was lying on her back, her chest rising slowly as she tried to pat Pearce away. "It's okay, I'll be okay."

"The hell you will," Pearce said and stared at me. "Do your thing."

"My thing?" My gaze went from Pearce's furious stare to Offord, trying haphazardly to shove a smile my way.

"Fuckin' save her or you'll never hear the end from me," Pearce's hands were clamped around Hazel's leg as a flesh tourniquet.

"I'm not a doctor." I shook my head.

"We know that dipshit, fix her." Pearce jutted her jaw at me, her glare increasing.

"I don't know how." I focused on Hazel, her skin greying as I watched. "I'm sorry I don't know."

Hazel lifted a hand and patted my leg. "It's okay. I'm okay, I'll be okay, don't worry about me."

"Fucking do your voodoo witchy shit and heal her or else," Pearce said as sirens screamed towards us.

I stared at her. What freakin' witchy shit was she talking about. I peered back at Hazel, she was slowly fading away, the energy surrounding her fading to that blue-grey people got before they passed over.

"I'll try."

"There is no fucking try Driver, heal!" Pearce snapped, tears flowing down her cheek. "Heal her."

I grabbed Hazel's hand and smiled at her. "You're going to be okay."

"Always," Hazel said with a wan smile as she closed her eyes and let out a long exhale that rattled.

I closed my eyes and drew myself into the netherworld.

"Sorry I have to meddle again," I said to the darkness. "It's not for me, a friend needs help."

There was no answer, so I reached out towards the veil. Hazel's form was blurry, as if in two minds about going through. I grabbed her hand and drew her away.

"You're needed back home, this is not the time to be slacking on the job."

"I'm okay," Hazel replied.

"I know, let's go back before Pearce cries herself into a stupor."

"Pearce? Crying? This I got to see, that woman doesn't know what feelings are, except rage, obviously," Hazel said with a chortle.

"Apparently, she does, she's hidden it well. She's crying right now actually."

"Why?"

"Oh, some reasons, let's go see why, huh?"

"Can I come back?" Wonder filled Hazel's countenance .

"Later, not now, we have to get a look at Pearce crying first, come on, we'll miss it."

"I'm okay," Hazel said, straightening up a bit and turning away from the veil. "This is some freaky shit. Typical Wayland, weird stuff happening all the time."

I shot her a big smile. "Yep, all the time."

I opened my eyes to see us surrounded by paramedics. Pearce was yelling at them to hurry and fix her friend while shooting them death stares. I sat up straighter. Hazel coughed again and then opened her eyes.

"You crying?" she asked Pearce.

The look on Detective Pearce's face was priceless as she faced her friend. "Fuck no."

"You are, why the hell do you have emotions all of a sudden? You going through the pause?" Hazel's voice was weak as paramedics shoved lines into her arms, trying to keep away from Detective Pearce's sharp gaze.

The smell of her blood sat heavily around her. I worried for a split moment that it would send Pearce over the edge, but she was too worried about her friend to even twitch towards the patch that was congealing beside her friend.

"No, I'm not going through menopause, you fuckin' scared me that's all, it's tears of fright," Pearce replied.

"I'm okay," Hazel said and then glanced at the paramedics, her eyes widening as a smile formed on her lips. "Handsome."

"Stop flirting and get better you dolt." Pearce threw herself over Hazel's chest in an awkward no arm hug. Pearce still had her hands on the wound stemming the flow.

"Pearce, are we friends?" Hazel asked, still smiling at the paramedic who was pushing fluids into her arm.

"No. I've got no friends," Pearce replied, as if it was part of a long-time argument.

"Yeah, you do, you've got me." Hazel closed her eyes again with a sigh.

Pearce furiously stared me down, as if she was ready to tear my head off if Hazel died.

"She's stable," the paramedic said. "We need to transport her."

Pearce stared at him for a moment and then realised she was still lying across Sergeant Offord's chest and pushed herself upright to standing. "Sorry, please help her."

The paramedics nodded and the others came forward to roll Hazel onto the stretcher.

I stood away from the scene as police swarmed out of the building with Tucker handcuffed and hooded. Pearce gawped, her eyes turning red, fangs extending. I reached out and grabbed her wrist.

"Don't, not here," I whispered.

"He's a dead man walking," she replied.

"Trust in the law."

"Not here, I won't," she snarled.

"You are the law."

She faced me, a gamut of emotions flying across her features before she settled on determination. Tucker was in for a terrible time. Pearce then dropped her gaze to my hand, which still clenched the short blade I'd created in the closet.

"You want to hand that over?" she asked.

I glanced down and then sighed. The metal flowed out of form and into thick, wide bracelets on my arms. "It's okay, I think I'll keep it for a while. Never know when I'll need it."

She nodded as the crowd of placard wielding elderly citizens started gathering around the police chanting something. The police pushed their way through towards a waiting patrol car, trying to keep Tucker from their grips.

I turned back to scan the rest of the square when Tucker screamed as police started yelling and then people in the crowd yelled in horror.

"What the fuck?" Pearce said as both she and I spun around to face the commotion.

Tucker's hands were still handcuffed behind his back and his hood slowly melting off his head. His clothing melted off him.

"He's on fire." I ran towards him.

"There's no flames," Pearce said, keeping up.

"Witch fire. My grandmother's here, she set him on fire with witch-fire. You can only see it at night." I tried to push through the screeching crowd to get to Tucker before the damage was done.

"Shit," Pearce said as Tucker dropped to his knees, blisters forming in big swathes over his chest and shoulders, the stench of hair and flesh burning had people gagging and vomiting as they raced away from the scene.

The police stood baffled at the scene.

"Move back," Pearce yelled, holding up her badge. "Everyone back."

"What do we do?" a young constable said from nearby.

"Get these people out of here, someone get a fire extinguisher.

"Won't work," I muttered under my breath as I formed the incantation that would stop the fire.

"Get these people away, it could spread," Pearce yelled.

The crowd appeared to notice her words and with almost a single thought they all stepped back, letting Pearce through. I followed her and released the spell onto Tucker as his head popped like an over inflated balloon all over Pearce. His body sagged to the ground with a wet thud as his blood boiled, coming out of the remaining arteries.

"Fuck me," another officer said.

The crowd screamed and ran. I hadn't got there fast enough.

"You do that?" Pearce asked wistfully as she wiped goo from her face.

"No, witch-fire. I didn't stop it in time." I carefully stepped around the scene.

"Damn. Remind me to stay on your good side." She flicked bits of Tucker off her fingers. "This is messed up."

I surveyed the scene and whispered. "How come the police were here so fast?"

"That's something I'd like to know," Pearce muttered. "I didn't give them the warning."

"Great."

I stood back as Pearce took control of the scene. An officer had handed her a towel to get the most of the gunk off her, but she needed a shower. The stench of the lotion the vamps had made her use was nothing compared to the scene of the burnt flesh and hair that had coated her from head to toe.

Pearce came back over to me when the forensic team turned up. "Better go home. Today is not the day for a shoot-out."

"She was here, had to be, you can't cast witch-fire without being close. I didn't feel her though, why couldn't I sense her?"

"I don't know. We'll look at the CCTV footage and go from there," Pearce replied.

"You need to shower."

"I need a new life, right now though I'm it until another senior officer graces us with their presence," she said with a definite snarl. "You go home, there's bound to be trouble here and there it is."

News vans had rushed to the scene and now were setting up across the street. What we needed. Once they realised who the shooter-slash-dead man was, they would be ferocious. I wondered if the mayor knew his son had exploded. He'd chosen to get involved in Blood Witch territory he deserved the fate coming to him. Pearce wiped more of the gunk off her chest with the towel that she'd been given, I hadn't the heart to tell her there was a string of some sort of tendon or brain matter hanging off the back of her head. I figured it was best not to say anything right then.

I glanced over my shoulder and saw Mistress Kable and a couple of older witches' step sideways to allow Cole to stride towards us. The look on his face was terrible. I didn't know which person he was angrier with, me or Pearce, he appeared ready to fight both of us for our stupidity. If we hadn't been here, then maybe Tucker would still be alive. Not for long, he'd outlived his usefulness and was bound to be eliminated by my grandmother sooner or later. Cole's icy blue eyes flashed with Sigma power.

Pearce's face darkened, her fangs dropping low and her hands bunching into fists.

"You'd better call off your wolf or I'll show him what a real fight is," Pearce growled low.

Blue flashed in Cole's eyes as if he'd heard her threat.

"He's not my wolf, he's his own person," I replied. "He's not here to fight you, it's me he wants to scold."

"Lover's tiff?" Pearce asked.

"Something like that." I stood and faced him.

"You want to tell me what happened?" Coles eyes were still full of carefully held fury.

"We came downtown with some senior citizens, Tucker tried to shoot me and ended up getting arrested, then got burned by witch-fire and his head exploded all over Pearce." I spoke as calmly as I could. When I put all the pieces together, it was one of those days you wouldn't write home about.

"He shot Offord, nearly killing her," Pearce said.

"Are you okay?" Cole asked. His gaze skimming over my body quickly before veering towards the mess that was Pearce. His nose wrinkled and he let out a little sneeze.

"I'm fine, thanks," Pearce said. "Just had a head explode all over me and no one in command seems to be coming around to take care of shit they're supposed to."

A few police officers trying to control the scene sniggered at Pearce's statement.

"The mayor is on his way," Cole said his voice quiet and gruff.

"He shouldn't, his son hasn't been tagged yet," Pearce replied.

"Your Captain is about two blocks away," Cole replied.

"Fucker," Pearce said under her breath.

Cole arched a quizzical brow. I touched him on the shoulder and he dropped whatever he was going to say.

"I need to get back to the house, the journos are here and they'll make a big issue when the mayor's around."

Cole nodded and indicated the way to his car. I looked at Pearce over my shoulder, my neck cracked at the movement. I needed to see a chiro or masseuse or something soon.

"You sure you'll be okay?"

She harrumphed. "Been doing this a long time. Get out of here before you cause a scene."

I nodded and set off with Cole. I had to get back to Josie, once word got out that witch-fire was used the first people they would blame would be her and the Coven. Even if we proved video evidence that they weren't near the incident, humans would still blame them. Unless we let them know that a Blood Witch was in the area. But the panic that would ensue from that proclamation wasn't what I wanted. To most humans Blood Witches were a myth. Something supernaturals used to blame away their problems. Unless, of course, they'd had an encounter with a Blood Witch and then they realised all the nightmare tales were true.

"Say it." I waited in the car's quiet as Cole drove us to the house.

"You went to force a showdown and nearly got Sergeant Offord killed, not to mention all those onlookers. The placards were a nice touch," Cole said.

"I didn't organise that, Pearce was working it."

"We know you have to face her, but I'd rather not lose civilians," he said.

He was right. It should have been her and me, no one else.

"How the hell did Tucker know I'd be there, who set me up? I'd only went there with Pearce as she made it up."

"Your grandmother has people everywhere. Tucker might have been stationed there and someone else might have been stationed at other places. Who knows? He's dead and she's still out there," Cole replied.

"I want her gone. Why can't I have an ordinary life? I want to live a quiet life."

Cole let out a grunt as he turned the corner to Coven House. "That's what most sane people want."

"She's not sane. She thinks she can gain immortality through the Fae, there's a reason they were banished from this plane of existence."

He pulled the car up. I'd forgotten that tomorrow was Sarah and Benji's big day. The house looked spectacular.

"I'll have to enforce the wards." I scratched at the back of my neck. I pulled my fingers away and saw a smidge of blood on them. "Damn it."

"That's not yours," Cole gritted his teeth.

"I need to shower and change." I tried not to think of whose blood it was.

"Is that an invitation?" Cole's voice dropped slightly into an almost growl. The effect on my body was immediate and his pupils dilated in response. He wanted me. I wanted him.

"I suppose it could be."

We made our way up to the house; the lights glittered throughout, sounds of laughter and glasses clinking could be heard as Cole opened the door for me. I waved hello to the crowd of young witches who were dressed up in their witchy best weaving garlands for the ceremony tomorrow. My grandmother had picked the worst time to descend on Wayland. I wished she'd waited a week. I hated that all this mess was marring what should be a wonderful time in Sarah and Benji's life.

Benji sat a little away from Sarah, his eyes were focused on her. TJ his friend was hovering around two other young witches offering them wine and nibblies. Hope stamped all over his face. The boy had it bad.

Josie spotted me and frowned. "Where'd you go?"

"Had a few things to do downtown, need a shower, I'll be back in a bit." I hurried towards my room.

Cole followed without a word, holding my hand. The heat from his skin sent shivers down my spine. I needed to get under the water and wash off any traces of gunk.

I opened the door as Cole put his hand on the small of my back. The shivers were definitely in full bloom, rolling down to my knees. I don't think Cole realised how much I needed him and what his touch set off inside me. I leaned sideways to tell him my thoughts when his eyes flared blue in agitation as his body shifted into battle ready.

"Oh, you're back," Rory said from inside the room.

I spun back around and saw his royal cockiness lying on my bed as if he owned it.

"What are you doing?" I stepped in front of Cole so he didn't do or say what I sensed he wanted to.

"You abandoned me here, remember? I was waiting for you and Pearce to come back, but ugh, you do pong," Rory replied, patting one of my pillows into submission.

"I just." I started and then shook my head. "I'm having a shower."

"Are you inviting me in?" Rory asked with eyes full of mischief.

Cole growled as his fists clenched, readying for a fight.

"No, not a chance in hell." I put my hand firmly up to Cole's chest. "You both need to go into the kitchen and help Josie with the preparations for tomorrow."

Rory sighed dramatically and then stood with the ease of a vampire, fluid and not quite human. He walked over and pulled something out of my hair. "Smells familiar? Do I know?"

"Tucker, exploded, dead, end of story."

"There's a story to be had," Rory said.

"Go, help." I pointed towards the door.

Rory put his hands up in defence. "Fine, fine. Where's Pearce?"

"She's dealing with the fall out." My hand was still firmly pointing to the door.

Rory eyed me speculatively then glanced over to Cole. "It could have been fun."

Cole took a step closer to him, his face passive, his hands still clenched.

"Don't, he's trying to goad you," I whispered.

"Ah well, you'll never know now," Rory replied and left the room.

"Dick." I shut the door and locked it. "I need to shower. You can come in or you can go keep an eye on his royal stuffiness."

Cole lifted me up and carried me into the ensuite without a word, then shut and locked the door behind us.

"He's got super hearing like you, he'll know if we do anything." I pulled my shirt off.

"I don't care," Cole replied.

"I do, he gets under my skin and that will give him another thing to tease me about."

Cole stopped helping me undress and peered at me. "Are you ashamed of us?"

My breath hitched. "What? No."

The look he gave me was pure sex. "Then it doesn't matter what he hears. I'm here, he's not."

"Is this a pissing competition?" My heart lurched the words. Was this all I was to him? A way to get one up on the vampire king?

Cole leaned in and kissed me solidly, wrapping his arms around my bare torso, his hot chest against mine.

"There is no competition. This is you and me," Cole replied softly. "Only you and me."

My body responded with a half lurch of my heartbeat and my groin caught fire. His touch set my skin ablaze with hormonal fluctuations. I wanted him, he most definitely wanted me, I ran my hands down his sides, tracing the tattoos that told a story of pack life. I leaned into him and kissed him back as he turned the water on to the right temperature.

"We need to get this gunk off you, the stench of that man shouldn't be a part of what I want to do to you," Cole's voice was a rumble in the water's downpour.

***

It was an hour later when Pearce came striding through the front door.

"Hello to you too, Detective." Josie's words were well and truly slurred.

"Is everyone off their nut?" Pearce stepped away from several young witches who were singing at the top of their lungs some new song they'd heard on the net.

"Yes," My body was more relaxed than it had been for several weeks.

"What's got you so content?" Pearce's acerbic tone cut through my good mood like a scalpel through paper. Then she peeked into the kitchen where Cole was cooking something that smelled amazing. "Oh."

"What oh?"

"I see you two." She pointed her finger back and forth and then spotted Rory flirting outrageously with a few of the young witches. "What, dickheads here too? You didn't?"

"What? No." My words came out with a stutter, my stomach roiled at the thought.

"Pity, it would be interesting to be the meat in that sandwich." Pearce let out a cackle as she watched me trying to figure out what she meant. "You are so naïve. Hilarious."

"I see you washed that man out of your hair." I tried to not think about what being in that wolf/vampire sandwich would be like and failing miserably.

"Eww, don't remind me. The mayor is unhappy and threatened the police captain with a few things if he didn't get the witch who did this to his son. Never mind the fact his son was found to be the shooter and openly admitted it. Nope, he's now stuck on the fact a witch killed his son and he's blaming you," Pearce said matter-of-factly.

"He's scared because he knows my grandmother will do the same thing to him. He chose his lot, he'll have to live with the consequences."

"Not before he stirs up enough shit to drown the entire Coven in it," Pearce said.

"He can wait until after tomorrow, we've got a wedding to go to." I let out a long breath and heading into the kitchen.

Cole plated me up a portion of the food and pointed at the table without a word.

"Yes, okay." I grabbed a fork and took my assigned seat.

"Dominance games? Of course, you'd be into that," Pearce said to Cole with a nasty twinkle in her eye then focused on me with that same look. "Sandwich."

I almost choked on my first mouthful. "Shut up, shut up, shut up."

She let out a hearty laugh and stole some of the food from the pan, then shot Cole a look of challenge. Cole's demeanour darkened as he shook his head and came to sit by me.

Josie took that moment to slide into a seat on the opposite side of the table from me. Her fist was tight around the neck of the bottle of spirits she was consuming.

"Shouldn't you water that down or something?" Pearce asked Josie with a wince as Josie belched.

"Tomorrow we will, tonight we don't," Josie said.

"Well, you might want to hold off until I give you my news," Pearce said as she made her way to the table with her own bowl of food. With a nod to Cole and then a wink at me, she sat. "Thanks for this."

"The food or the ability to eat it?" Rory said with a snide tone moving to the end of the table.

"Both." She picked up the fork and shovelled a mouthful in. She sat back and chewed slowly and loudly with a smirk directed squarely at him.

"Idiot," Rory muttered and slumped back in the chair.

"I suppose your little adventure brought new problems to our door?" Josie asked Pearce as she put the bottle down on the table.

"Grandma torched Tucker, exploded his head," Pearce said in between mouthfuls. "Garlic. Love it."

"Tucker's dead?" Josie asked with a genuine smile.

"Ask me how," Pearce said.

"I'll bite," Josie said.

Rory shook his head.

"Witch-fire!" Pearce said and then let out a cackle. "Fucking blew his head up. Who knew?"

"Witch fire?" Josie's mood changed in an instant.

I had sat quietly trying to eat my food without calling attention to myself, but now I was facing Josie, in her Coven leader tone.

"Yes. Lillith Dorchasa unleashed witch-fire on Tucker. He didn't stand a chance."

"You said you could have stopped it," Pearce said, downing her last forkful of food.

"If I had made it in time, yes, he still would have died but not as...horridly?"

"Great, does his father know?" Josie asked.

Pearce nodded. "Yep, he's blaming the witches."

"What's he trying to do?"

"He and the captain were having a stern argument when I left. They're both up shit creek without an inflatable toy and now they are facing the consequences of getting involved in a Blood Witch's machinations. Good riddance, I say," Pearce said.

"We have a wedding tomorrow, nothing is going to interfere with that," Josie declared.

I held my hands up. "I'm going to redo the wards tonight, no one who is not invited will cross the threshold, no matter how powerful they are."

Josie let out a guttural noise then scratched at her nose. "There's so much to do, we have the cake, the food, the flowers are done. The ribbons are ready and consecrated. Benji's grandmother has been given the right to come out of hospital for the ceremony. Nothing is going to stop this."

"It'd be the perfect time to attack," Detective Pearce chimed in.

Rory tsked at her words. "Nichole, they don't need that."

"I was just saying." Pearce held up her hands before stepping back from the table. "I need more of this food. I should hire you as a cook wolfman, you're halfway decent."

Cole shook his head, then ignored her, focusing his gaze on mine. I placed a hand on his leg, Pearce would take every opportunity to goad him. She did it to everyone.

"Sandwich," she whispered.

25

The rest of the night was spent trying to mitigate any issues that might arise with Tucker's death and the thought of my grandmother interrupting the wedding. Cole accompanied me while I walked around the outside of Coven House, strengthening the wards. Come hell or highwater Sarah and Benji's big day would not be ruined by my grandmother or the mayor or anyone. These wards would keep out everyone not invited. My issue was I hadn't seen the list of those who had been invited, but I was too tired to deal with that. I eventually made it to bed, Cole had to go do pack things, so I rolled myself up in my blankets and dove deep in to sleep.

When a person is exhausted and tries to sleep, they close their eyes and it's morning already. I woke up feeling like I hadn't slept a wink. All I needed was five more minutes of sleep, or another ten hours would be perfect. Rolling over, I saw that it was actually eight o'clock in the morning. I had slept. The clock was proof even if my body refused to believe it. I showered again and set my hair in curlers the way Josie had ordered me to. I was not officially part of the bridal party, but by association I had to look my best, or something like that.

Josie had hung my dress up in the closet, I got to wear midnight blue, the bride would be in black and silver, Josie was in a deep emerald green and the girls were in shades of forest green. The backyard did look amazing. Having white witches in the house meant the flowers were blooming even out of season. Tiny solar lanterns had been strung throughout the foliage, giving the appearance of fireflies. It wasn't the season for them, so we compromised.

I left my room wrapped in a robe and smiled as I surveyed the house. Even through all the giggling going on last night and the heavy drinking, the witches of Wayland Coven had outdone themselves. I suspected more than a little magic had flowed, fixing the house up. The kitchen was overflowing with food; the cake was still in the second fridge hidden in the pantry. It was a marvellous creation, three-tiered, dark blue icing with gold embellishments starting at the top and tapering out to the bottom. It reminded me of a deep night sky. The embellishments floating on the icing like stars and was large enough to feed a hoard. Sarah and Benji couldn't agree on the type of cake they wanted, so they threw the decision over to Dana, whose parents owned a bakery on the other side of town. She nailed the assignment. I would have to remember to tell her that later on.

"Good morning." I moved carefully around Josie who stood head in hand hunched over the kitchen bench.

"Not so good, don't talk so loud the medicine hasn't kicked in yet," she muttered.

"Someone shouldn't skull liquor from the bottle?" I grabbed the toaster down from the cupboard and set it up a little way from her.

"It was necessary," she replied, still not looking up at me.

I shrugged. I was happy. The only issue I had today was feeling like I had had no sleep. A hangover would make me miserable. "You ready for today?"

She glanced up and took another swig from the glowing mug in front of her. "I will be, give me a few minutes."

"That looks tasty." I pointed at her mug and grimaced.

Josie's medicine often tasted like the vilest fluids that ever graced the planet but they did work. The more disgusting the taste the faster the fix. From the look of Josie's face as she sipped, that one was going to work extremely fast.

"It's working, that's all that matters," she whispered, her voice ending with a croak.

"I'll stick with not downing bottles of wine the night before the wedding. Where's Sarah?"

"The girls left for the salon an hour ago, they'll be back in a little," she replied and put her mug in the sink.

"Do you think Benji will be okay?"

"He'll be fine, but his friend might not." Josie held up a little vial of glowing liquid. "I've got this just in case."

"Always prepared," I gave a little jump as the toaster popped.

"Speaking of which, how're things going?" Josie said.

"Fine." I scraped butter across the crispy browned bread.

"Want to talk about it?"

I frowned. "What?"

"Oh enough. You, him, shower? You're not quiet, I think I might have to sound proof your room if he stays over," she replied.

Heat rose in my face. "Oh."

"Yes, oh, oh, oh," Josie replied, then giggled. "You should see your face right now."

"Well, it's been a long while." I busied myself with my food. I hated that my skin burned with the fury of a hundred suns right then. She knew. I knew she knew. And I knew I'd never live this down.

"From the sounds of it he's taken care of business." She snatched a piece of my toast from my plate.

"Stop asking me questions, it was good, but we've got things to deal with today. Why is my love life so important?"

"You look happier, sated. He's good for you. Although Pearce kept laughing about sandwiches after you'd gone to bed, what's that about?" Josie's mood had picked up. Teasing me always brought her back to a good mood.

It was like old times, when we'd run the café together. I shook the thoughts out of my head.

"Pearce mentioned something I won't think about." I bit into my toast and lost the battle to not thinking about wolf/vampire sandwiches.

"Oh, you, Cole, Rory?" Josie said in a singsong tone.

"Shut up."

Josie tipped her head to the side as if the weight of the thought was too much for her brain and then started giggling.

"What's this then? Did I hear my name used in vain?" Rory asked, coming up from the lower room.

I choked trying to swallow my food too fast. "You're here?"

He turned around the room, as if looking to see who I was talking to. "Of course, both my safe houses were destroyed, your gracious leader allowed me the use of the lower levels until this whole shebang is over. It is lonely down there. I could have used some company to keep me busy."

"Cut the sleaze act Rhuairigh," Josie said.

"Where are Raoul and Joseph?"

I hadn't seen either for a few days and that was worrisome.

"They are around, they're good at not drawing attention to themselves," Rory replied.

"If my grandmother got hold of them, the amount of power she would get would be enormous."

"They're fine, we've had a few foreign visitors to our city and they're running interference," Rory replied, dragging a chair out to sit beside me.

"The vampires are still sniffing around?" Josie asked. Her tone not quite hiding the alarm we both felt.

Rory nodded, picking up a grape and rolling it around in his fingers as if he longed to bite but knew it wouldn't satisfy. "If someone would stop making day-walkers, we wouldn't be in this mess."

"They'd still be here, you've grown too powerful for their liking your majesty," I snapped back.

He shot me a grimace and dropped the grape onto the table. "Be that as it may, I do need to get a better outfit and things for this wedding tonight."

"Did you need Pearce to go out, seeing as though you can't stand the day?" Josie asked

"I was hoping Lucy would be kind enough to walk me to another place I need to go." He draped his arm over the chair to his left and leaned slightly back.

"She's got things to do here to prepare for tonight," Josie replied.

"You can spare her for an hour." His tone was soft and soothing, as if he was trying to cast a spell on her to comply with his wishes.

"I can feel your magic Rory, cut it out." Josie brushed her hair away from her face as if he was another annoying customer she had to serve.

He shrugged and then threw her a wistful smile. "It never hurts to try."

"Don't try it on the leader of a powerful witch coven," I reminded him tapping him on the shoulder.

"Got to keep the old hand in, never know when I'll need it." His toothy smile made him look like a crocodile who's caught his dinner entering the murky waters where he lay.

"Keep your hands to yourself."

He held his hands up, his smile never wavering. "I only put my hands where you want them to be."

"Sandwich," Josie murmured.

Rory's brow furrowed. "Pardon?"

"Fine, I'll go with you to get your outfit your majestic-ness. Where are we going?" I shoved past Josie who giggled in return. She would be the death of me, or at least the embarrassment of me. I wondered if someone could die of embarrassment. I mean anything was possible. The thought of a supernatural sandwich with his highness and Cole was something I could not afford to entertain. Distracting wasn't the word for it.

Rory's face showed he knew he was the butt of our joke but he hadn't quite worked it out yet. He would keep pestering us now to find out what she meant. For a man of his age, he was sensitive to how people perceived him. I wanted to strangle Josie for it, but I only had Pearce and my awful imagination to blame.

Rory gaze rolled over my body a smirk forming on the side of his lips as if I was an open invitation for his imagination to run wild. "Would you like to change? I'm all for this look of relaxation, it brings many things to mind, but we will be in a semi-public place, you might want to cover up that luscious body of yours."

I looked down. I was still wearing the robe but it was barely covering parts I didn't want seen. "Fine, give me five minutes."

"At your pleasure," Rory replied. His smile stretching into a full-blown leer.

I wondered if his sleaziness was genuine or if he was acting human to put both Josie and me at ease. He'd been undead for centuries and over time vampires lost their humanity. The subtle little movements humans make when they're standing around waiting for things. The blink of an eyelid, the fidgeting of the fingers on a shirt sleeve or the flickering of their gaze left and right in boredom. Vampires did not need to move in this way and many who chose not to became almost statue like when they weren't engaged in having to move towards or away from things. Like automatons ready for a battle.

It took me a little longer than five minutes as I had to send a text to Cole to let him know what I was doing and reminded him that I would see him at the wedding later.

I threw on a pair of dark woollen pants that fit snuggly and a navy long-sleeved shirt with a black wool coat over top. I pulled my hair up in a bun at the back of my neck to keep the curls I'd started for the wedding from unravelling. I would have to get Josie to work her magic on my hair later.

"I'm ready, let's go." I offered my hand to Rory and then asked, "where are we going?"

"To the museum basement," he replied.

I frowned, but he held up his hand before I could ask a question.

"I have things stored there and as I'm the largest donor to the establishment, they let me have my area there. I often gift things for display which keeps them happy."

"Does anyone else know this?"

"No, just the museum director." He took my hand.

"We might have to go in and out of the shadows, it'll hurt you more than me."

He shot me a slight grimace and then took my hand in his. "I've been hurt before."

I shook my free arm and inhaled. The movement into the shadows took a bit of energy, but moving through them bodily with another person in tow was like wading through thick thigh deep mud. I needed more food if I was going to keep doing this. I wondered if there was a protein smoothy that had enough calories to replace the energy I was burning and decided I'd stick to chocolate and doughnuts. The thought brought back a twinge of regret that the Sugar Shack had burned down.

"I think you should invest in re-opening the Sugar Shack." I pulled him through another round of shadows.

"What on earth were you thinking about to Segway into this conversation?" Rory asked with a grunt at the end. We were moving as fast as I could manage, but it still stung, flowing through building shadows.

"I need sugar and I was thinking about doughnuts. I miss the food. You could give them a loan to rebuild either there or establish somewhere else until the insurance kicks in."

We stepped out of the shadow within the dreary depths of the museum.

Rory stopped and glanced around, getting his bearings. "Would it make you happy?"

I sniffed the air; it was stale, but not dusty. There were rows upon rows of shelving, similar to the curiosity shop he had before the bombing. "Yes. And it would mean a lot to the community."

"You're that hungry for doughnuts?" He replied, reluctantly letting go of my hand.

"Their works burger if you must know. And their double caramel chocolate doughnut was worth the money."

Rory shook his head. "I don't think I miss food."

"Did you want me to make the changes so you can eat again? I mean then you could find out why the works burger is so damn good." My gaze skimmed the room trying to identify anything that might indicate where exactly I'd brought us out. "Grilled pineapple."

Rory stilled. His eyes wide after half a breath's hesitation he replied, "Don't tempt me."

"Did I bring us to the right area? I can't see any clothing."

Rory glided across the room towards a shelving unit that held crystals and other knick-knacks. "This is the place. Give me a moment."

I followed him and studied the crystals on the shelf. It was obvious to my untrained eye that these weren't quartz or amethyst. I spotted several uncut rubies, aquamarines and a dazzling fire opal that was nearly fist size. I was tempted to touch a few, but knowing Rory they would be warded with nasty surprises. I kept my fingers away.

The shelving moved sideways as Rory flicked on a light behind it, showing a deep stairwell.

"We're going down there?" I asked with a sigh.

"I'm going down there, you stand watch," Rory replied.

My eyebrow arched. "What's down there you don't want seen?"

Rory shot me a frown.

I crossed my arms.

He had stilled again, no movement from his chest, his eyes turning red as he stared directly at me.

I gathered darkness to me, several of the crystals vibrating in reply to my magic.

The hum brought Rory out of his daze as he shook himself. "Of course, there's nothing down there that you can't see."

"I can wait here, probably for the best." I stepped back.

Rory appeared to be two minds, one wanted to explain himself and his reluctance for letting me down into what appeared to be the start of catacombs, the other wanted to see the mayhem ensue. After the briefest of moments, his face registered my words and he nodded then took off at speed towards the darkness. I let out a slow breath and let my gaze travel around the room. Only the crystals appeared to have any magic stored within them. The rest of the things were clutter he'd kept with him over the centuries. The sentimental old thing was secretly a hoarder. I picked up a tunic that had definite fifteenth century vibes and wondered if he'd been a part of Tudor England at any stage. I reminded myself to ask him if he knew Shakespeare. Someone as old as him must have spent some time with famous people. I was deep in contemplation of an old leather-bound book about sprites and sprigands when Rory came strolling back up the stairs. His clothing was impeccable. But his eyes betrayed a haunted shadow, which he was not ready to share. Everyone deserved to have their secrets.

"You look nice."

He nodded to me and readjusted his waistcoat. The dark coat he wore over the black three piece fell back into place once he was happy with his fit.

"Shall we?" he asked, holding out his arm for me.

"Now it's my turn to get ready."

"Do you need help?"

"Rory." I threw us into the shadows and jumped back to Coven House.

"Argh," he said as we landed in the spell circle inside the basement of the house.

"Sorry, I can't waste time shadow jumping, I'm tired, hungry and need to get ready or Josie and Sarah will kill me."

Rory bent over and took a large breath, with his hands firmly planted on his knees. "That takes a lot of getting used to."

"It hurts, it's draining and that's why more people haven't worked out how to do it." I pushed greying strands of hair back from my face. I was running low on energy and my body was ready to stop me in my tracks if I didn't feed it. My stomach took that opportunity to sing the song of its loneliness.

"You need to eat." Rory straightened his jacket.

"I need sugar."

He stared at me and then sighed with a dramatic flair that should get him an award. "Fine, I'll support the rebuilding."

I frowned and then his words clicked in. "Good. Emerald and Marty deserve good things. They've always taken care of me."

"Go, go." He shooed me away with his hands.

26

I took the stairs as quick as my body would allow and headed to the freezer. Luckily the thing was stocked with ice cream and other delectable goodies. I made myself a banana mint smoothy and drained it quickly. My stomach slowed the gurgling down, but I was still feeling like a newborn velociraptor and headed to the main fridge. Sugar or protein? Luckily for me, Josie had stuffed the fridge full of sliced meats and homemade guacamole. I pulled some out and made meat wraps.

"You need to go get ready." Josie came down the stairs from Sarah's makeshift bridal room.

"I will, I spent a bit of energy and needed to feed the monster," I replied, patting my now happy belly then a glint of wrapping paper caught my eye. An entire table outside on the patio was filled with glittering paper and ribbons and bows. "Ooh, that's a lot of presents."

"You need to stop doing things for everyone else and start focusing on getting ready." Josie's tone betrayed her worry, she sighed. "The guests sent their presents over early so they didn't have to handle them tonight."

"Who brought the big one at the back?" I tried to get a better look.

"The pack sent one, Mistress Kable has the one that looks like a picture, there's one from the Coven, of course it's the biggest, can't have anyone outdo us," Josie said with a smile. "No, stop making a mess everywhere."

"I will. What time are we starting?" I put the rest of the food back in the fridge.

"We've got two hours. Not enough time to make you not look like you need fourteen hours sleep," she replied, tapping me on the shoulder.

"Righto mum, I'm going." I slumped my way to my room.

The dress was beautiful and Josie was right, I did look like a mess. I took myself into the bathroom and hid under the shower for longer than necessary. It'd been a few days since I'd shaved my legs and even though I knew no one would see them under the layers I was about to don, I took time to make sure I was presentable. My hair, as predicted, took longer than anything else. I was of two minds to cut it shorter. It would make it more manageable, but then I couldn't be bothered. I sent a spell to dry and curl it. It had been over a decade since I'd used my magic in such a way, but it had been second nature to me once. The curls were way too tight, so I brushed my hair and caused the whole thing to become a frizz ball. The image reflecting at me was so ridiculous I could stop laughing.

"You okay in there?" Josie asked, knocking at my bathroom door.

I opened the door in my underwear, my hair extending from my head like a brown balloon.

"Oh, my hells, what have you done?" Josie asked, stepping back, her bathrobe tied tightly around her waist, her own hair still up in curlers that threatened to fall with every movement.

"I'm rusty on the magic." I let out another chorus of chortles that made the whole situation much funnier than it should have been.

"You doing okay Lucy? You're over tired. You've got the sillies."

I held my hands up in surrender. "I don't know how to fix this." I waved at my hair and then at the world around me. "I can't fix any of this and people need me to."

Josie put her arm around my shoulder and directed me to sit on the edge of my bed. "You don't have to tonight. Just let me fix your hair. One thing at a time."

I nodded not trusting myself to say anything.

Josie busied herself putting a brush through my hair and going back and forth from my bathroom for calming mousse and other concoctions to soothe my wild mane. It was nice to be pampered, but I did need sleep. I was running on an empty tank and would have to eat something more soon. Taking Rory through the shadows twice was harder than I realised. All for a suit. I was of two minds to tell Josie about the secret stairs incident but then forgot to when she stood back and smiled.

"That looks good. I can't do much about the shadows under your eyes, but at least your hair looks presentable," she said with her hands on her hips.

"Thanks. You need to go take care of yourself. I'll put some makeup on and get dressed then come help get things ready."

"Don't fall asleep, I mean it."

I waved her off and headed back to the mirror to apply make-up. She was right about the bags and the sallowness of my skin. I needed extra concealer. I chose a pink eyeshadow shade with dark smokey combo to take some of the focus off my weariness. I would have worn false lashes, but they were too fidgety, so I put on a couple of layers of mascara and called it quits. Luminous red lipstick set my look well and I struggled out of the bathroom to put my dress on.

I'd opted out of high heels for this wedding and strapped small silver spikes to my legs in case I needed them. Iron didn't affect the Fae, even though stories said it did. They couldn't stand silver because it was an inert metal. Iron could hold a magnetic charge, so was useless against them. Silver stopped magic flowing freely from within them and if I stabbed a Fae with it, it would hurt them badly. In the right place, it would kill them outright. I didn't think any Fae would try to crash the wedding, but I would be ready. I stepped into my dress and zipped it up. I couldn't help myself and gave a twirl, watching my skirt billow out. The silver and navy panels flared out like petals in the wind. I could never be called pretty, but this dress helped a lot towards that label.

I strode to my top drawer and pulled out several silver chains I had, pinning them into my hair. People would think of them as embellishments or adornments. Only those who knew me knew that they were weapons if I so chose. I closed my eyes and opened them in the spirit realm. It wasn't more than two heartbeats before Death appeared next to me.

"To what do I owe the pleasure?" Death's tone was soft, almost kind.

Kindest in Death was not something you would consider real. Death was abrupt, painful, sudden, ongoing, but never kind. I wondered if he'd been studying humanity again, trying to figure out how to fit into the role of parent.

"I'm about to take part in a wedding. I think she will attack there. Will you be ready?"

"I am everywhere. I would spare you this pain if I could, but it must be done," Death replied.

The sinking sensation of the inevitable pulled at my limbs. I would do what I had to do to keep my friends safe. I would do what was needed because no one else could. I would do it even though I wanted so much more from life. Not trusting myself to speak I nodded. I would do it.

"You have everything you need."

I opened my eyes back in my world and grimaced. It would have been nice if Death had complimented my dress. But then I realised how stupid that remark sounded. Vanity was never a good fit. I opened my door and stepped out into the chaos of the wedding build up.

I was soon roped into setting up the food tables and then was sent to find the groom. He was on the grounds somewhere. My ward had let him in.

"You doing alright?" I asked Benji when I found him pacing back and forth down the side of the house.

The look he shot me was a mixture of worry and fear. "What if she doesn't show up? What if I'm out of my league. No, I know I'm out of my league. What if she realises that and then doesn't want to marry me? What do I offer?"

I grabbed both of his hands in mine. "Stop. Settle. She loves you."

He scanned the area as if wanting the plants to swallow him whole. "I don't know. I'm not good enough for her. She's a witch and I'm a security rat."

"Hey, you're a damn good security rat, so hold it right there."

He shook his head.

"Your grandmother is inside and the witches are doting on her. She's here. Sarah's in there ready to go. How about you take a breath and get married?" I still held his hands, but they no longer shook.

"I know. I hope I can live up to her view of me." He pulled his hands back and rubbing at the back of his neck.

"That's what this is about, you two work together to make a future."

Benji glanced around, then quickly back to me. "Where's TJ? Did you leave him near the drinks table?"

"I think he's too busy trying to chat up two bridesmaids to go near the alcohol."

Benji chortled. "Such an idiot."

"I remember an idiot not so long ago trying to impress the women."

"There you are." Marg strolled towards us. "I don't know if you know this Benji but the wedding needs a groom to work."

He shoved his hands in his pants pocket and nodded. "I'm just. I don't know."

Marg laughed. "You're freaking out, everyone does. I thought I'd give you my present early."

Benji frowned. "You don't have to do that."

Marg gave him a hug and then held out an envelope. "I do. It's about time."

Benji gingerly held the envelope. "You've done so much for me. Giving me a job and all that."

"Go on, open it," Marg said, winking at me.

He opened the envelope that held a single piece of paper within it. Benji's frown deepened. "What?"

"The light here is dim, come on, let's take it around the back where the light is, you can read it there." She looped her arm around his and walked him towards the back of the yard where the ceremony would take place.

I followed along, happy knowing that Marg had him under control.

"This is too much," Benji replied, his hand shaking the paper. "You don't need to do this."

"It's only a promotion, not like I'm giving you a house or anything," Marg replied.

Benji stared at her, then flicked his eyes towards me and back at Marg. An ear-splitting grin appeared on his face as he engulfed her in a hug.

I arched an eyebrow at her.

"He's management now. Needed someone to take over my spot so I can finally do something with my life," Marg replied.

I congratulated Benji as he took off with the paper still in hand, dragging Marg towards his grandmother who was seated at the front of the ceremony.

I felt Cole step out of the house and move to me before I saw him. The rest of the guests were taking their chairs and a hush was falling over the crowd. Cole smiled as he took my hand in his.

"You take my breath away," he murmured so only I could hear.

I was pretty sure any supernatural in the crowd who was concentrating on us would hear him, but I didn't care.

"Do you like it?" My voice was breathy.

He took my breath away and set my nerves alight. He was dressed in a two-piece navy suit, black shoes and belt. His cologne was woodsy, with a hint of citrus. He'd trimmed up his beard and was looking at me as if he couldn't wait to tear my dress from me.

"Don't look at me that way," I whispered.

"I was thinking," he replied, with a hint of a smile.

"Well, don't think that right now, we've got a wedding to go through." I nodded towards the others.

"I can't help myself," he replied.

Josie stopped my reply by dimming the lights in the yard as music echoed through from the house. I pulled at Cole's arm so that we took our seats towards the back of the ceremony.

TJ stood next to Benji, fidgeting with the cufflink on his sleeve. It appeared TJ was the one getting married not Benji, with the amount of nervous energy the kid was putting out. Benji bumped his elbow into TJ's side. TJ shot him a look of frustration. This was probably the first and most likely the last time the former gangster would ever wear a suit this formal. I hid my smile as the two bowed their heads in a heated discussion with TJ eventually dropping his sleeve and wiping the sweat off his brow with the back on his hand.

The music changed again and the guests rose as one. For a non-traditional wedding, there were still a few traditions that Sarah had wanted, including being walked down the aisle by a loved one. There was no priest standing behind Benji, instead Sarah's father had taken on the role of officiant as an ordained marriage celebrant.

I craned my neck to watch the first of the witches walk down the aisle. They were barefoot and bedecked with floral crowns. White witches were one with nature. Blood witches never married. They saw no use to the male donor after conception. There was a binding ceremony they would use to ensure that the witch conceived quickly, but as far back as I can remember there were no unions like this.

Cole squeezed my hand, bringing me back from my thoughts. Josie and Sarah were coming down the aisle arm in arm. Josie let out small sparks of magic to sprinkle rose petals in front of Sarah's feet as she walked. I shot them both a gigantic smile, but they were too focused on getting to Benji to notice. When Josie handed Sarah over to Benji, she sent a little thunderclap off above the stage. TJ fell backwards, almost toppling himself with a squeal. Benji grabbed his arm, steadying him as the guests chortled and relaxed.

The ceremony then continued, with each of them promising to support and love each other. Sealed with a kiss, we clapped and laughed as glowing butterflies were released from above them. The couple had to go back into the house to sign official documents, so Cole and I sat back down in our seats while the rest of the guests quietly mingled between themselves afterwards.

I scanned my wards with a bit of my magic. Still strong. Tonight, would not be messed with.

"Didn't she look lovely?" Marg said as she plunked herself down next to us.

"She would look beautiful in whatever she wore. But the whole thing is gorgeous. Even Benji scrubbed up okay, don't tell him I said that."

"He's going to do well," she said, plucking at her small hand bag.

"You're finally retiring?" Cole asked.

Marg shot him a rueful glance. "Something like that."

I squinted at her. "Marg, what are you doing?"

She let out a long breath and then shrugged one of her shoulders. "Oh, you know. Been thinking about fixing some things."

"But you're handing over the management to Benji," I reminded her.

"I know. But the city's been under terrible management for a while now and I thought well someone better fix this before the world turns to garbage," she said.

"You're running for mayor?" I couldn't contain my genuine shock.

Marg was busy, I'd never seen her not working. Swift Security was the company it was because she kept it afloat.

"I think you'll do well," Cole said, keeping his hand on my lower back.

"Thank you. I'd like to think all these years of running a company would help me clean up some of the stink that's been coming out of the mayor's office recently," she replied.

"Does he know?"

Marg let out a giggle. "He does, in fact he was vocal in denouncing my bid, right before he found out his own kid had his head blown off. That was interesting to see. You have anything to do with that?"

Cole shook his head.

She craned her neck to focus on me with an over plucked eyebrow raised.

I sighed. "I didn't blow him up. I was there but couldn't save the idiot."

"Well, there are a lot of concerned citizens like me who've decided enough is enough and I'm running," Marg declared. Her face set in a mixture of determination and annoyance. Marg cleaned up messes, she would do a good job, but I worried that her taking on the role of mayor would put her firmly in the sights of some of the more nefarious parts of the city.

"I will let the pack know. Our votes are yours," Cole replied.

"Who's voting now?" Rory asked, sliding into a chair beside Marg. "Hello Margie, you stirring up trouble again?"

Marg's face darkened for a moment. "Enough of that, you slimy old git. If I've told you once, I've told you a million times, the answer is no and always will be."

"Is there some history here?"

Marg shook her head slightly. "His majestic-ness can't take no for an answer."

"All I offered was to help you out financially and to this day you still treat me unfairly," Rory said with no bitterness to his words.

"I have managed well without your help," she replied.

"You were in a hard place at the time," he countered.

Marg leaned over and patted him on the jaw. "And I still didn't need you."

"And yet I need you," he replied with a pleasant smile.

I was about to ask more, but the happy bridal couple came back out and the band struck up a lively tune.

"Now this is the good part," Marg said. "Time to get merry and eat amazing food."

27

I was still holding Cole's hand when a tingle of fear flew across my stomach and lodged into my spine. I spun around, searching for the source. Someone had hit my ward. Someone with ill intent.

Cole's eyebrow raised, but he stayed silent as I scanned the yard. The ward alerted again. Someone was trying to cross. Why now? Anger surged up, erasing any fear factor within me. I dropped Cole's hand and walked purposefully towards the house.

"What's going on?" Josie said as I passed her.

"I'll deal with it, you go make sure everyone's happy." I waved her away.

Cole loomed beside me, our strides in sync. He didn't say a word, he didn't have to. I knew he had my back no matter what. I was glad I had strapped the silver to my thighs and had so much of it in my hair. If I had to fight, I'd make sure whoever was trying to harm the coven would pay.

Cole stepped forward and opened the front door. Down at the gate, the mayor and several police officers waited, unable to open the latch. My ward flashed green again as he slammed his fist into it.

I let out a breath and muttered, "Humans. I was ready to fight wraiths to the death and it's a bunch of humans."

"Steady." Cole took the front steps two at a time and striding down the pebbled driveway with me.

"I'll play nice," I murmured back.

Cole placed his hand on the small of my back as we faced the police.

"Mr mayor, how nice to see you this evening. You were not invited to the wedding, so I'm surprised you're here disturbing the ceremony."

"You." The mayor pointed his finger at my face. His hand came nowhere near me, the ward did a good job at protecting us.

I moved so I could see the Police Captain. "Sir, is there a reason you are here?"

He gritted his teeth and then spoke crisply. "We believe someone at this event was responsible for the death of Tucker. We need to take several people in for questioning."

"At a wedding. You do this now?"

"We have a warrant, signed by a judge. If you choose not to comply, we will have to use force," the captain replied.

I blinked once, then sighed. "You demand that you interrupt a supernatural wedding ceremony to arrest people you think killed a man who admitted to attempted murder of a police officer? And you think you can use force on supernaturals and survive?"

Cole's hand around my waist squeezed once and I dropped my hands.

"Can I see the list you need to talk to?" Coles voice was neutral, as if he was a bystander.

The mayor continued to stare daggers at me. If he could punch me in the face, I think he would have. I stared back at him. This pathetic man had taken up with my grandmother, hoping to secure power and money. The absolute farce of him thinking he could ever best her.

"None of these women were at the scene," Cole stated.

"They are wanted for questioning in regard to the death," the captain replied, his tone on edge.

"They will comply with your demands in the morning, Captain, at a reasonable hour and with legal representation," Cole replied, not giving an inch. His voice was still neutral but his jaw set.

"No, they will come out here now. I will see the killers hung," the mayor snarled.

"If you want the witch who killed your son, you know where to find her." My voice was barely a whisper. "She will kill you too, you're already dead. Never get in bed with a blood witch. They don't leave anyone to tell the tale."

The major slammed both fists against the ward and, as he did so, several large shifters emerged out of the darkness behind them. The police officers who up until this point had appeared disinterested grabbed their weapons, fear etched into their faces.

"We will comply with your request at a reasonable hour Captain," Cole replied. "If you insist on continuing, I cannot guarantee your safety or the safety of the officers here."

"You are abominations, you should be wiped off the face of the earth," the mayor said, slamming his fist again as if this time he could crack the ward with pure determination alone.

"Control you man," Cole said to the captain, ignoring the other man's antics.

Two officers surrounded the mayor and pulled him away from the gate. The shifters didn't growl, didn't move towards the group, they stayed there, looming in the dark, their eyes aglow as shifters did on full moon nights. The eerie sense of being sized up for dinner was a nasty sensation. Too bad it was all show. The shifters wouldn't attack, Cole had let me know they were on our perimeter in case we needed them. I had tried to tell him we didn't need them. The coven could fend for itself fine, but I'm glad he'd not listened to me.

"We will comply with your request first thing in the morning," Cole said.

"What's going on?" Mistress Kable asked from behind us, her arms flapping as she took the stairs fast, making several of her metal bangles clank loudly as she came towards us. "This is a wedding. How dare you interrupt."

I pivoted so I could shoo her but noticed the horror on the mayor's face. What the hell?

"This doesn't concern you," the captain said, folding the paper back up in his hand.

"Why not? You think you can come here and interrupt things?" she said again, her voice dropping in tone.

I grabbed Cole and pulled him away from the witch as she exploded into power.

"No, no." I stumbled back. Cole steadied me, and I was glad of his bulk.

Both Cole and I were scrambling back as Mistress Kable threw a massive spell towards the mayor and the police captain. My ward obliterated in an instant.

"No," I yelled as the shield that kept the house safe cracked and then shattered.

Mistress Kable turned to focus her evil attention on me, her face contorting and her eyebrow raised in a familiar arch. "I'll deal with you in a minute."

Gone was the façade, as my grandmother Lillith Dorchasa, Blood Witch Queen, stood before me, not two metres away.

"She killed Kable, she killed her. She's been wearing her likeness. Shit." I scrambled to my feet. I pointed at the police and the shifters who stood dumbstruck. "Run. Fucking run."

Cole burst into his sigma wolf form in an instant, the tatters of his clothes dropping to the grass beside him as wraiths poured towards us from the storm drains.

My grandmother had been here all along. I was such an idiot. I peeked over my shoulder to see Josie and several other witches' stream from the house.

"Go, get them out of here, she's here! Get them out," I screamed as I pulled my magic towards me.

"I told you not to interfere." My grandmother shed the visage of Kable and standing tall. Her grey hair streaming behind her as her blood magic swelled around her like a cape. "You can't do anything right."

The police officers opened fire as she stepped towards the men. Wraiths surging towards them with terrifying speed. I transmuted the metal I held into two machete-like instruments and grunted.

Cole burst forward intending to take Lillith to the ground but was tumbled to the side by two wraiths that tried to drain him. I leapt towards him, swinging and decapitating them, covering Cole in goo.

"Sorry."

Lillith saw me, her face darkened as she sent her wraiths towards me. I closed my eyes for an instant and pulled at the magic that kept them bound to this earth. Her hold on them was hard, I figured out quickly that I could not take her the way I had taken Esmeralda.

I swung again as Cole joined me in slaughtering as many as we could. I could hear the screams of the guests from the backyard. Wraiths were everywhere. My grandmother had spent a terrible amount of energy and she would stop at nothing to get her way.

Lillith stood over the mayor's husk, pulling the last of his energy out of him.

"Stop, grandmother. Stop this, you need to stop," I yelled at her.

She ignored me and advanced on the police and the captain. The shifters ran towards the back of the house through the side lane. Cole ripped through another wraith and growled at me as I stood, trying to make sense of what Lillith was about to do. I took one look at him and ran with him through the house to the backyard.

To my surprise Jessie was in the yard with Lauren and Brad gathering guests to them. Jessie grabbed Benji's grandmother's arm and disappeared into the shadows. The rest of the guests were being herded through a makeshift hole in the back fence and were running away. Jessie returned and grabbed another guest, pulling them through the shadows. I ran towards Lauren.

"Stop her. She'll wear herself out. Take her when she comes back and go. She can't be here, my grandmother would drain her in an instant and I wouldn't be able to stop it." My machetes dripped goo onto the flower petals strewn across the lawn.

Lauren nodded at me while Brad and Cole ripped into more wraiths that had made it into the yard. Rory and other vampires were helping behead several further towards the fence line. I spun and faced Cole.

"We have to get the vamps out of here, she'll use them."

"We've got things under control, find the portal and destroy it," Brad said. I figured he was interpreting the thoughts Cole was projecting.

Pack had some advantages, including telepathic communication. I scratched at my scalp. The portal was here. She brought it in. "She's got it here."

"How did she get through?" Brad said as Lauren wrapped her arm around Jessie who was clearly exhausted and ran through the back fence with her. Jessie was struggling weakly to break her hold, but by the time they disappeared it seemed like she had accepted her mother's decision.

"She has Mistress Kable somewhere, she couldn't have assumed her form if the witch was dead," I replied.

"Did she bring the portal?" Brad asked.

I glanced over at the gift table, most of the presents had been stomped on in the panic that had ensued. The large one at the back was still intact.

"The present." I ran toward the table.

Rory heard me at the same time my grandmother strolled out of the house and sped towards the table.

"Don't," I yelled as Lillith reached out with her magic and seized him, lifting him off the ground.

I threw my own magic at her and hit a shield that surrounded her. Rory screamed as she drained him. Without thought, I threw my machete at my grandmother with all my force as Detective Nichole Pearce tackled the Blood Witch Queen from behind, sending the two of them tumbling down the stairs.

Rory slumped onto the ground as Nichole pushed herself off Lillith and half scrambled and ran towards Rory, lifting him up in a fireman's hold and racing towards the back fence.

"Looks like it's you and me," Lillith said, pushing herself up to her feet.

"You don't have to do this. You're making a terrible mistake, there is not immortality the Fae are lying," I said, scanning the yard.

Cole and the other shifters were still engaged in fighting off the last wraiths that my grandmother had with her. Raoul and Joseph were in the fray. They were noticeably bigger than they had been, as if they'd taken some kind of vampire steroids and had hit the gym. I couldn't focus on them as my grandmother used her magic to lift the portal out of the pile of presents and brought it to her.

"I have waited a long time for this," she sneered at me.

"The Fae are parasites, any magic they have, they stole. There's no immortality spell, nothing that they can offer except death and enslavement." I took a hesitant step towards the portal.

"So crafty, I'd wondered who my daughter had lain with to sire you, always the disappointment." Lillith Dorchasa's voice was filled with contempt as she stood tall beside the portal, slowly tearing the wrapping paper open.

"Maybe to you, but you don't matter."

"Such a stupid chit of a girl, could never master the spells, couldn't even perform the simplest of magics. My daughter gave her life so you could come into the world," she hissed.

"Your daughter hated you so much she made a deal, her life freely given," I replied.

If I could get close enough, I could melt the portal before she powered it up. The shield she held would eventually run out of power and I could strike. Behind me, growls emanated as the shifters had demolished the last of the wraiths and turned their attention towards us.

"So interesting that you would attract the attention of a sigma. Maybe you do have some power after all," Lillith said.

"You tried to kill me once, it didn't work. You should not try to open the portal, all you will get is pain."

Cole stood next to me, Brad and his larger-than-life wife Lauren on my left. Behind me, the witches chanted. Lillith's eyes widened when she saw Lauren.

"Where did you get a dire wolf? I thought we'd killed the last of their kind centuries ago," she asked.

"Some are born, some are made."

Lillith's gaze flickered over the rest of the crowd. "You can stop the chanting. White magic has little power against ours."

The haughtiness in her tone and the imperialness in her stance bugged me. She'd spent her life thinking her magic was the most powerful. She had no idea of what other magic could do.

"Always the snob." I stepped towards her. "Give me the portal."

Lillith stared at me and shook her head. "Come and take it."

I took another step forward and carefully waved my hand downwards to ask the rest of those with me to wait. I had to give her the chance to not go through with her plans. Maybe she could see reason. Cole didn't think so, he growled low and menacing. Brad joined in, but it was Lauren's deep rumble that drove through my bones. She carried the echoes of my father's power in her voice. Well, there was something you didn't see every day.

"Ah, death magic, no wonder she's been kept hidden." LIllith sized Lauren up with new praise. "How did you ever manage?"

"A girl's got a trick or two."

28

―·―

"T he youngling, she walks shadows, I saw her, chased her a few times, but she was too quick," Lillith said. "I must make sure I get her and study her. Anomalies are quite rare amongst these specimens."

"You can stop this."

"You never got away from me," she said.

I frowned.

"You thought you'd left it all behind, but I knew every step you took. I sent your grandfather to keep an eye on you, to make sure no one else found you before I was ready." She placed her hand on the portal.

"I died, you told everyone I was gone. You knew I hadn't."

She shrugged one shoulder. "It seemed best. The council were hellbent on opening a portal and sharing the power."

"So, you killed the council and now it's all yours."

"It took a while, yes. I had to make several deals with the witch hunters. They came in and decimated the council. Some of them put up a good fight, but in the end they died. I took their power for mine, those that were still alive afterwards and I had a hell of a time killing a few of the hunters. They're all gone by the way. My wraiths feasted well," she said.

"Now no one will oppose you."

"Those who try are doomed to fail." Lillith pricked her finger with her magic and letting her blood slide down the portals side.

"Harrold was my grandfather." I stepped to the side.

"He had outgrown his usefulness. My mother was right, I should have got rid of him after conception, but he kept an eye on you for me and that was enough," she said.

"Is it hard?"

She frowned at me. "What? You always were a queer one. Never asking the right questions."

"Is it hard, being so alone? No one in this world would care if you lived or died. You have eliminated anyone who could ever care about you. Your own daughter died to make sure you would never gain the power you wanted."

"My daughter made a foolish mistake. You are the result. You always have been a disappointment," she spat.

"Did you at least ask her who fathered me?"

"I didn't need to, some stupid male who had no hope of creating an offspring as powerful as I needed. I'd spent years working out a match for her and she threw it away." Lillith let her blood drip down the other side of the portal.

The silver pulled the blood into itself and a dark swirling mist started in the centre. She was powering up the portal. Only certain bloodlines had the right combination of magic and blood rights to use the portal. Olivia had drummed these words into me since

I was old enough to mumble. The Dorchasa line was a direct Fae descendant. That's where we had got our powers from. We alone could open the portal to the next realm. We were the chosen few.

"And now you're trying to open this to gain immortality for what? For who will you live? You have no line left."

"I don't need any," she replied, as the portal faded.

"Looks like you do." I pointed at the portal sputtering. "You might need to feed it more."

She snapped out a large tendril of her Blood Magic towards me, intending to slice into me. My blood definitely would open the portal with a bang. My Dorchasa side had some magic, but my fathers side would rip the portal directly open. I countered her strike with a tendril of my own that I wrapped around hers and pulled her towards me. She wasn't ready for me and I made her drop her hold on the portal.

"What?" she stuttered.

"I don't think Harrold did a good enough job of spying on me for you. Doesn't look like he told you everything."

Cole shifted wide to the right side of me, while Brad and Lauren went left, intending to flank us. The white witches led by Josie behind me finished their chanting and a ward blazed up in a wide arc around the two of us. Whatever came through the portal would be trapped long enough for us to deal with it. Olivia spun around, looking with wide eyes at the now encapsulating dome we were in.

"How?" she asked. "White witches don't have this power."

"Yes, well. I get involved and I make mistakes, as you say. Sometimes though, what seems like a mistake turns out to be helpful.

Especially when you need power to trap a blood witch," I replied. "Go on, test it."

Lillith narrowed her eyes at me and then, without warning threw a strike of magic at the ward. It held. It was soft in spaces, but the ward held. "You, you taught them this. But you have no magic."

"How long have you worn Kable's form?" I kept my tone soft, inquisitive.

"Long enough to know you shouldn't have this capability," she said.

"So only a day or two. I wonder how you captured her. Mistress Kable is a crafty witch."

"She tried to save someone and ended up trapped instead. She did put up a fight, but she's useless to me now."

Josie was running through the house. Kable would be close. Stashed somewhere nearby, if we had any chance of saving her Josie and the other witches needed to be fast. I wondered if one neighbour had a basement similar to ours. That's where I'd stash her.

Once the witches had set the ward, they would need help powering back up. They couldn't help me in the fight. So, it was down to me, my grandmother and the three shifters. I had hoped to spare Cole and the others the pain of fighting a Blood Witch, but I could never push them away.

"You are right. I didn't have magic, proper blood magic. Even though I cried myself to sleep as a child, hoping that I could make you proud. What a fool I was. Nothing will satisfy you."

"You have done something." She steppped back to the portal and dragged it upright again. She sliced her hand deeper and poured her blood into the silver.

"Keep going. By the time you drain out, you might open it without me."

"You did open a slice the night you pretended to die. If the council had drained you properly, we could have opened it enough for our purposes," she replied, her tone as parched as a pavement in the midday sun.

"Yep, I'm sure I did, but it wasn't my witch blood that did the job."

She arched an eyebrow and opened her right hand up, pouring blood from both hands down the portal as she stood behind it. "You are of no consequence anymore. I don't need you."

"Probably not, but you still haven't asked the right question Lillith." I used the same tone she'd used a hundred times on me when I got things wrong.

"And what is that?"

Her contemptible sneer used to be scary to me, but now I stared at her. Taking a deep, emotionless look, I saw the scared woman she really was. She needed power to protect herself and she had lashed out at those that would have been kind to her all her life. She'd known nothing of love or kindness. She'd surrounded herself only with those that had the passion for power and authority. Such a waste.

"How is it possible that a witch like me could bring back the dead, create day walkers, dire wolves and shadow walkers, all with the touch of her blood?" I tilted my head to the side and tapped my foot the way she used to.

"Only death has that power," she snarled.

"Bingo." I threw my hands up and clapped once. "My mother was amazing. Only she could have made a deal with death and got them to agree. She did it to stop you. Once she knew what you and the council were up to, she realised that death was the only power strong enough."

Lillith shook her head. "My daughter could not have. She didn't have the power."

"No, she didn't, that's why she agreed to bring me into the world, she sacrificed her own life to do so." I pulled at the magic the earth was so eager to provide.

Cole and the others stepped away from me, still in the ward in case they were needed to fight anything that got through the portal, but far enough away that they would not be affected by my magic.

"That's preposterous, she didn't have it in her," Lillith replied and started chanting under her breath as she stared me down.

"She did. My parent says hi, by the way. They've known about your plans for a long time and they were willing to help out. You can't break the fabric of reality without consequences." The magic built up behind me ready for me to meld, however I wanted.

"You're a metalsmith and you can use some blood magic, but badly, that's it. I had you tested repeatedly. You failed, all of it," she said and continued pushing her blood into the portal.

"You didn't test me with the right magic. No one in the council could have known what I was, not even you. But that's okay, now for the last time I'm asking you to stop. Stop trying to open this idiotic thing. You can still save yourself."

"You foolish girl, you have no idea what I can do," she said.

With a sigh, I stepped closer. "I'm sorry Grandmother. I know you want power, but it comes at a cost. I hate to do this, but you won't stop."

"What do you think you can do? Nothing," she spat and pushed more of her power towards the portal.

Dark swirls continued through the portal as light seeped out of cracks in the mist.

"I can do this." I pushed my magic into the portal.

The portal flared to life. Lillith stepped back her hands still gripped the portal frame.

"What? What are you?" she asked. "That's death magic you're wielding. How? She tricked me? How do you have death magic?"

"I tried to warn you. If you open the portal, there's only one way to stop it. I'm sorry. I tried to stop you." I poured more of my parent's power into the portal.

Through the cracks in the mist, a long spindly arm reached out, splinters for claws on the end of its hand scraped at the air in front of the portal. Lauren let out a base growl, death magic swirling through her voice. The hand hesitated as a shoulder and part of a head tried to push through.

"Lillith Dorchasa you are condemned. You have opened the realm to evil, you cannot abide here further." I intoned the words Death had told me to and added in my own quiet voice, "I am sorry."

"What?" Lillith screeched as her blood spilled from her into the portal, her hands and wrists now a husk the portal stealing her magic and soul away.

"I tried to warn you. Death would have been easier. You must go through, it's the only way." I pushed my magic at the portal.

Lauren lunged and snapped at the creature trying to make its way into this world. It flared back and lost grip on our reality, tumbling back into the portal. Lillith stood on trembling legs, her face contorted with agony.

"No, they promised power, immortality," she said looking around her in desperation.

I started forward, how could she possibly be so naïve? "No, they promised none of that, you heard what you wanted. They cannot give, they only take. Good bye. I'm sorry you chose this."

Cole snapped at another arm coming through the portal. Brad and Lauren were ready beside him.

I opened myself up and poured out every ounce of magic I held into the portal as it sucked Lillith Dorchasa, Blood Witch Queen, into the mist as a dried husk of a human. The portal flared brighter.

"Save yourselves," I shouted to Cole and the others. "Run."

The ward shattered around us in a green flash. The portal flared again, the screech that came through was unearthly and sent shivers through my bones. I kept pouring out my magic. Brad and Lauren turned and ran, a few vampires who'd been on the periphery of our fight ran as well, their red eyes trailing in the distance. Only Cole remained. Liquid seeped from my eyes I wiped my hand to push it away and came back bloody. This hurt. I couldn't stop. Death had told me what I had to do to save the world and I would not stop.

"Go Cole, you can't be here, you'll die," I whispered as I dropped to my knees.

Cole, still in wolf form stood by me, propping himself under my arm as a support. I pushed more power into the portal; it flared again. The screeching reached a crescendo. I thought my eardrums would split and then, in a moment of extreme disappointment the portal failed. It sucked back in on itself. The metal warping into a small ball of misshapen metal and I fell back on the ground, dragging Cole down with me.

"It's done." My vision failed as my body was sucked deep into the void.

29

Small voices chittered around me. If this was death, then I was going to get cross with my father. He'd lied to me. Death had said it would be peaceful. The voices continued chittering and I wanted to swat them away, but I couldn't move my arms.

"I don't know, the doctor didn't say how long she'd be out," a female voice said close to my feet.

A deep rumble echoed through the room followed by shuffling of feet.

"Don't growl at me, I told you we're doing the best we can. I can't help, no one can, it's up to her," the voice said again.

I wanted to tell them to be quiet I was trying to be dead here and then it hit me. If I was dead, then I wouldn't hear the squabbling. I was still alive. Ha. Who knew? My parent had told me that it would require everything I could give and maybe more to shut the portal once my grandmother had started the process. But I hadn't died. Now if only I could tell them to shut up.

I tried to open my mouth, but I didn't have enough energy to even do that. My finger was far too heavy to lift. Since when did my fingers get so heavy? I had a nap and let them argue through.

Eventually they'd stop and I'd give them a piece of my mind but right then I really needed sleep.

A sharp jab struck my arm again. I blinked my eyes open. The room was darkish and blurry. I tried to slap whatever was poking my arm away, but my right arm wouldn't cooperate.

"Shhhhhtttoop." My voice came out sloppy, there was something in my throat that wouldn't let me speak. It hurt.

The person jabbing me dropped my arm with a little screech. I couldn't tell if they were a male or female, but they appeared to be in uniform. Was I in hospital? A light blinked over my bed and then footsteps raced towards me.

"How long has she been like this?" an authoritative voice asked.

"She said stop," the other voice replied.

"That's a good sign. We'll run some more tests," the first voice said.

I tried to grab hold of the hand of the person standing next to my bed but could only move my fingers a little.

"Hello Miss Driver, glad you're back with us. Say nothing, we've got a breathing tube in for you. We'll get that out in a minute, it'll be better once it's out. You gave us quite a scare," the authoritative voice said.

I blinked twice in response. My eyes were still blurry, I could see that there was no light from the window so it must have been late at night. Bugger. I needed to get up and get home. We had to fix so much.

"We'll need to extubate and remove the orogastric tube as well," the voice I had decided was the doctor replied. Her tone was one of calm authority, used to being in command.

There was a pinging in the background that could almost be the beat of a club song. Steady rhythm, I could dance to it. Oh damn, I was supposed to dance at the wedding. I'd promised Sarah. With a sigh, I closed my eyes again. Thinking was hard.

"Miss Driver? Miss Driver? Can you cough for me, big cough right now thanks," the Doctor said, "that's it, a bit more?"

I coughed like she asked. If I followed her instructions she would stop pestering me. All I wanted was a nap.

"That was perfect," the Doctor replied, as if I'd spoken.

"How long will she be like this?" Cole's voice rumbled from the left of my bed near the window.

"It's hard to say, this is good. She's on the mend," the Doctor said.

I waved my hand in his direction to get him to be quiet, the woman was trying to do her job, not her fault I'd almost died trying to save the world. She's a doctor. My heart leapt as he took my hand in his, the warmth of his skin eased some of my fear. I was alive. I was in hospital. Cole was here. I was safe. Not dead. Not dead at all. Boy, would I have a word with my parent when I saw them next. I had believed I would die shoving my grandmother through the portal. The worst would have been to be dragged into their realm. I would rather die in this one than live in the other. Lillith Dorchasa chose her fate. I tried to warn her.

"Who'd you warn?" Coles voice was soft.

"Lillith, she's gone," I whispered.

"She's gone, you did it. You saved everyone," Cole said.

"I don't know about everyone," Rory said from the other side of the room.

"I've told you before. I'll let you stay here, for her safety, but if you upset her, both of you are outside," the Doctor replied.

"Do you know Detective Pearce?" Rory asked.

"Who?" the Doctor replied.

"Never mind," Rory grumbled and went quiet again.

I squeezed Cole's hand and opened my eyes. I tried to smile, but my mouth hurt and my throat was sore. I managed a nod and then dropped back into sleep.

I was awoken by someone shaking my shoulders. The nerve.

"Come on Driver, I know you're faking it. No one gets to sleep all day and night for four days in this place. Get up, we've got work to do." Nichole Pearce's voice dragged through my slumber like fingers down a chalkboard.

"Piss off," I hissed, refusing to open my eyes.

"Ah, you're not dead. Good to know," she replied, with what appeared like a genuine happy tone.

Pearce was happy, someone would be in trouble now.

"You said that out loud Driver. Have you lost your inner monologue?" Pearce replied, more waspish.

"You are annoying," I replied with a cough. My throat was on fire.

"Oh, yeah, sorry, here's some water, they said you'd be groggy," Pearce said.

I opened my eyes to find her standing over me with a cup in hand.

"Give me a break." I pushed myself into a slight sitting position.

"You want me to fix the bed?" Pearce offered.

"Stop being nice, I can't stand this. If this is the bad place then I repent, send me somewhere the devil isn't."

Pearce stared at me for a microsecond and then let out a false laugh. "You're funny. Not. Sit up, drink the freakin' water so we can let you know what's going on."

I sat up and then regretted it. My head spun and nausea rose in my gullet.

"Drink this, it'll stop the spewing feeling," Pearce said distaste clear in her tone.

I took the cup and sipped at the liquid. It wasn't as bad as Josie's brews, so I guessed I was definitely in a human hospital.

"What's happened?" I asked after my throat eased.

"Lots. Your boyfriend and his royal arseholiness were almost at blows over your care. The good doctor kicked them out. Josie is fixing things with the Coven. Marg is officially the mayor of Wayland City. They held a snap election when both the mayor and police captain were killed."

I leaned back onto my pillow. My teeth were fuzzy, I wished I had a toothbrush handy. "Is everyone okay?"

"Some people were hurt. A couple didn't make it," Pearce said her tone uneasy.

"Who?" I closed my eyes.

"Mistress Kable, she put up one hell of a fight, but in the end her injuries were too great," Pearce replied patting me uneasily on the arm as if to take some of my pain away.

"My grandmother would have taken part of her skin and sewn it into her own to maintain the deception to fool my wards."

"Josie and the other witches gave her a proper send off, Marg made the city pay for the funeral and all that."

I nodded and needed a moment before I spoke. "Did Sarah and Benji and the others make it out okay?"

"They're good, Benji is now manager of your workplace. I'd start looking for a new job if I were you. I'm sure he'll want to give you all the shit shifts because your grandmother spoiled his wedding. Someone chucked a decapitated wraith into the cake. Goo sprayed all over it. So that was a bit of a fizzer."

"I'm sure we could make a new one."

Pearce let out a chuckle. "They've already planned a late reception, there'll be cake and good food and a live band."

"Am I invited?" My voice cracking on the last word, so I took another sip.

"I think so, the Sugar Shack is catering, they're back up and in business. Seems his arseholiness can do some things right."

"Works burger." My mouth watering at the sound of those words.

"You're not allowed anything yet," Pearce replied and turned to face the door. "Oh looksy, it's Tweedle dumb and dumber."

I glanced past her as Cole and Rory strode into the room, both jockeying for main position.

"Put it away boys, she's half dead and isn't interested, unless you have a works burger then she might be your friend," Pearce said. "Or is it a sandwich she's after?"

I choked on the water I was trying to swallow and glared at her.

"Anyway, I have to go do some stuff," she stated to the air.

"Now you're police chief?" Rory said.

"What?" I asked, reaching out to her.

She avoided my hand and shrugged half-heartedly. "They needed someone to step up. I'm next in line so I got the gig, for now. Unless his royal nastiness here mucks it up for me."

Rory glowered but held his tongue.

"Wise," Cole said.

"Sandwich," Pearce said and disappeared at vampire speed through the hallway.

"What is her issue with food?" Rory asked as if he was not expecting an answer.

"She's police chief of Wayland City," I stated and then giggled.

"What?" Rory asked, moving closer with vampire grace.

"I worry for the underbelly of this city, they don't know what's about to descend upon them."

"Raoul is out of the chop shop game. She's already made ultimatums to several of our kind who were doing dodgy business, those who survived your grandmother anyway," Rory replied.

"Any news on the vamp council?" I set my cup on the bedside table to my left.

"They know that we were dealing with a Blood Witch and that we successfully defeated her with help from both the shifters and witches," Rory replied.

Cole stood next to me at ease but with a slight tension to his eyes.

"And they're going to leave you alone?" I winced at the tightness in my throat.

"For now. There are other pressing matters, someone devastated the Witch Hunters throughout the state, there are no active ones left. They think this might be something new," Rory replied.

"Did you tell them it was her?"

He shook his head. "They'll figure it out one day. It'll keep them away from us for the time being, though."

"That's good." I dropped my head back on my pillow. "What happened to the portal?"

"It's a melted wreck, we've taken it to a secure location and no one will ever see it again," Rory promised.

"Good, good."

"After all the excitement, what are you going to do with yourself now?" Rory asked.

Cole frowned, his body stilling as if in readiness to tackle Rory should he need to.

"I thought I'd nap a bit more, I'm so tired. After that. I don't know."

"You've still got your magic?" Rory asked, slinging himself in the chair beside my bed as if it was a well-used throne.

"I guess." The hesitation hit me. I'd used everything and if Cole hadn't grabbed me, I would have given too much. Did I still have my magic? "Pass me something metal."

Rory reached over and handed me a teaspoon from his coat pocket. I sent him a quizzical look, he shrugged as if it was normal to have a spoon on yourself at all times for royal vampires. You never knew when the next cup of tea would appear out of nowhere.

I pulled the metal to me and sure enough it flowed. I let out a long breath that I had been holding. Still got it.

"Yes, we can see you can change metal, what about the other stuff? Our esteemed coven leader was worried," Rory said.

Cole rubbed my forearm and remained quiet.

"I don't know, got anyone you want me to bring back from the dead?" My tone was anything but kind.

"Can you still wield it?" he insisted.

I tried. I dropped my eyes and pulled at the magic. Nothing came. I tried again. It was gone. I'd lost it. I didn't know how to feel. I'd hated having it all my life and now that I'd started using it a lot, I missed it. It was a curse and a blessing.

"I can't. It's not there." Shock echoed through my voice.

Rory stood in contemplation and then sighed with relief. "All for the best."

I closed my eyes again, trying to pull deaths magic to me, or at least transfer myself through the shadows. It was gone. I was still on my bed, feeling more alone than I ever had.

"She's had enough," Cole said. The warning tone eminent in his voice.

Rory held up his hands. "It's fine. I'm going anyway. Call me when you need me."

I nodded and then lay back. "It's gone Cole. I can't get into the shadows."

He stared directly at me, muscles in his jaw flexed as if he wanted to say something, but he sighed and said, "Maybe not now, give yourself time."

I grimaced. "What if it doesn't?"

"We'll deal with that when you're ready," he replied.

After a long silence, he pushed a strand of hair off my face. "You scared me."

"I'm sorry."

"Don't do that again," he said.

"I'll try not to," I replied. "You know me, though. I act and not think at times."

"I can't live without you."

I held his hand in mine. "Thank you for not giving up on me."

He leant over and kissed me gently. "I'll always be here."

"What now?" I asked.

"Now we spend the rest of our lives together," Cole replied with a smile, his eyes glinting with his power.

"That'd be nice," I said. "I'd like to hide somewhere no one can find me for a little while. A nice beach, little ocean hut, or up in the mountains where you have to hike a long way to find me."

He smiled again as he waited for me to clue in on his words. I blinked slowly.

"Did you say together?"

Cole reached into his pocket. "I know this is cliché and it's not how I wanted to do this, but."

I watched him pull out a ring box made of black leather. He opened it up and inside was a single deep set emerald ring on rose gold.

I stared up at him.

"I almost lost you, I won't let that happen again. Will you stay with me forever?" His voice shaky.

"I," I stammered.

"Just say yes," Jessie said from the doorway. She was surrounded by several people, including Josie, Sarah and Benji who had the biggest grin on their faces.

"How'd you get here?" I asked her.

"Lucy, say yes, please," Jessie said.

I glanced back at Cole who still stood holding out the ring and then back at the rest of the group who appeared to have known this would happen. Back up dancers at the ready.

"Yes. Of course, yes, do you really want to marry me though? I mean I come with baggage," I said as he slipped the ring on my finger.

"We all do, but you need him and he's lost without you, you should have seen him moping about," Jessie replied flopping on the edge of my bed in a dramatic re-enactment of Cole's misery.

Cole leaned forward, ignoring the tenacious girl and kissed me soundly.

"Eww," Jessie said and was shushed by all the adults now crowding into my room.

The rest of the morning rocketed by. I was discharged from the hospital into Cole and the witches' care. I had let Jessie know not to shadow walk without talking to me first. I was worried that now I couldn't do that she might get lost or something might come for her.

It wasn't until that night when I was tucked soundly in Coles big bed with his amazing blankets that my body started to gain a sense of energy. Pearce had come through with the works burger and had argued soundly with Cole that as police chief she had every right to step into his home and deliver the saviour of mankind's burger to her regardless of his feelings. I thought it was a bit much, but the burger was delicious. Pearce had stepped into his house with no compunction to stop. I wondered about the vampire myth of invitation only. I'd have to ask Rory about that. It could have just been that Pearce doesn't give a shit about rules, magic or otherwise and she could go where ever she damn well pleased.

I snuggled closer to Cole. I could hide here forever. I had family. The witches, the shifters and even the sometimes-arrogant vampires, they were all part of my messed-up life. Cole rolled over and pulled me into his arms. The wind squalled outside, another one of Wayland City's typical winter nights where everyone in their right mind was tucked up safely in bed snuggling with the ones they loved. Including me.

The End.

ACKNOWLEDGEMENTS

I'd like to thank my family, for their patience, encouragement and enthusiasm.

Rory O'Brien again for letting me use his name but not his moustache.

Nichole Pearce, for inspiring a hard-arsed detective who has almost a good resting B face as her. Although she'll never keep up with the invective language. A true master.

Hazel for lending her name and enthusiasm. Anmarie for her encouragement, it means a lot. Maths is witchcraft and I will die on that hill, especially circle theorum.

Sarah Waites of Illustrated Book Cover Design, for the fabulous cover.

To my CYA conference family who've helped me all these years and who have on occasion reminded me with rather threatening emails to stop procrastinating and get it done.

About the Author

Raised by obsessive readers, I've found myself drawn to stories that can whisk me away from the normal world. Nothing better than a good book and a quiet place to read. I'm currently juggling raising teens, teaching Science full time and trying to tackle my TBR pile, which keeps growing because there's so many amazing authors out there. In between all this I write, probably as a way to deal with life, but also because I lose myself in the words. I hope the worlds I create can help someone else escape for a little while too.

You can catch me on TikTok under @sylviejanes0 (I locked myself out of my original account) and Facebook under Sylvie Janes.

Also By

Magic Rises

Blood magic is an abomination.
Those who wield it work dark deeds.
Never let a Blood Witch live.

My name's Lucy Driver, I work three jobs to make ends meet. I've perfected the art of being entirely normal, hiding in plain sight to protect myself and those around me. The witches think I'm a dud, the vampires have ignored me and the shifters don't think I'm worth their time. But when a Blood Witch appears in my city attacking supernatural children, I have to risk exposing my secrets to stop the witch's plans.

No matter the outcome, the life I've carefully crafted for myself in Wayland City is forfeit. If I'm lucky I can stop the Blood Witch before other, more deadly, supernatural forces discover my secrets.

I've never been the lucky type

Magic Rises is the first book in the Magic Returns series. It's full of vampires, shifters, and witches. If you enjoy urban fantasy stories with a plenty of action, snark and a kick-ass heroine, then you'll love reading Magic Rises.

MAGIC RETURNS
Ding Dong the Witch is Dead.

In real life, when you kill a wicked witch no one gives you ruby
slippers.

No happy munchkins jump around singing questionable songs
about your greatness.

No yellow brick road pops up to help you on your way to a happier
life.

It's just more of the same. More days spent working to scrape a
living and more hustling through life in search of better times.

More slog, less singing and dancing.

My name is Lucy Driver. I stopped the Blood Witch killing children in my city. A Witch Hunter has been sent to investigate. If he
finds out I was the one to kill the witch, he'll stop at nothing to
take my life.

Only problem is, I don't know who he is and unless I can figure it
out everyone I care about is in danger.

Magic Returns is Book 2 of the Magic Returns series. It's full of vampires, shifters and witches.

If you enjoy urban fantasy stories with a plenty of action, snark and a kick-ass heroine, then you'll love reading Magic Returns.

www.ingramcontent.com/pod-product-compliance
Lightning Source LLC
Chambersburg PA
CBHW031423240626

47154CB00001B/170